BEGINNINGS

sheryl m. malinics

adventures in extreme grace series

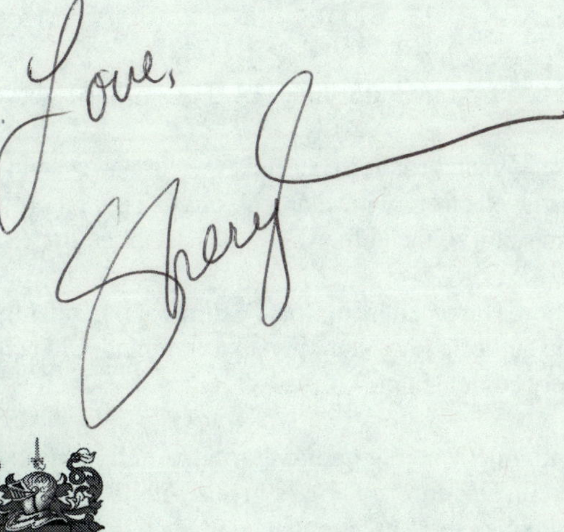

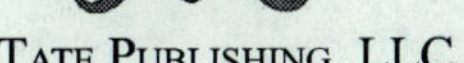

Tate Publishing, LLC

Published in the United States of America
by Tate Publishing, LLC
127 East Trade Center Terrace
Mustang, OK 73064
(888) 361–9473

ISBN: 1–5988616–4-6

DEDICATION

This book is dedicated to the memory of my father, Arlen Peahl, who gave me the gift of stories from his own childhood, and who had a wealth of untapped writing inside him.

It is also dedicated to the memory of my mother-in-law, Ann Malinics, one of the most well rounded readers I've ever known. She also gave the gift of a love for reading to her son, who is this reader's kindred spirit, and also my husband.

ACKNOWLEDGMENTS

My first acknowledgment must go to an incredible woman who has given me most of who I am and what I have. Life wouldn't be nearly as good without her involvement. Thanks, Mom!

I would also like to acknowledge the true motivators behind this book. If it wasn't for you reading my silly stories about bathrooms and encouraging and egging me on with my writing, I never would have had the courage to attempt publication of any book.

Back in the fall of 2001, circumstances threw us together from across the state and we quickly became an awesome group of women, known as the MoMPIEs (Moms on a Mission-Pioneers In Education). Our commonality was the desire to acquire the best in education for our children, and our goal was to make cyber charter schools a reality in our state. From legislators, to the governor, to the Secretaries of Education (both Federal and State), we plowed our way through endless phone calls, letter writings, editorials, and even a rally in the state capitol building. We lost the battle with the PDE for our own school, but the war was won and cyber charter schools are now established and have credibility in our state.

So here's to you all: Beth, Carrie, Carol, Diana, Deb, Diane, Eeni, E'lisa, Gayle, Gillian, Jeanie, Karen, Linda, Lisa, Lynn, Melly, Mia, MJ, Nicki, Patty, Rose, Shari, Shawn, and Susan.

Perhaps we are no longer needed as a bunch of "in your face" activists for our children's education, but we have gained so much more as a result of that season of our lives. Now, we're sisters, and I thank you from the bottom of my story-telling heart.

FOREWORD

George Washington said that if men were angels, we wouldn't need government. The governing principles in the Bible are there for our benefit, and if we will only give heed to them, our lives become a much simpler and more beautiful walk. The author has captured this principle in great detail in this, at times serious, at times humorous, look at a group of newly converted teenagers in a world filled with tests at every turn. Leaning to walk in the Saviors' footsteps is the business at hand for these very human and lovable teens. Come join in the beginning of the adventure as these teens experience an extreme journey in their walk with the Savior!

Diane Laverty
Fellow MoMPie and a busy mother of 5

Character synopsis

Rev. Carl Ganderson- The Pastor of the Community church, and the father of 4 children; Dale, Diana, Steve and Kristen.

Kelly Ganderson-the wife of Carl Ganderson, and mother of his children.

Dale Ganderson-the first-born of Kelly and Carl. He is 16 years old. He is tall, with blond hair and warm brown eyes. Dale is arguably the most vocal of the BBG's, but nonetheless, the others look to him for spiritual insight and wisdom that seems to be beyond his years. He plays the guitar, and occasionally the keyboard.

Diana Ganderson-the eldest daughter of Kelly and Carl. She is 15 years old, tall, with long blond hair and green eyes. She is considered the quiet one of the group.

Steve and Kristen Ganderson-younger siblings of Dale and Diana

John Baker-the father of Paul, Megan, and Joshua. He works with an architectural firm.

Patty Baker-the wife of John Baker, and the mother of Paul, Megan, and Joshua.

Paul Baker-the eldest Baker child. He is 16, sturdily built, but not as tall as Dale. He has brown hair and brown eyes, and normally is considered the calmest and most unflappable of the BBG's. However, he is anything but calm when you put him in front of a keyboard. He can also play the guitar.

Megan Baker-the only daughter of Patty and John. She is 15, petite, with bright blue eyes and short brown hair. She can be vocal and adamant about things she feels strongly about, but she is loyal to her friends and is the most emotionally open and sensitive member of the BBG's.

Joshua Baker-the youngest Baker child. He is 13 years old, and also the youngest BBG. He is as tall as his brother, and looks a good deal like him, with the same brown eyes, but is a blond. He is extremely thoughtful, and can be rather quiet. However, when he does speak, the other kids listen. He has a lot of good things to say. He plays the guitar very well.

Peter Bradford, III-a wealthy businessman, and the father of Pete, Beth, Andy, Jon, Suzi, and Micah. In his business dealings, he has to deal with government officials, and some celebrities, but he prefers the quiet country life.

Emma Bradford-a debutante, wealthy in her own right, the wife of Peter Bradford, III, and the mother of his children. She is poised and gentle, but runs the mansion with a sure hand. She insists on manners in her children, and is teaching them to be at ease with all types of people.

Pete Bradford, IV-the oldest son of Peter and Emma. He is 16, tall, with piercing gray eyes and brown hair. He is considered the most responsible of the BBG's. His music instrument of choice is the guitar.

Elizabeth Bradford-the oldest daughter of Peter and Emma. She prefers the nickname of Beth. She is 15 years old, is tiny with blue eyes and beautiful auburn hair, usually tucked into a ponytail. She is also an outspoken member of the group, but she claims the title of most adventurous as well.

Andrew Bradford-the second son of Peter and Emma. He is 14 years old, with gray eyes and light brown hair that streaks to blond in the summer. He is energetic like Beth, but is more reserved and responsible. He is the group's drummer, but can also play the guitar.

Jon, Suzi, and Micah Bradford- the younger siblings of Pete, Beth, and Andy.

Dave Smith-the ever patient youth group leader. Community Church was his first pastorate, and he started there the year Pete, Paul, and Dale started in the Senior High youth group. It was a crash course in real life outside of his schooling, but Dave managed to come through with honor and the respect of all the members of the Sr. High group. The fathers of the BBG's trust Dave with the most valuable things in their lives, which are their children. Although younger than the BBG fathers, Dave is especially close to them and often looks to them for guidance.

Anne Smith-the wife of Dave and co-leader of the youth group with him.

BEGINNINGS

INTRODUCTION

Many years before the start of this story, a young couple by the name of John and Patti Baker came to live in a home that had been in John's family for generations. It was a stately, old, stone home, built in the early 1800's. It had a shining history associated with it, being used at one point as a stop in the Underground Railroad. The following generations that lived in the house after that kept the small, secret room behind the fireplace in an upstairs bedroom as a testimony to their family's stand during the great Civil War. John Baker himself was an architect, with a love for history. He and his new bride lovingly kept and maintained the home, adding only an extra bathroom, and converting the old kitchen garden into a comfortable patio, complete with the original low stone wall surrounding it. As their married life went on, children were added at a fast pace to the household. Three children were born within 4 years to the couple, and the old house rang with children's laughter and footsteps once again.

When the Baker children were still small and not yet in school, the Ganderson family moved into the parsonage across the field from the Baker's home. The Bakers had faithfully attended the church across the field from their home for many years, and now welcomed their new Pastor and his family to the area. John and Patti were especially delighted to find that Carl Ganderson, and his wife, Kelly, had children the same ages as their own.

The two families became fast friends. By the time that Patti and Kelly sent their oldest sons off to kindergarten, their children were inseparable.

Carl was a good Pastor, and the small Community church grew and flourished under his care. John became an elder in the church, and for several years, they ministered together, watching the church and their children grow.

Shortly after their oldest children turned 9, the farmland across the street from the church, the parsonage, and the Baker home was sold. John, Carl, and their wives began praying for the new owners of the land. Rumors about a wealthy man and his socialite wife building a summer home on the land flew around the tightly knit community. The Bakers and the Gandersons feared the influence that the new owner's children might have on their own country raised kids.

The kids were already watching in awe as the house went up across the street. It was an enormous mansion, and try as their parents might to keep them away from the house, the kids daily went over to explore the large home after the workmen had quit for the day. Even after the doors were put on and were able to be locked, the Baker and Ganderson children made it a point to at least look in the windows to see the progress each day. When the inside construction no longer held their interest, they watched the swimming pool being put in, and then the gardens being landscaped. Finally, three of the largest moving vans the kids had ever seen pulled into the circular drive of the mansion, and unloaded all of their contents. The next day, the kids saw people moving about in and out of the house, and they hurried over to ask if there were any new kids to play with. They were disappointed to find that they had encountered the household help, and not the owners themselves.

Their parents continued to pray. They were frightened by how enamored their children were with the wealth that was already displayed. The next week, the kids were playing in the church's playground that sat between the church and the parsonage when 2 mini-vans pulled up in the circular drive. This time, they watched carefully to see who was getting out. The first van was empty, except for the driver and a woman passenger. Disappointment fell on the little group watching from across the street, but their faces turned into big smiles as the second van's passengers tumbled out. First, a man and a woman got out of the front seats. Then the side sliding doors opened, and out tumbled 5 children! To the Baker and Ganderson children's surprise, that wasn't even all of the children who would live in the big house. They watched as the man reached inside the van, and carried out an infant car seat with yet another child in it! However, since it was supper time, Kelly and Patti were able to keep their children from rushing over that day to immediately introduce themselves.

The next day, however, the poor mothers had no rest until they had packed some of their garden harvest in baskets, and put Carl in charge of 3 month old Kristen Ganderson. The baby slept peacefully as he worked on his message in the den, and the mothers took the older children over to welcome the new family. Both women gave each other anxious looks as they crossed the street and walked down the long drive. They almost turned around completely when their knock was answered by a man in a suit, who was obviously a butler, and not the owner. Their children, however, were not intimidated in the least, and pushed ahead of them, asking politely if the man had any children to play with. The butler smiled and relaxed, and invited the mothers and children inside. They stepped inside the large, round reception room, and once again, Kelly and Patti felt the urge to run away and never return. They felt small and ridiculous standing there in the grandeur of the room, dressed in shorts and T-shirts and carrying farm baskets. The children, as brown as nuts from the country sunshine, chattered excitedly, looking for all the world to their mothers like simple country urchins, with breakfast crumbs still on their shirts.

In just a few short minutes, everyone heard thundering footsteps coming from somewhere upstairs. Patti and Kelly had to smile as 5 rambunctious youngsters fairly flew down the grand, curving staircase after rushing across the balcony to get there. Following them, at a more sedate pace, and coming from a downstairs hallway, were a friendly looking man and woman. Kelly looked at the Bradford children's clothes, and breathed a little easier. The kids were dressed in jean shorts and nice T-shirts. The man introduced himself as Peter Bradford, and his wife as Emma. The Bradford children had already enthusiastically introduced themselves to the other children, and they were all chattering happily. When Emma introduced her children, they stopped giggling and talking long enough to say polite hellos to the other women. Some of Patti and Kelly's worries over the type of influence these children might have on their own youngsters melted as they realized that the Bradford children had beautiful manners for as young as they were. Emma then took the women's baskets, thanking them profusely for their gifts of produce. After some more pleasantries, Peter excused himself, and went back to his office. The children went upstairs to see the Bradford children's bedrooms and playrooms, and Emma invited Patti and Kelly to come back to the kitchen with her to give the produce to the cook.

That was the start of a life-long friendship between all three families. The Bradfords were solid believers, and quickly joined in the work of the Community church. Far from the rumor of a wealthy family's summer home, the Bradfords built their home there as their permanent residence. They wanted to take advantage of the country atmosphere and the somewhat slower pace to raise their children. The three oldest Bradford children quickly became another extension of the Baker and Ganderson families, and the kids formed a rather informal group. They called themselves the BBGs, an acronym for the first letters of their last names, Bakers, Bradfords and Gandersons.

While Peter Bradford's business dealings brought him into the company of well known celebrities, and his wife's family's social standing brought them into contact with more celebrities and government officials, the Bakers and Gandersons found that they had no reason to fear him or his family's influence over their children. The Bradfords lived as simple a life as they could, and often asked for advice in parenting from the Gandersons and Bakers. Because of his humility, Peter Bradford joined John in the eldership of the church a year after moving into the community.

As the children became adolescents, their ability to blend in with their peers was some what hampered by their family circumstances. Paul, Meg, and Josh had to live with their home being an historical landmark and their family name emblazoned on street signs, libraries and even a school within the county. They were frequently called upon to discuss the history of their house in the classroom, which made it very difficult to remain unnoticed.

Dale and Di had a very popular community Pastor for a father. Carl was well loved in the community, and often spoke or offered the blessing at community events. He was also often called when the police or ambulance crew had an emergency to deal with that needed a Pastor's care. Everyone knew and recognized Dale and Di, and the children's term of 'life in a fishbowl' became quite accurate. It seemed as if everyone was watching them and if their behavior wasn't what it should be, their parents inevitably heard about it.

As for the Bradfords, no matter how hard Pete, Beth, or Andy tried to dress "down", or complain about their allowances or pretend like they had no more money than anyone else, everyone seemed to know where they lived, and which celebrities were likely to appear at their house on any given weekend. So like the other BBGs, the Bradford's had many sets of eyes watching them, with little hope of being "just like everybody else".

This unwanted celebrity status led to trouble in the young BBG's lives. They were often teased, or even ridiculed if their family's name happened to appear in the newspapers. Early on in their school careers, they developed a tough outer shell in order to cope and defend themselves. The older boys became the leaders of the little group, and often led the adolescents down wrong or dangerous roads. By the time the boys reached high school, they were a rather troublesome lot. Their parents' prayers became those of desperation at times, and it was with great hope that the church hired a youth pastor at the beginning of the boys' first year in high school. The youth pastor was a young man, with a young wife who was just finishing up her senior year in college. It was his first pastoral position, and as Carl, John, and Peter said many times after that, he certainly earned his keep by shepherding the group he was entrusted with. During his first year, he doggedly kept at the boys to mend their ways and turn to the only true way. He learned to listen to them, to laugh at their funnier antics, and to discipline them for their antics that weren't funny at all. By the time the boys were finishing their sophomore year in high school, however, Dave had been all but worn to a frazzle by the BBGs. Although they technically had too many demerits to go to the church network's spring youth conference that year, Dave felt a strong leading to allow them to come along anyway. He was going to be a keynote speaker there himself, and he dared to hope that something might get through to them there, away from home and away from the girls and younger boys. He was sorely disappointed with the first 2 days of the conference. The boys did not attend many of the meetings, and instead chose to wander the streets of the large city that was hosting the conference. Finally, during the final evening message, Dave arranged for each boy to sit with an unknown adult, separate from the other boys. He gave a powerful message, but his heart fell when he saw Paul and Pete rush out of the conference room the minute he finished talking. He couldn't find Dale at all, and figured he had slipped by his minder and left even before the message was over. Dave returned to his hotel room with a heavy heart. Moments later, however, he got the shock of his life, as he heard worship songs being played in the adjoining room, which was occupied by the three BBGs. Peeking through the partially opened adjoining doors, he realized that it was Dale who was playing those worship songs. Pete was on the floor, sobbing with repentance, and Paul was just about to join him. Dave quickly went to get Anne, his wife, and some of the other adults who had been praying diligently for the BBGs.

Dale had tried his best not to listen to Dave's message. He tried to focus on other subjects, tried to plan something big for the last night at the conference, even tried to mentally shut down his brain so he wouldn't think of anything at all. But a picture kept flashing through his mind, like reruns on the TV. It was the picture of a judge, seated behind his bench, staring angrily at a defendant who stood before him. Standing beside the defendant, with his arm around the defendant's shoulders, pleading to the judge on behalf of the defendant, was Jesus. Dale had tried to blink that picture away many times. He knew about sin, and he was very well versed on repentance. He knew about Jesus. He prayed, sometimes, especially when he needed help getting out of a tight spot, and he was in church most every Sunday. He angrily defended himself by saying that he had paid the price for his sins at the hands of his earthly father and mother. But he couldn't shake the knowledge that there was an eternity waiting for him. And he knew well enough that there were eternal consequences to his actions in the here and now. He knew his repentance had been shallow most of the times, and it was usually repentance from being caught, not for the action itself. He suddenly realized that Jesus was taking and had taken the consequences of his sin upon Himself all of those times. If he was nothing else, Dale was a loyal friend, and the thought of anyone taking his punishment for him, hurt his heart to the core. Tears had not come to Dale's eyes for a very long time before that evening, but now they began to flow out of the sorrow that his heart was bearing. The adult sitting beside him gently took him to a room off of the conference room and let him cry until he was spent, and the sweet presence of the Lord filled Dale's heart.

Meanwhile, Pete and Paul had rushed back to their room after Dave had concluded his message that night, and were waiting for Dale to join them so that they could walk the streets of the city one more time. When Dale arrived at their room, Pete and Paul's mouths flew open. Dale looked as if he had gotten into a tussle with someone, as if he had already been out on the streets without them. His eyes were puffy and bloodshot, his hair was tousled and plastered to his head with sweat, and his face was red and blotchy. Pete and Paul immediately demanded to know who had done that to Dale. They too, were loyal friends, and if someone was big and strong enough to do that to Dale, they weren't going to let it go unnoticed. Dale was still in a state of euphoric shock, and sort of stumbled into the room. He immediately went through the adjoining doors to Dave and Anne's empty room, picked up Dave's guitar and brought it back into the room he shared with Pete and Paul. Pete and Paul knew that Dale could play the guitar, in fact, they both knew how to play and had their own guitars themselves, but the music that came from Dale's playing was some that they had never expected to hear from his hands. They sat on the bed dumbfounded, listening to the worship music he was playing and singing. The message of the first song went straight to Pete's heart. He suddenly realized that while he had everything a teenager could ask for in the material realm, he still had a large void in his life that money was not taking care of. He knew that his mother and father did not have that void, and he had secretly longed to know what they had that he didn't. When Pete looked at Dale, he noticed that the battle scars were fading. The red splotches on his face were gone, and his hair was drying, but Dale looked different somehow. Pete looked a little closer, and when Dale raised his eyes to look back at his friend, Pete saw for the first time that Dale's eyes had softened to a warm brown, capable of melting any heart. The hard, steely eyes that had challenged everyone were gone. With just a few simple words of his own, seemingly spoken as an afterthought while he played, Dale told Pete that it was Jesus he was looking for, and Pete's heart was shattered into a million joyful pieces as he met the Friend Dale had talked so briefly about.

Paul was now worried and confused. He had never seen Pete fall apart quite like that before, and Dale's actions were more than just a little out of character for him. Dale suddenly switched songs, and for a moment, Paul listened to the new lyrics. For him, it was a matter of control. Paul needed to be in control, needed to have a plan, needed to protect himself. It was easy to count on his friends' loyalty, but in the end, he realized that counting on them was simply a part of his plan. He was not a risk taker without a plan, and tonight those character traits translated themselves in Paul's mind, into cowardice. He was afraid to trust anyone else with himself. At the point that Dave peeked in, Dale was speaking to Paul about being afraid. Again, it was just a few short, meaningful words, but Paul knew that he had never, ever, spoken about being afraid or shown fear to anyone. He had to know who had told Dale, or how he had known that Paul thought himself a coward. When Dale shrugged and told him that it was Jesus, Paul's heart fell as well.

What a joyous ride home that turned out to be! Everyone was so excited about the dramatic turn of events, and the obvious changes in the boys. Everyone that is, except for Beth, Meg, and Diana. They were furious. It made no difference to them that the boys still did most of the same things, going to movies, going out to eat, and going to the mall, which they had done before the conference. To the girls, it seemed as if the thrill of life had been sucked out of them, when actually it was only the thrill of forbidden treasure that had been taken away. Even when their parents rewarded the boys' changes in attitudes with driving permits which very quickly turned into driving licenses, the girls refused to give in or be impressed. Grieving over the potential in her own mind for a long, boring summer and the loss of her long standing friendship with her brother and Paul and Dale, Beth asked her father to send them all to the shore for a week. Peter agreed, and made arrangements for a young couple in his employ to take the teens to the beach house he had rented for the summer. It started out as a long and dreary vacation trip, and it looked for a while as if it was going to be the funeral of the BBGs as a group as well. The girls were just not giving in. They wanted the old Pete, Paul and Dale back and nothing else would satisfy them. The boys made a point of doing everything that they had done the previous summer, but it was their heart attitude that the girls didn't like. There was no sneaking into 'R' rated movies, they saw movies that were popular, but open to their age group. They did not make attempts to stay on the beach after it closed by hiding under piers and behind dunes, they left the public beaches at the appropriate time, and used their own private beach for campfires and late night strolls. To the girls, it simply wasn't 'fun' any more. After many shouting matches, slammed doors, icy cold stares, and long silent meals, Di made it a point late one night to interrupt the boys' talking in the living room to sever her relationship with them. Instead, however, she ended up being introduced to the same friend that had made such a difference in the boys' lives. The next evening, as the boys and Di sat in the living room talking, Meg came in to accuse the boys of meddling in the girls' affairs and for getting Di 'over to their side'. She was as angry as any of them had ever seen her, and yet, by the time the night was over, she too had fallen in love with the new Friend they had introduced her to. Finally, Beth could take it no longer. In a dream, she saw herself as being left behind from all the others. She woke up early and disturbed that morning, and took a walk on the private beach to clear her head. Paul was also awake, and followed her, and introduced her to the friend they had all spoken about so lovingly. The ride home from the shore was much different than the ride down, with unity all but restored to the group. Shortly after they arrived home, Josh and Andy came into the saving part of grace as well, and then the BBGs were complete. Their lives changed from the inside out. They were still the energetic, fun loving group they had always been, but now there was a genuine love between them and a hunger that Dave had a hard time trying to fill with his messages to the youth. The most astounding part of their transformation, however, was their music. It had ceased being a sign of rebellion, and took on a Christian tone. From there, it went to worship songs, and from there it took off on a life of its own. They no longer did it just for something to pass the time or to entertain others. It became a very real part of them, something they simply needed to do.

This is where the BBGs find themselves as the story begins. I invite you to read on, and enjoy the adventure!

CHAPTER 1

On an early summer Sunday morning in rural southern Pennsylvania, the open windows of the Community church allowed the sweet scent of flowering trees to come into the sanctuary. The regular worship song period had just ended, and a group of teenagers were setting up to give the congregation the first glimpse of their musical talent. They did 2 songs that the congregation clapped enthusiastically along with, and then they quickly set their guitars in the guitar stands and found their seats in the first long pew. To any visitors in the congregation, the teens were an obviously delightful, talented group. To the regular worshipers who came on Sundays to hear the message and participate in worship, the teens were also easily recognized as the children of the Pastor and the two elders. To those who knew the families of these teens well, however, this morning's debut was nothing short of a miracle. For several years, the friends of the families had prayed for the teenagers, but had seen little in the way of answers. Then, just a few short months ago, life had changed for the teens, and they had given friends and family alike a wild but wondrous emotional roller coaster ride on the start of their new lives with the Lord.

The group consisted of three 16-year-old boys, Dale Ganderson, the Pastor's son, and Pete Bradford and Paul Baker, sons of the church's two elders. Also included in the group were the boys' younger sisters, who were all 15-years old; Diana Ganderson, Beth Bradford and Megan Baker. Wrapping up the group were the younger brothers, Andy Bradford, age 14, and Josh Baker, age 13.

They lived their lives in the fishbowl of the church and community, which everyone agreed was not easy to do. The community well knew the children of a popular Pastor, a millionaire neighbor, and the children of a family whose lives in the area had spanned the generations back to the revolutionary war. Many in the church family also knew their Pastor and his two elders well, and with that, knew their parenting styles. To those close family friends who sat in the congregation, it sometimes seemed as though they were living through a chapter of a Tom Sawyer type story. Those friends knew what it meant when the Pastor gave a certain look in the direction of his children on a Sunday morning. They knew that the children were expected to behave properly in the church service, and that there would be consequences if they didn't.

This morning, however, there was no doubt about the look on the Pastor's face as he approached the microphone. Beaming at the teens, he made several announcements, and then, as if he could not hold his joy in any longer, made an announcement of his own.

"I know we don't have Special Music here on a regular basis, but I hope you'll forgive me when I say that the music we just heard this morning was really, really special music. Thanks, guys, for giving us those songs," he said.

The teens were sitting close enough to the front to see the tears misting in the Pastor's eyes. As the congregation applauded, the Pastor motioned for the teens to stand up. With flaming faces, they faced the congregation and received the applause.

It was obvious to everyone there that they were well loved by their parents and friends alike.

The church family was not alone in their affection towards the teens. Some of the BBGs were officers in their respective classes at school, and they were all good teammates in the several different sports that they were involved in. But for all the love and acceptance that they did receive, life in a fishbowl is never easy, and there were many, many eyes on them wherever they happened to be. While word about what they had done only occasionally made its way back to their parents, the fact that they had been caught by someone whom they were sure to run into again, at church or a social gathering, was difficult for the teens to bear for any length of time. That pressure often drove the teens to confess to their parents quickly, instead of taking the risk that someone else would beat them to the story.

For now, though, school was out for the summer and the older boys had just gotten their driver's licenses. They had just spent a week at the shore where the girls had found the Friend the boys had spoken so highly about. Andy and Josh had followed suit just days after their return home. Their parents were still in a state of euphoric shock from the changes in the teens' lives, and all seemed well in the world and in the fragrant breezes that wafted through the church that morning.

After the service, Dave Smith, the young youth Pastor, approached the group as they stood outside the doors to the lobby.

"Hey, Pete, Paul, Dale! How about working up a worship set for youth group tonight? Maybe about 6 songs?" he asked

"But, Dave, that's your job," Dale said.

Dave laughed. "Yes, and it's one job that I would gladly give up to some qualified kids," he replied.

"Do you really think we're qualified?" asked Pete.

"I certainly do, and this morning proved it. Will you give it a try?" Dave asked.

Dale looked at Pete and Paul, who nodded.

"Sure. We'll give it a try tonight," said Dale.

"Great. Paul, if you want to play the keys, you can. I'm just looking for more of what I heard this morning," Dave said, smiling at the kids' genuinely surprised faces.

"Okay, we better get working on it, then. Come on guys," Dale said, and the group waved to Dave as they headed across the parking lot to the Ganderson's home.

As they sat on the patio picnic table and benches, trying to decide the afternoon's activities, Paul suddenly said, "Well, we need to put some thought into this worship tonight, gang. The best place I know for quiet thinking and praying is the rocks on the lake. We might as well take a picnic with us while we're there, huh?"

Pete laughed. "I've never known us to need an excuse for a picnic before, but, hey, I'm game. I'll see if I can borrow the van this afternoon," he offered.

"We can stop at the Pizza Place and grab some subs and chips. We have a bunch of soda cans in the downstairs fridge. I'll grab some of those," Meg put in.

"And I just baked 2 pans of brownies. I'll grab one of the pans!" added Diana.

"Yummy!" replied Pete. "I'll grab the paper towels and the garbage bag. If I can get the van, I'll meet you all back here in 15 minutes," he said, starting off in a trot to his home across the street.

"Wait! What if your parents are using the van?" called Di.

"Uh, I'll see you sooner. We'll just do the picnic in our backyard!" he called back over his shoulder.

"I'll call you if we aren't coming back with the van," Beth said as she hurried after her brother.

Meg hurried home to get the sodas with Josh. The rest of the teens piled into the Ganderson's kitchen while Di cut her brownies and put them into a large plastic bag.

"Hey, Dale, Go upstairs to my room and grab my backpack, OK? You guys will have guitars to pack, so I guess it'll be up to us girls to haul the food," Diana said

"We do have Andy and Josh, you know. But if you really want to carry the food, I'll go get your pack," Dale suggested.

"Thanks, but if you're volunteering those two, why don't you get your pack? I hardly think they want to be seen wearing a hot pink backpack," Diana giggled.

"Geesh. All right, you win. It's my pack. I just hope your brownies are light and fluffy this time," Dale said, disappearing up the stairs to his room before Di could throw the wet dishcloth she had in her hand at him.

Pete and Beth arrived back at the Ganderson's home in their van just as Meg and Josh stepped onto the Ganderson's patio. Meg handed Paul a bag.

"Here, Paul. Mom says not to go charging through the woods in those clothes," she said.

"Thanks, Meg. I'll be right back down. Dale, can I use your room?" Paul asked as he headed towards the stairs.

"Sure, Paul. Andy, do you want to change too?" Dale answered, looking at Andy.

"I guess I should have gone home," Andy said, looking down at his clean khaki pants and nice polo shirt.

"Moms are all programmed the same, Andy. Here are your clothes," Pete grinned as he handed his brother a bag of clothes as well. The kids all laughed, and Andy followed Paul up to Dale's room.

Finally, they were ready to go. After a quick stop to grab some subs and chips, Pete turned the van towards the nearby state park. After picnicking and practicing some worship songs, they rested on the rocks jutting into the lake for some time before returning to the church.

That evening, as Josh and Andy walked by the Sr. High youth room, Dave noticed them looking into the doorway with long, wistful faces. He spoke to one of the other youth leaders, and asked him when Andy and Josh would be eligible to move up to the Sr. High group from their Middle School group.

"Andy should be joining us this fall," the other adult answered, "but Josh is only going into the 8th grade. He has another year to go yet before coming over here."

"Wow. That's going to be tough on that group of friends, isn't it?" Dave asked.

The other adult agreed that the separation would be difficult for the BBG's.

"How many 8th graders do we have over there? Are there a lot of them?" Dave asked.

"I don't know, but I'll go check on it for you," the other adult said, and left to speak to the Middle School leaders. He came back shortly afterward, and said, "Bottom line, Dave, is that they expect to have 24 kids over there this fall. Seven of those will be in 8th grade with Josh."

"Man, I hate to split the BBG's up, especially at this point in their lives. Josh needs the older kids right now. Let me talk to Carl first, but maybe we can work something out," Dave said thoughtfully.

Later, after youth group was over, the teens walked to the Pizza Place for their usual ice cream treat. Dave found Carl sitting on a bench near the children's playground, watching his youngest daughter playing with some of her friends. After some pleasantries between the two friends, Dave asked Carl what he thought about the possibility of giving the 8th graders a choice between the Sr. High group and the Middle school group. He explained Josh's position, and why he thought it was important to keep him with the rest of the BBG's.

"Well, Dave, I'm all for it, as long as we still have enough 6th and 7th graders to keep a Middle School group going. Why don't you talk to the Middle School kids and see if there is an interest in moving up a year ahead of time.

Maybe we can make it on a case by case basis. Find out the answers there, and then report back to us at the Leadership meeting on Thursday night, OK?" Carl answered.

Dave nodded, spoke with Carl for a few more moments, and then found his wife and went home.

On Wednesday night, Dave approached the Middle School group, and told them a little more about the Sr. High group. He talked to them about the possibility of giving the 8th graders a choice of staying with the Middle school group or moving up to the High School group in the fall. He asked them to think about it, and then let him know at the end of the meeting if they would be interested in doing that. When he returned to the Middle School group after both meetings were over, the response was as he had hoped it would be. Josh was the only 8th grader interested in joining the older group that fall.

The next evening, Dave brought that information to the adults attending the Leadership meeting, and they agreed unanimously that Josh should be allowed to move up to the Sr. High group with Andy that fall.

The BBGs were playing their guitars up in their tree house behind the parsonage when the Leadership meeting broke up. Dave walked over to the benches situated around the playground with Carl Ganderson, John Baker, and Peter Bradford, and the men sat for a while listening to the music coming down from the tree in the corner of the yard.

"They've really found something special," Dave said, quietly.

"Yes, it's like candy to my ears," agreed Carl.

"Thank you Lord, for hearing our rather desperate prayers," put in Peter Bradford.

"And now, just keep the fire burning, Lord," added John Baker.

When the teens had finished singing, they climbed down from the tree house, and were quite surprised to find their fathers and Dave praying on the benches surrounding the playground.

"These adults get weirder every day," joked Andy.

"I agree," said Meg, laughing.

The men heard them, and finished their prayers with a chuckle.

"Come here a second, guys," said Carl.

"We're only joking, Dad," said Dale, glancing at Andy.

Carl laughed. "You're not in trouble. We actually have some good news for you," he said.

The group then approached the men expectantly.

"We've decided to let Josh move up to the Sr. High group this fall with Andy," Dave said, and was totally unprepared for the whooping response that followed.

"I'm glad you approve," laughed John Baker.

"Dad, you just don't know! It's another answer to prayer! Just last Sunday, at the rocks on the lake, we all prayed for a way for us to be together this fall!" Meg said, jumping up and down.

The men looked at each other in amazement.

"Dave, did you know about that?" asked Carl.

Dave shook his head no. "I thought my idea was an original one," he replied, and then added, "but I'm glad to know I was hearing the Lord's voice, even if it was without me knowing it," he chuckled.

The ecstatic teens all hurried home with their fathers, none of them happier than Josh. He was only 13, but he had always managed to keep up with Meg and Paul, making him seem older than what he was. Although Dale and Di's younger brother Steve was only a year younger than Josh, there was a wide difference between the two boys in the eyes of the BBG's, and Josh definitely belonged with them. Josh had been worried about Andy moving up to the Sr. High group without him, fearing that the other kids would forget about him. He needn't have worried at all. In spite of the 3 year age difference between him and the oldest boys, they all looked at Josh as an equal.

The next morning, the sun was shining brightly as Diana hung laundry on the clothesline in her backyard. She waved a wet towel in Meg's direction as Meg stood and stretched in her family's garden. The peas and strawberries were coming in fast and Patti Baker was busy freezing both of them with Meg's help. Every morning, Meg went out and gathered ripe berries, took them inside, and then went back out to pick the peas. While her mom capped the berries and cleaned them, Meg shelled the peas. Most mornings found Di doing the same chores in their family's garden, but on laundry mornings like today, it was Steve's turn to harvest the crops. Di could see Steve picking the peas from their trellis now, and she was glad that Kristen could help shell the peas this year. That meant that today, when the 3 loads of laundry were washed and hung on the line, she was free to do what she wanted for the rest of the day until the early evening when the clothes had to be folded and brought in again. Today, in between laundry duties, Di intended to go over and spend the day with the other BBGs at the Bradford's home.

Dale had the lawn tractor out and was cutting the grass around the church. After that, he'd get the trimmer out, and then this evening, he'd water the flowers around the outside of the church building. Everything would look bright, clean and green for Sunday.

Josh and Paul were busy painting the white picket fence around their backyard. They had finished half of it yesterday, and intended to finish the rest of it today before lunch.

Di went into the house for the last basket of clothes, chuckling. Seeing her friends and siblings working, she wondered what Pete, Beth and Andy were up to that morning. It was certainly not laundry, or gardening or home maintenance. She giggled out loud at the memory of Beth's futile attempts to do chores. The woman who came every day to do the large family's laundry was indignant with Beth for following her around and wanting to learn how to do the job.

"Miss, you'll never have a need to do laundry. Can't you just go learn fashion design or something if you're interested in clothes?" the poor laundress had finally pleaded. Frequently after that, on laundry days, Beth would come over and join Di or Meg, and attempt to learn how to be normal, as Beth put it.

When Beth had inquired about putting in a small vegetable patch in her backyard, the gardener was aghast.

"Dig up a perfectly good grass to put in vegetables that will simply encourage weeds? I think not, Miss," he said.

Of course, if Beth had mentioned any of this to her parents, they would have surprised the gardener, the cook, the laundress and the other employees by telling them to go ahead and teach Beth the skills she was longing to learn. But instead of complaining to her parents, Beth simply found her answers at her best friends' homes by helping them. At the young age of 15, she had no desire to marry into money, and instead, had a feeling that one day, she would need the knowledge she was gaining at the homes of her friends. However, she did spend time with her mother, learning the art of running a large home with servants. She wanted to be able to help her mother with her chores, like the other girls did, even if her mother's chores involved very little physical work. Beth was even becoming quite adept at flower arranging, putting together menus, keeping track of cleaning the large house, and having the proper workmen come in to do needed maintenance work.

Diana decided that Pete was probably on the computer, going over sites and updating them or gathering information for his father to analyze.

Andy was likely to be going over budgets and calling merchants to order and purchase household goods. Diana giggled again. No merchant would ever let her buy something over the phone, let alone someone a year younger than her. However, Mr. Bradford had personally sent letters out to everyone he did business with, authorizing Pete, Beth or Andy to make purchases under a certain amount. Nobody seemed to have a problem with that over at the Bradfords.

CHAPTER 2

When Dale was finished with the grass trimming, he got out the hose and washed off the lawn tractor and blade that he had used earlier to cut the wide area of lawn around the church. Carl Ganderson was working on his sermon in the church office, and happened to glance out the window. Seeing his oldest son hard at work, he decided to take a break from writing his Sunday message and go outside. Dale saw him coming out of the church, and greeted him cheerfully.

"Hi, Dad!" he said.

Carl smiled at his son's greeting. Just a few short months ago, Dale's response to his father's coming outside would have been drastically different. Back then, Dale would have been nothing but defensive at the appearance of his father. He would have demanded to know what he had done wrong that had brought his father outside to check up on him.

"You know, Dale," Carl said as he put his arm around his son's shoulders, "you will never know how proud I am of you and how happy I am with this brand new son I've acquired."

Dale laughed and started to roll up the hose.

"Gee, Dad, I didn't know Mom was pregnant again," he said with a grin.

Carl laughed, too.

"Bite your tongue, Dale. Kristen is the last of this Ganderson family. Seriously, though, son, the Lord has really turned your life around. I'm proud of you for allowing Him to work in you like that," he said.

Dale finished with the hose, and then turned to face his father.

"Does it really show on the outside, Dad? I only feel different on the inside," he asked.

"Yes, Dale, it does show. You can't hide what's inside of you. What's in your heart will eventually flow out of not just your mouth, but your actions, your eyes and your facial expressions as well. You are a changed man," Carl answered.

Dale looked down at the ground while he dug in his pocket for the keys to the tractor. Finding them, he looked up at his father, smiled and said, "Thanks".

Carl patted him on the back and then walked back into his office. Dale hurried to put the tractor away and change into his swimsuit. He was hungry, and he didn't want to miss any of the lunch served around the Bradford's pool.

At lunch time, with all their chores done, the teens gathered at the tables on the deck around the Bradford's pool. They began to eat the BLT sandwiches the cook had brought out, along with a bag of BBQ potato chips, and fresh carrots. During the meal, Beth reminded them all of the volleyball game scheduled that evening with another church's youth group. The Sr. High kids played in a church youth volleyball league, and Andy and Josh normally tagged along to act as ball boys.

"Who are we playing tonight?" asked Pete.

"The team that was undefeated last year," replied Diana.

"Oh, man, you mean that team that has all those rough kids on it?" asked Paul.

"That's the one," said Diana.

The kids moaned, but then quickly forgot any thoughts of the other team as they finished lunch, cleaned their tables up, and returned to the pool for an afternoon of swimming fun. Later that afternoon, they separated so the Bakers and Gandersons could go home and finish their chores. Dale needed to water the flowers around the church as well as the family's garden, and Paul needed to water his own family's plants and vegetables. Diana needed to fold the clothes that were drying on the clothesline and take them inside.

Back at the Ganderson household, Kristen, the 7-year old baby of the family, had a friend her age over to play for the day. Being the baby of the family, she was pampered by all of her siblings, but Dale especially had a soft spot in his heart for her. When Dale started to water the plants, Kristen and her friend romped and teased Dale as he worked, baiting him to squirt them. Finally, when he was finished, Dale turned the hose on Kristen and her playmate. He intended only on getting their feet and legs wet, but the playmate mischievously found the faucet to the hose and turned it on full blast. The powerful surge of water caught Dale off guard, and the hose leaped in his hand. It shot the water right at Kristen's face.

"Ow! Hey, Dale, stop!" Kristen cried as the water stung her face.

Dale quickly turned the hose away from Kristen, but managed instead to turn it, full blast, into the open window of the church's kitchen.

"Yikes!" he exclaimed, as he turned the hose again, this time making the water hit his father in the back as he came out of his office.

"Hey!" Carl exclaimed as Dale frantically dropped the hose and lunged for the faucet, getting himself soaked by the flailing hose. As the water slowed to a trickle, Kristen and her friend started to laugh at Dale, shaking his dripping hair like a dog.

"Dale? Want to tell me why you gave me that impromptu shower, mopped the church's kitchen floor, and got your sister and her friend drenched? Didn't you think before you put the water on so high?" Carl asked.

Dale knew his Dad was annoyed with him.

"I didn't," he started to say, and then noticed Kristen's friend's face start to crumple into tears. "I didn't realize the pressure was so strong," he finished lamely.

Kristen and her friend grinned at him for not squealing on them.

Carl looked at the silent exchange between his children, and then said, "Well, Kristy, you had better go find some dry clothes for you and Jenny. Mom just called and said that supper is ready, so be quick, now."

Kristen and her friend ran for the house.

"And you'd better get dried off and then clean up the church kitchen mess, Dale," Carl said to his son.

Dale looked at his watch. He wasn't going to make that volleyball game if he didn't hurry.

"Sure, Dad. We have a volleyball game tonight, so could you ask Di to make me a sandwich to take with me, please? And tell Mom I'm sorry that I won't be able to eat with you guys?" Dale asked before sprinting across the parking lot and into the house.

Carl laughed in spite of his wet shirt.

"Sure, Dale," he called after his son.

In spite of hurrying as fast as he could, though, the youth church bus pulled out of the parking lot just as Dale gathered up the wet towels in the church kitchen. He ran the towels over to his house, put them into the washing machine, and then grabbed his sandwich from the kitchen counter on his way to the garage.

"Oh, man, I need the keys!" he exclaimed to himself as he reached the family's mini van and realized that he didn't have the keys. He then tried to slow down a little, and walked back into the house to find his father while he ate his sandwich.

"Now, don't go racing over to the game, Dale. No volleyball game is worth your life or even a speeding ticket. Understand?" Carl said as he handed Dale the keys.

"You're right, Dad, and don't worry! I'll be careful!" Dale said, trying not to sound rushed.

Kristen and Jenny met him at the garage when he arrived for the second time.

"We're sorry," they both said sincerely.

Dale stopped to give them both hugs. "Don't worry about it girls. Now get far away from the car, OK? I want to get there before they finish all three games," he said, and grinned at them as they ran, giggling, out of the garage and to the playground.

Dale drove safely to the game, which was being held on the lawn of another church, and arrived just after the finish of the short devotional time held before each set of games.

"Hey, Dale, aren't you disqualified from playing because you missed the devotional?" a large boy from the other team sneered at Dale. He had heard rumors of Dale's conversion, and had made it his goal for the evening to feel him out and see if the rumor was fact. Upon hearing the boy's words, Dale was crestfallen. He knew the rules, and unfortunately, the unruly boy was right. Dale looked over at where Dave stood. Dave smiled over at him and said, kindly, "Don't worry, Dale. Your Dad explained every thing to me, and said you'd be a little late. Mr. Bently and I have decided that it's OK for you to play."

Dale sighed, and took his position on the team. He helped the other BBG's and their team win the first match. Then the other team won the second match. In the final match of the evening, Dale found himself face to face across the net from the boy whose wise cracks had tormented him all evening, starting with the question of his eligibility to play at all.

"Heard you found religion," the boy sneered again at Dale. Dale said nothing in response. In fact, he had not answered the boy's taunts all evening, which by itself was a feat that Pete, Paul, and Dave found amazing. Dale's lack of response alone should have told the boy that Dale had indeed changed.

Suddenly, the ball was on Dale's side. Meg set the shot up from the third row. In the second row, Pete put it up for Dale's spike from the net. Dale jumped for it, but suddenly felt a stabbing pain in his shin when the boy across the net kicked him. Dale grabbed at his shin, and the spike was lost. The ball then fell easily to the other side and they returned it. Dale stood painfully by the net, and when the ball came to him again, he tried once more to spike it to the other side. This time, in an apparent misjudgment of Dale's move, the boy on the opposing team crashed into the net, hitting Dale fully in the chest. The boy hit Dale with enough force to knock him to the ground, and as Dale fell, the other boy laughed and sneered again. All the frustration of the evening, and the physical pain he was feeling burst into Dale's consciousness as he hit the ground, hard. He raised both fists and slammed them into the ground with anger. Before he could even think about it, the words, "D— it, Phillip!" had escaped from his mouth.

Immediately, the other youth group leader called, "Foul language! Son, you're out of the game."

Dale was shocked. "But didn't you see what he did?" he asked.

Mr. Bently, the other team's youth group leader, shrugged.

"Volleyball is a rough sport, and accidents can happen," he said nonchalantly.

"Yeah, like accidentally being undefeated last year. Guess we all know how that happened, now don't we?" Dale said angrily.

"Arguing with the ref is a technical foul. One point to the Walnut Grove team," Mr. Bently said, and then added, "Now will you leave the game or will it be a forfeit for your team?"

Dale glared momentarily, then got up and walked off the field. On his way back to his car, he brushed past Dave.

"It's OK, Dale, I saw what happened, and I've been listening to the kid's taunts all evening. Don't worry about it," Dave whispered as Dale walked by him.

Dale barely looked at Dave to acknowledge his support. Instead, he went and sat in his car, resting his head on the steering wheel.

"God! I blew it again! I let him get to me. I am so sorry for my temper," Dale prayed, and then closed his eyes and waited for his emotions to calm down.

After the game, which Dale's team rallied and won, a much calmer Dale joined his team to shake hands with the opposing players. When he reached the boy who had spent the evening testing him, he shook hands with him and said, "I'm sorry, Phillip. I had no right to lose my cool with you."

Phillip looked unbelievably at Dale. The Dale Ganderson that he knew last year in school was not the apologizing kind. Phillip knew that he had been taking a big risk by teasing Dale like he did. Had the rumors of Dale's conversion been false, Phillip realized that he could have expected retaliation in some form or another after the game and away from the eyes of the youth leaders. Instead, there had been no verbal come backs at all to even the most vile of Phillip's taunts, and now Dale was apologizing for being angry over the physical abuse Phillip had heaped on him.

"Uh, sure Dale, me too," was the only thing Phillip could think of to say.

Dale smiled inside. He knew that Phillip was confused about his actions, and just knowing that gave Dale more pleasure than the act of physically decking him ever would have given him.

After going through the team's line, Dale walked over to where Mr. Bently and Dave stood.

"I apologize for my outburst. I really am trying to learn how to control this temper. Obviously, I'm not as far with it as I thought I was," Dale said to the men.

Dave put his arm around Dale's shoulders. "You're forgiven, Dale," he said, smiling.

" I was a PK too, so I understand," Mr. Bently added, and then said, "I saw how Phillip baited you tonight, and you handled yourself pretty well until you reached the boiling point."

"Thanks," Dale smiled at the men, and then went to join the other kids standing around a table full of drinks and snacks.

The other BBG's noticed that Phillip was now quiet with his taunts, and that he stood apart from the crowd and ate his snack with a wary eye on Dale and his friends.

"What did you say to him in the team line?" asked Pete.

"I apologized for reacting the way I did," Dale said with a grin.

Pete laughed. "Way to go, Dale. Get even by messing with his head," he said.

"Hey, it worked, didn't it?" Dale replied.

Pete shook his head and smiled, and then walked over to talk to some other friends. Both teams talked for a while and then the groups began to board their buses to go back to their churches.

"Want to ride along and pick up the pizza and movie with me?" Dale asked Pete and Meg, who were standing with him by his car.

"Sure," Pete said, and then called over to Dave. "Dave? Meg and I are going to ride home with Dale!" he said.

Dave shook his head no, and walked over to the 3 teens.

"Youth Group Rule number 59 states: He who comes on the bus, goes home on the bus," he said in a voice that sounded vaguely Asian.

"Aw, Dave, that's so that kids don't go off with their friends without their parents' permission. You know our parents wouldn't mind if we went home with Dale," Pete said.

"Please? You know us," Meg added.

"Really, I'm sorry, guys. There are a million 'what ifs' to every rule. I'm flexible for good reasons, but not for every whim that hits you," Dave explained.

"Great. Just great," mumbled Dale, as he opened the car door and got in.

"We'll meet you in the church's parking lot," said Meg, leaning into the open window.

"Sure," said Dale grumpily. Meg walked over to the bus and got on, and Dale started the car and drove to the Pizza Place by himself. He picked up the 2 pizzas and the movie they had planned to watch that evening at the Bradford's home, and then drove home. When he pulled his family's car into their garage, the rest of the group sat waiting for him on the Ganderson's patio. Dale gave the pizzas to Pete and the movie to Beth, and then went inside to give the car keys back to his father. Finally, the group walked across the street to the Bradford's. They went immediately into the spacious family room and opened the pizza. The cook had placed some paper plates, napkins, cups and a gallon of lemonade on a side table for the teens, and they hurriedly filled their plates and took their seats in front of the TV. Andy put the movie in and turned on the VCR, and the teens settled in to eat their traditional Friday pizza and watch their movie. About 20 minutes into the show, Peter Bradford buzzed into the room on the intercom.

"Dale, can you pick up the phone? It's your dad," Mr. Bradford said as his voice floated into the room.

Dale picked up the family room's phone extension, while Pete pushed the talk button on the intercom and thanked his father for the message.

"Yes, Dad?" Dale said.

"I think you'd better come home, Dale," Carl Ganderson said.

"Is something wrong, Dad?" Dale asked, fear creeping into his voice.

The rest of the BBG's in the room heard the fear in Dale's voice, and stopped the movie. They turned and watched Dale as he continued his phone conversation. His face grew cloudy as he heard the next words his father had to say.

"Everyone's fine here, son. But I just got a phone call from an angry mother about you. She came to the volleyball game to pick up her daughter, and she says you exploded on a play and swore at one of her daughter's teammates. She was terribly unhappy that her daughter was exposed to such poor sportsmanship and language in a church league," Carl said seriously.

"But, Dad, Dave will vouch for me. I got out of the game and later apologized to the kid for my outburst. Did the mother manage to mention that?" Dale said.

"You got out of the game? How about getting kicked out of the game and then earning the other team a technical point for mouthing off to the ref?" Carl said.

"I see she did manage to touch on all the bad highlights of the game," Dale said angrily, and then added, "I also apologized to Dave and Mr. Bently, who was the ref who gave me the technical foul."

"Dale, I didn't really call to discuss the matter. I called to ask you to come home, now. Ask Paul to walk Diana home after the movie," Carl said.

"Dad, the movie just started. I paid the price for my dumb actions at the game," Dale pleaded.

"But you didn't pay my price, Dale, and it's going to cost you more than a missed movie if you argue about it any further," Carl said sternly.

"All right. But life in this fishbowl still stinks," Dale said angrily, and hung up.

Turning to face his friends, he said, "Well, this just ends a perfect night. I'm being recalled because some woman called Dad and complained about what I did at the game. How did she know who I was, and why can't I just be Joe Schmoe, the anonymous kid?" he groaned.

Pete and Paul got up to see Dale to the door.

"Hey, Paul, will you walk Di home after the movie?" Dale suddenly remembered to ask.

"Sure, Dale, and don't worry. We can always rent this movie again," Paul said.

"Yeah, don't take it so hard," added Pete.

"Good night. See you guys tomorrow," Dale said.

He walked slowly down the long driveway and across the street to his own home. When he came into his own family room, he found that his family was also watching a movie. He grabbed a handful of popcorn from the bowl on the coffee table and sat down beside Steve to watch it with them.

Carl looked over at his son, and said, "Dale? I'd prefer that you go to your room."

"My room?" asked Dale in an incredulous tone.

"Your room, or my den. With me," Carl said pointedly.

"I'm going, I'm going. There's a law against double jeopardy in this country. I wish it applied to this family," Dale grumbled as he picked himself up off the couch and walked up the stairs to his room.

About an hour later, Carl also went upstairs to Dale's room. He found Dale lying on his bed with his headphones on and his eyes closed. Carl tapped him lightly on the shoulder, and Dale jumped.

"Sorry, Dad, I didn't hear you," Dale said, taking off the headphones.

"I can see that," Carl said with a smile. "I'm sorry for breaking into your own personal concert, but I just wanted to say good-night. I also wanted to make sure you're not still mad at me before I turn in for bed," Carl said.

Dale smiled and said, "No, I'm not mad anymore."

"I'm glad for that, Dale, and I am sorry that you and Diana and Steve and Kristen have to live with the community's eyes watching your every move. But you know, getting better at controlling your temper isn't going to come by just saying a few words. You're only going to learn to control it by practice. If you don't get any practice, your self-control isn't going to get any stronger. Understand?" Carl said gently.

"You're right there, too, Dad. I just think I over-practiced tonight. From Jenny's prank, to Phillip's abuse, to Dave's refusal to let Pete and Meg ride home with me instead of on the bus, to being recalled from the Bradford's house just as I was getting into the movie; it's just been a very bad night," Dale sighed.

"You have taken the brunt of things tonight, haven't you? I'm sorry for that, Dale, but the end result is that you're getting stronger," Carl said sympathetically.

"Maybe so," grinned Dale, "but I need a break from all this practicing."

"Well, good night, then, Dale. Sleep well," Carl said as he patted his son on the back and left the room.

"Good night, Dad," Dale replied as he put the earphones back on.

Chapter 3

On Saturday morning, Carl, Peter, and John had breakfast together at a local diner. While they were eating, they discussed the idea of taking their families on a camping expedition. Since all the men were able to take a few days off from their jobs the following week, they decided to leave on Monday morning and return home in time for the evening church service and youth group meeting on Wednesday. To make it easier, they chose a familiar campground that was only an hour's drive from their homes.

When the fathers returned home later that morning and announced the trip, the teens were ecstatic about the news. They loved camping, especially when the three families camped together, which they frequently did. The kids all pitched in to help ready their family's camping gear for the first camp-out of the summer.

The Gandersons owned a pop-up camper, which Dale and Steve aired out. Diana helped her father air out the tent that Dale and Steve usually slept in.

The Bakers also used a pop-up with a tent for the boys. The Bradfords, on the other hand, had a self contained camper that slept all 8 of them and was pulled by a large van.

Bright and early on Monday morning, Peter Bradford pulled his van and camper out of his driveway. As soon as he passed by the Ganderson's driveway, Carl pulled his vehicles in behind, and then John Baker brought up the rear. The camper caravan made it to the campground without incident, and the children all helped to set up camp after the men pulled into their designated spots.

With the work done, the BBG's packed themselves a bag lunch and set off on foot for some of their favorite trails. They spent the rest of the morning and the early afternoon hiking and rowing on the small lake tucked into the woods of the camping area.

That evening, Dale, Josh, and Pete brought out their guitars and the families enjoyed a sing-a-long around the campfire before heading to bed.

The next day, as the BBG's explored, they ran into some kids they knew from school, who were camping in another section of the campground with their families. Although the BBG's didn't know the other teens well, they agreed to go along on a hike with them. As the teens walked and talked, one of the other kids offered the BBG's a cigarette.

"No, thanks," Beth said for all of the BBGs.

"C'mon, I know you guys smoke," said one of the other boys.

"Not anymore," Diana said emphatically.

"Yeah, we quit last February. Pete almost got pneumonia, and we got a look at his lungs," Paul said.

"I'd be a blimp if I didn't smoke," argued one of the other girls.

"Better blimp than dead," mumbled Beth.

The group walked on in companionable silence until they reached the part of the trail that ended at the small lake that the BBGs had rowed on the day before. They all decided to eat their lunches there, and when they were through, they hiked back to their own campsites.

While the BBG's were hiking, their mothers took the younger children to the pool. They left the men sitting and relaxing in their lawn chairs at the camp site. Although Patti Baker did not have any younger children, she tagged along with Emma and Kelly anyway.

"Well, I must say, it does feel good not to have any young ones to keep from drowning anymore," Patti joked with her friends.

"I will loan you any one of mine at any time," laughed Emma. All three of the mothers were really very devoted to their families, but because they were such close friends, they were able to have and share a sense of humor between themselves about the difficult work of child raising. The truth was, that over the years each mother had provided childcare and babysitting services to all the BBGs and their siblings on occasions that were too numerous to count.

Several hours later, while the younger children were still swimming, the BBG's returned to their campsite. They decided to get their guitars out of their campers and jam for a little while. Going to his family's camper to get his instrument, Pete walked past his father, who was sitting in a chaise lounge with his eyes closed. As Pete passed by, the distinct smell of cigarette smoke wafted from his clothes to his father's nose.

Peter Bradford opened his eyes at the smell and noticed Pete walking by.

"Pete?" he said, looking at his son intently.

"Yeah, Dad?" Pete answered.

"Come back here a second. You too, Beth and Andy," Peter Bradford said seriously.

Hearing Peter's serious tone, the other two men opened their eyes and watched the three Bradford children gather around their father. Suddenly the breeze brought the smell to the other two fathers as well, and they listened intently to Peter's conversation. They were fairly certain that whatever the Bradford children were doing, their own children were involved with as well.

"What did you guys do this morning?" Peter asked his children.

"We ran into some kids from school, hiked up to the lake with them, and ate lunch," Beth said.

"Why, Dad?" Pete asked. He knew from the serious look on his father's face that something was wrong.

"Why? Because I'm worried that all of you have picked up some of your nasty old habits again," Peter answered.

Beth, Pete, and Andy looked at each other blankly, trying to figure out what their father meant.

"All of us, Dad?" Andy asked, thinking hard.

Meanwhile, Paul had walked over and was standing beside Beth. Just then, the wind blew towards him, and he caught the strong smell of cigarette smoke from Beth's hair. He immediately knew what Peter Bradford's concern was.

"Oh, Mr. Bradford, that smell isn't from us, honest! The kids that we met from school were smoking like chimneys. We don't do that anymore, at least not since we got to see Pete's chest x-ray, and your friend gave us some of those special cigarettes to try," Paul said.

Peter Bradford relaxed and smiled. Earlier that year, the BBG's secret smoking habit had been caught on an x-ray intended to check for pneumonia in Pete. Peter had been in New York City on business at the time, and had run into a friend who was in the process of getting a patent for a cigarette that was meant to be used by people wishing to quit the habit. The taste and smell of his cigarette were almost like that of a regular cigarette, but gave the smoker a feeling of nausea soon after the first draft was taken. Peter had invited the man and his wife home with him to try the product out on the BBGs. It had worked marvelously, and all the BBGs had immediately stopped smoking. They knew that Mr. Bradford still kept a pack of those cigarettes in his desk drawer at home in case they were ever needed again.

"The kids you were with?" Peter asked.

"Yeah, Dad. The kids we were with. But not us, ever," Pete said adamantly.

"Well, then, hit the showers, all of you. You're about to knock us out with that smell!" Peter Bradford said, relaxing and sitting back in his chaise lounge again.

The BBGs scrambled for their shower bags, and hurried to the bathhouse.

"Whew!" exclaimed Beth, as she, Meg and Di got ready to jump in the showers. "I thought we were goners!" she continued.

"So did I!" giggled Meg.

"Me, too!" put in Di.

That evening after supper, the BBG's school friends walked up to where the BBGs sat with their parents under a large screen tent that was placed over the picnic tables.

"You guys want to go for a walk?" one of them asked.

"Mom, is it OK?" Di asked for all of them.

Kelly looked over at her friends. Since neither of the other mothers voiced any objections, she answered for all the parents by saying, "Go ahead, but take your flashlights, and mind the curfew. Be back here before then."

"And remember our camp rules!" put in Carl.

"Thanks!" all the BBGs yelled. They ran to get their flashlights and then joined the others.

"Do you guys want to go to the arcade?" one boy asked as they walked along the gravel road.

The BBGs agreed, and played several arcade games before stopping and getting sodas to drink. They were sitting around the picnic tables in the building talking, when suddenly another crowd of loud teenage boys came in.

"Oh brother. Here's trouble," whispered one of the girls sitting with the BBGs.

The loud group of teenagers headed right for the BBGs and their school friends. The BBGs recognized the stony defensive look in the other groups' eyes, and knew by the saunter in their walk that they were a troublesome bunch.

"Hey, where's the excitement?" one of the new boys asked.

"Not here," replied Dale, hoping to avoid trouble.

"Well, let's make some, then," someone in the loud group suggested.

"Sorry, we're just on our way back to our campsites," said Pete, trying to get out of the situation in a calm manner as well.

"Oh, come on. The night's still young. I bet you'd like to come along, wouldn't you sweetie?" one boy asked as he planted himself in front of Diana.

"No, she wouldn't," answered Pete, getting up and moving to stand between the boy and Diana.

"Let the lady answer for herself," the boy insisted, pushing Pete aside.

"No, thank you. I've got to go," Di said. She was angry at herself, because she thought that the boy had singled her out because he could tell she was the weakest link. In truth, the boy had thought nothing of the sort. He picked Di because he liked Di's tall form and friendly face.

"Well, how about you, then?" he asked Meg, who was seated next to Di on the picnic bench.

"Nope. Gotta go," Meg said, standing up and pulling Diana up with her.

"You?" the boy asked as he looked at Beth.

"Not on your life, bud. Now isn't there someplace else you could haunt?" Beth was very agitated and was getting impatient with the whole scenario.

"Ooooh! A live wire! Come on, hon, just take a little walk with us, please? You'll have a better time with us than with these wet noodles," the boy said, smiling at Beth.

"I don't think so. Good night, gentlemen," Beth said defiantly, and got up from the bench and started to walk towards Di and Meg who were now standing over by a counter.

The boy clearly did not take Beth's rejection well. He got up and planted himself in her path.

"Not so fast," he said.

Beth angrily watched the friends who had invited the BBGs to the arcade in the first place quickly and quietly slip out the door. While the teenage boys' attention was focused on Beth, they had jumped on the opportunity to leave unnoticed. They didn't seem to mind leaving Beth and the other BBGs to cope with the bullies by themselves.

Beth then looked back at the boy, still planted in front of her.

"What do I have to do to make you understand? I'm not interested in your excitement. I'm due back at my campsite now. If I'm late, I'll be grounded, and I really, really hate that. So please, step aside and let me go," she said, pushing the boy.

"Mommy's baby's afraid of being grounded?" the boy sneered. "With as feisty as you are, I'm surprised that you let her ground you," he finished, stepping in her path again.

Beth sighed and looked at her watch. It was already 15 minutes past the campground's curfew.

"OK, you want to take a walk? Then walk us back to our campsite," Beth said.

At that moment, a maintenance man walked into the arcade. The BBGs were relieved to see him enter and announce to the teens that the arcade was closing.

"Let's go, guys," Beth said

"Good night!" Di called to the workman.

"Night now," the workman answered, waving.

As the teens left, the workman became concerned about their large number and the tense mood that seemed to surround them when he walked in. "It's past curfew," he thought to himself, "I'll just ring security to make sure they get back to their sites okay."

Outside, the teenagers' debate continued. The one boy still blocked Beth's path. Finally, Beth said, "I'm done talking already. Come on, guys, let's go," She ignored the boy's attempts to block her way until he finally put his hand on her arm. At the sight of this, Paul bristled. He had a special place in his heart that had Beth's name on it.

"Let go of her," Paul demanded, rather than asked, and took a step towards the bully.

"Why?" the bully taunted.

"Because we said so," said Pete, moving to stand beside Paul.

"You want some action?" the bully asked.

"Not that kind of action," Dale said slowly, and then added, "All we want to do is to get back to our campsite before we get caught breaking curfew."

What the bullies did not know was that when Dale spoke softly and slowly, it didn't mean that he was backing down. All the BBGs knew that instead, it was a sign that Dale was heating up, and fast.

"Well get going. What's stopping you?" the boy said, gripping Beth's arm harder. The girls groaned inwardly. This boy did not know Dale at all, and was making a big mistake by reading him totally wrong.

"You have your hand on one of us," Dale said evenly, but in a softer voice than he had used before.

With a nearly imperceptible nod from the boy holding Beth, two of his friends grabbed Pete and Paul's arms behind their backs, and then the boy holding Beth pushed her roughly into a third boy's arms. Everyone's eyes then went to Josh and Andy. The leader of the bullies watched them for a few seconds, and then decided that they were harmless enough and did not need to be contained like Pete and Paul. Having settled that matter in his mind, the bully looked directly at Dale, and challenged him to do something about the situation. In response, Dale smiled innocently at the leader. His eyes, though, were following Meg and Di as they silently moved behind the boys who were holding Pete and Paul. Dale's smile seemed to infuriate the challenging bully, who repeated his challenge.

"Well, I don't know, maybe I should just go on home," Dale mused.

He was stalling to give the girls time to get into position behind Pete and Paul's captors. Beth looked intently at Dale. She was not at all fooled by his cowardly pretense. Instead, she tried to read his facial expression for the plan that she knew he was hatching.

"Or, I could do one or two other things," Dale hedged.

With those words, it only took a second for the recognition that he was looking for to appear in Beth's eyes. As soon as he saw it there, he said, "Three! Do it now!"

In a split second, Meg and Di simultaneously kicked the backs of the boys' captor's knees, causing them to buckle and making the bullies fall forward. They released Pete and Paul with howls of pain. At the same time, Beth used her elbow as a battering ram into her captor's stomach, making him double over with pain and release her. The screams of pain from his friends caused Dale's challenger to look towards them for a second. That was all the time Dale needed. When the boy looked back to Dale, he met Dale's fist square in the nose. The punch sent the boy sprawling to the forest floor, with blood trickling from his nose.

"Security's coming!" yelled one of the bullies, and most of them hobbled back into the dark woods as best as they could manage. Their leader, however, was left sitting, stunned and still on the ground, holding his nose.

The BBGs stood around the bully as the security officer, speaking on his walkie-talkie, hurried towards them. A slow grin spread on the officer's face as he saw who was sitting on the ground.

"Brian? Are you at it again? I see you picked the wrong kids this time, and they dished it back to you. You better get home and tend to that nose, son, or you'll be looking like Rudolph the Red Nosed Reindeer in June. Be sure to tell your other buddies that I know who they are this time, and that their dads will be getting curfew fines just like the one your Dad is getting," the security officer said sternly.

Dale put out his hand to help the boy get up. "Hey, I'm sorry, Brian. I just lose my temper when someone starts bothering the girls. Where is your campsite? Can we walk you home?" he said sincerely.

Brian just stared at Dale.

"Do you want to meet somewhere else on better terms, like tomorrow?" Dale tried.

Brian laughed in spite of the pain in his nose.

"Do you really think I want to see the guy who broke my nose? And what do you want to see me again for? You beat me, now get on with your life, and leave me alone," Brian said angrily.

"Oh, it's not broken," Dale assured the other boy. "And I didn't beat you. I was only protecting my friends and my sister. We'd all like to see you again, as long as you behave yourself with the girls, that is," he added.

Brian refused Dale's hand and got up himself. Unable to resist trying to figure the BBGs out, though, he agreed to meet them at the amphitheater at 10 the next morning. He then turned and walked slowly down the road to his family's campsite.

Dale watched Brian leave, and then looked at his watch. "Oh, man!" he cried. "It's almost midnight! We'd better get running, fast!" he said.

The security guard stepped up to Dale, and said, "Not so fast, buddy. I happened to see the whole thing. Now I know Brian, and I know how he can start a fight. And I'm glad that someone finally took him on, and knocked a little wind out of him. But, it is definitely past curfew, and I did witness a fight between you guys. There is a fine at this campground for breaking curfew. Even without the curfew fine, though, the fight itself is grounds for you and your parents to be removed from the campground. Tonight," the guard said solemnly.

"If you know that Brian starts fights, why is he still here? Why hasn't he been removed?" asked Beth, still angry with the whole situation, and starting to feel as though the guard was treating them unfairly.

"Well, I guess you don't know Brian very well then. His parents own a permanent site in 'C' area, and they are also part owners of the campground. His dad knows how he acts, and doesn't ask for special favors, but that doesn't mean we can remove him from his own land. Now, come on, let's get you kids home to your parents," the security guard said as he got back into his golf cart, and started it up. He drove slowly alongside the quiet BBGs until they reached their site.

Their parents were in the screen house finishing a game of cards when the teens arrived. Noticing the time and the security guard escort, Peter, Carl, and John got up and went out to meet them.

"Are you the parents of these kids?" the security guard asked the men as soon as he got out of his golf cart.

"Yes, sir," answered Carl.

"Well, then I'll return them to you. They seem like a nice bunch of kids, but I ran into a couple of problems tonight," the security guard said.

"I can bet one of the problems is that it is seriously past curfew," said Peter.

"That is the first problem, yes, sir," the security guard answered.

"Is there a fine, or how does the campsite handle curfew breakers?" John asked.

The security guard chuckled. "This is their first offense, and we only give warnings to that. The real problem is the reason that they are late getting home," he said.

"Oh, and what was that?" Carl asked.

The BBGs stepped back a few steps into the shadows. The guard noticed this and realized that he was talking to parents who were not going to brush their children's antics aside. He felt pleased about this, and tried to soften the blow he knew his words were going to cause.

"Let me finish the story before you jump on the kids, okay? You have to understand the background to the situation before you can appreciate what your children did," the guard said.

"What did they do?" Peter asked.

"They were in a fist fight," said the guard.

"A fist fight?" asked John, Carl, and Peter together. This brought Emma, Kelly, and Patti up off the picnic benches to stand beside their husbands.

Dale held his head in the palm of his hand.

"I'm a goner," he whispered to Pete who stood beside him.

"You and the rest of us," Pete whispered back.

The BBG's parents listened intently as the guard told them about Brian and his friends and their method of having fun with the other young campers.

"Even though I don't know what started this whole thing, I can be pretty sure that your kids acted in self defense because of Brian's history," the guard added.

"What exactly did you see our children doing?" John asked.

The guard took a deep breath and told the adults about Beth, Pete and Paul being held hostage while Brian tried to pick a fight with Dale. Then he told them how the BBGs managed to extricate themselves from the situation.

"The thing that concerns me the most about this whole thing, though, is the way your kids acted as a team on a coded message from the one Brian was fighting. I'm not totally sure, but I really don't think this is the first time they've executed those maneuvers. And that really bothers me, to think that these kids who seem like good, decent kids and who have caring parents can also be practicing these moves on the side. Gangs are a real problem nowadays, and they aren't confined to the cities anymore, either. I hope your kids aren't involved in something like that," the guard said sincerely.

"Thank you for mentioning your concerns, and for caring about these guys. We'll take your words seriously, believe me," said Carl.

The guard nodded his head. "Don't be too hard on them. Like I said, I've never seen anyone walk away from Brian and his group with the upper hand. It's what we've all been hoping for over the last couple of summers," he said and then turned to the BBGs. "If Brian shows up to meet you tomorrow morning, I doubt that you'll get any flack from him. Just make sure there isn't any more fighting, understand?" the guard said sternly.

"No more fighting," Dale adamantly agreed.

"I'm terribly sorry about all of this, sir," Carl said sincerely.

"Well, like I said, I really believe it was in self defense on the part of your kids. I think that they did the right thing, and stuck together. They got themselves out of a very sticky situation, and I'd be proud of them for that, if I were you," the guard answered with a wink towards the BBGs.

"Good night, everyone," he said and got into his golf cart and motored away.

"Good night and thanks again," the men called after him.

"Come on down out of those shadows, guys, and let's take this out of the street," suggested Peter, as he turned and went back to the screen house.

The BBGs slowly followed their parents and found seats at the picnic table. They were horrified at what the guard had just told their parents.

No one spoke for several minutes. Finally, Carl looked intently at Dale and said,

"So according to the security guard, you're the mastermind behind all this?"

Dale winced. "Well, this time the challenge was to me, yeah," he said, and immediately regretted it.

"This time? There really have been other times?" Carl asked.

"Not many. Not recently," put in Pete.

"Pete and I actually stood up first, when the goon grabbed Beth," said Paul.

"You actually acted as an organized team?" John Baker asked his son.

"Dad, he had a hold of Beth. What were we supposed to do?" asked Paul.

"Well, I'm glad you defended my daughter, all of you," Peter said.

"But dear, striking people?" Emma Bradford asked.

"And having it down to coded words and teamwork?" added Kelly Ganderson.

"It wasn't a code, Mom, we just knew what to do. We've had self defense classes in gym, and we're all in the same gym class at school," Dale said.

"Dale and Diana, I want you two to head to bed. I've got a lot of thinking to do, and I want to talk this over some more with your mom and the others. I don't need to tell you, though, that I'm disappointed with what went on tonight. I had really hoped we had turned a corner here in our lives," Carl said seriously.

"I have turned a corner in my life," said Dale, adamantly.

"If Dad only knew how true that was," whispered Diana to Meg, who was seated beside her.

Meg stifled a giggle.

"Dale, look at what's happened recently. First, the volleyball incident, and now this," Carl reminded his son.

"I'm sorry, Dad," Dale said.

"So am I, Dale," Carl said, and then broke into a smile when he saw Dale's worried face.

"Get to bed, kids," he said, giving Dale's shoulder a squeeze.

John Baker and Peter Bradford also excused their children, and all the BBGs hurried to the bathhouse.

CHAPTER 4

"Oh, boy! Are we in for it, or what?" asked Di as she and the other girls got ready for bed in the bathhouse.

"I don't care. I still think we did the right thing," said Beth.

"Yeah, your Dad's happy enough that we saved your skin," Meg said, and then added, "I sure hope he talks some sense into our dads."

"I don't think that security guard had a lick of sense. How dare he suggest to our parents that we're a gang?" Diana said indignantly, as all the teens started back to the campers and tents.

"Calm down, Di. The guard was only calling it like he saw it. To him, that's exactly what we looked like," Dale said sadly.

"Oh, come on! Who would think that about us?" asked Beth.

"Anyone who didn't know us would," Pete said, and then added, "We really blew it tonight."

"How can you say that? Who knows what would have happened to me if all of you wouldn't have intervened?" Beth said angrily.

"Beth, think about how it started, and why he picked on you," Pete said.

"So you're saying all this is my fault?" she asked defensively.

"Oh, Beth, what I'm saying is that you challenged Brian. He had to do something to save face in front of his friends after you insulted him," Pete said.

"So it is my fault?" Beth pressed her brother.

"Beth, it's not totally anyone's fault. There were a lot of mistakes made tonight. I, for one, didn't have to hit Brian. We all challenged him at some point. There just had to be a way to avoid all of this at each step. Maybe we should have just invited him to walk us home to begin with. I don't know the right answer, but I do know that there had to be a better answer than what we delivered tonight," Dale said, sadly.

"I'm sorry, guys. Dale's right. I should have just kept my mouth shut from the get-go," Beth moaned.

Dale put his arm around her shoulders. "It's Ok, Beth. Like I said, it wasn't totally your fault, and we all learned something tonight," he said kindly.

By this time, the teens had reached their campsites, and each one tumbled into their own beds, with the hushed voices of their parents drifting in and out of the open campers' and tents' windows.

"I want to say right off, that even though I don't condone violence, I'm glad our children are well enough equipped to get out of situations like this tonight. Emma and I worry about the safety of all of them. There are plenty of strange people around who look for easy opportunities with well known kids in a community. The fact that our children stick together and stand up for each other is very encouraging to us. What does worry me, though, is their apparent experience in situations like this. How and when did they get this experience?" Peter Bradford said solemnly.

Emma Bradford's eyes filled with tears. "Peter and I moved out here so that our children wouldn't have to face the pecking order of the private snob schools like we attended, or the danger of the large city schools. I know Beth hasn't exactly grown into the gentlewoman I had hoped she'd become, but a member of a gang? Knowing how to purposely hurt someone?" Emma stopped speaking in order to grab some tissues.

"Oh, Emma, I know! I can't imagine Dale clobbering anyone. He hasn't done that at home since he and Steve were young boys. Where did they learn all this stuff, and where was I when they were practicing?" Kelly said, putting an arm around the friend sitting beside her.

"Are we like those parents whose children live these separate lives, and then when something bad happens, they just shrug and say, 'I had no idea' ? Is there anything else we don't know about our own kids?" Patti Baker asked.

"I think maybe we should ask some of the other adults that are around our kids a lot, like Dave Smith, or some of their teachers and guidance counselors in school. I'm not saying that the security guard wasn't being truthful in telling us what he saw, but he doesn't know our kids at all. He was seeing something from a totally different view than what we would have seen it. I think it would be a good idea to get the counsel of a few more people before we rush to judgment," Carl said.

"I think you're right, Carl. Before tonight, I would never have thought of my kids as being in a gang. We've just had an incredible couple of months with them, and maybe I'm wrong, but my gut is telling me that these are good kids. Good kids who just had a life changing event occur in their lives. I'd like to give mine the benefit of the doubt for a little while longer," said John Baker.

"Besides, how could such violent kids give us the worship we had last night? I know they weren't faking that, and they're not faking the changes that have been happening in their lives. I'm willing to say that maybe they messed up tonight in terms of the methods they used, and maybe Dale didn't have to hit this kid, Carl. Then again, he didn't seriously injure the boy, and the security guard didn't seem too concerned that our kids wanted to meet this bully again tomorrow. I don't think he thinks it's for another fight," Peter said.

Carl smiled at his friends. "Thanks, guys. I'll speak to Dave about the kids after the meeting tomorrow. Any of you want to contact a teacher or guidance counselor? We have several in our congregation," he asked.

"I'll speak to Lee Carson," said John.

"Then I'll speak to Cal Winters," said Peter.

With that consensus reached, the adults then got themselves ready for bed and turned in.

The next morning, the teens were up and showered before the adults. They sat in the screen house and talked about their plans to see Brian over their bowls of cereal.

“Let’s take our guitars,” suggested Pete.

“I was thinking that same thing,” said Josh.

“You guys finished eating?” asked Dale, suddenly standing up from the picnic table. “I could sure use a good prayer time,” he added.

The other teens were done, and so they all stood up, cleaned up their bowls, spoons, and cereal boxes, and put the milk away in the cooler. Then they walked over to the field behind the campers, where they had pitched the Baker and Bradford tents, and gathered together on the grass. The teens knelt or sat, and buried their faces in their hands. Tears flowed, as the teens once again cried out to their heavenly father in repentance and in petition for the boy whom they would soon be meeting with.

Meanwhile, Peter, Carl and John had gotten up, and were looking for the teens, hoping to talk to them some more about the previous night’s activities. Carl found them in the field first, and quietly went to gather the other men and their wives. After observing the teens for a few minutes, the adults returned to the screen house to eat their breakfast with the younger children.

“Well, that settles it for me. Unless Dave has some earth shattering news, or you guys come up with different evidence, I’m choosing not to believe we’ve raised a gang of violent offenders,” Carl said, pouring the milk on Kristen’s cereal.

“You’re right, hon. How on earth could we have ever entertained that idea, anyway?” Kelly Ganderson asked, and the other parents laughed and agreed.

When the teens were finished praying, they noticed that their parents and siblings were eating in the screen house.

“Well, let’s go face the music,” Pete said, getting up.

“Oh, man, I really don’t want to do this,” moaned Paul.

Dale, Pete, Andy and Josh first went to get their guitars, and then joined with the others going into the screen house.

“Good morning kids!” Carl said cheerfully.

Dale looked at his father, with his eyes still a little red, and his face still splotchy from heartfelt praying. “Is it a good morning, Dad?” he asked cautiously.

Dale’s face looked so sad, that Carl could do nothing but go over and envelope his son in a warm hug.

“Yes, Dale, it’s a good fine, morning,” Carl said, chuckling, and then added, “Sit down, gang, and I mean that only in the best BBG sense.”

The teens sat on the grass and waited, expecting a very stern lecture and some sort of punishment.

"Go ahead, Carl," Peter Bradford said.

"All right. I don't know what to think about you giving anyone a bloody nose, Dale, especially after that volleyball outburst," he started.

"I don't know why I clobbered Brian, Dad, it was just a gut instinct to try to protect Beth," Dale said sadly.

"Hold on, Dale. I know you did it, and I know that you're sorry you did it. I'm just saying that I'm not done processing all of this. Mr. Baker, Mr. Bradford, and I are going to be speaking with some of the other adults in your lives to try to get a better handle on things. I am going to tell you all that I don't like what I've heard in the last few weeks, especially about you, Dale, but as parents, we still want you to know that we are proud of all of you for sticking together and taking care of one another. We're proud of your commitment to the Lord, and we can see that you're trying your best to move in the right direction. We've decided that we are not taking any stock in a BBG violent gang theory, partly because of what we saw you doing in the field earlier this morning. However, the jury is still out over what to make of your actions last night. Dale, I've a good mind to take you out back, and tan your hide for punching that other boy, regardless of how poorly he was acting, and Diana, you deserve to be grounded for a long time for striking someone, as well. You both know that, don't you?" Carl asked his children solemnly.

"Yes, sir," Dale said humbly.

"Yes, Dad," Diana whispered back.

Carl smiled at the looks on his children's faces and continued speaking. "But somehow, I just can't get past the reason why you guys did what you did. Protecting each other is a good thing, and I surely don't want to punish that. You guys sure know how to mess up our parenting manuals, don't you?" he chuckled.

"Sorry, Dad," Dale mumbled

Carl chuckled again. "Lighten up, Dale. And that goes for the rest of you. We're not going to punish you for doing the right thing, even if it was in a questionable way. Now go find that guy with the swollen nose and befriend him. You've forgiven him, so now why don't you extend to yourselves that same grace? Stop beating yourselves up over this. All right?" Carl said.

The BBGs silently looked at each other, and then unanimously decided to get while the getting was good. They picked up their guitars and quickly headed out of the screen house, making the adults laugh at their haste.

The teens said nothing to each other as they made their way to a natural amphitheater in the campground. Although they did not express their thoughts out loud, each one was taking to heart their Pastor's words, and trying to forgive themselves for whatever errors in judgment they had made the night before. When they reached the amphitheater, Paul looked at his watch.

"Gosh! It's only 9:30!" he exclaimed.

Dale sat down on a log and pulled out his guitar. "Let's just play for awhile, then," he said thoughtfully. Josh, Andy, and Pete got out their guitars as the others found spots on logs to sit on. The group played and sang until it finally turned into heartfelt worship, and they became oblivious to the time or what was going on around them. Brian and 2 of his friends had arrived, and were sitting at the top of the amphitheater in the shadows, listening to the BBGs. Peter, Carl, and John had also come, but were sitting unseen in the shadows of the trees surrounding the amphitheater. The security guard stopped by for a few moments, and then left, shaking his head at the music he heard coming from the group down in the front of the amphitheater.

"I knew there was something different about that group," he mumbled to himself as he went on with his rounds.

At last, Pete stopped playing, and looked at his watch.

"Jeez, now it's 10:30!" he exclaimed.

Diana looked up from her worship, but did not see Brian and his friends making their way down the side of the amphitheater to meet them.

"I guess Brian's not coming," she sighed.

"Rats. I really wanted to see him," said Dale, putting his guitar back into its case.

"For what? Damage assessment?" Brian's voice floated in from the shadows along the tree lined side of the amphitheater.

"Brian! Thanks for coming!" Dale exclaimed, jumping up and offering the boy his hand.

Brian laughed, but this time gave Dale his hand for a shake.

"Who are your friends?" asked Meg, looking around Dale and seeing 2 other boys standing several feet away from Brian.

"You didn't really think I'd be stupid enough to come alone, did you?" Brian scoffed, still unsure about who the BBGs really were.

"Hey, it's no problem, Brian, but we'd like to call them something other than Brian's bodyguard number one and Brian's bodyguard number two," Dale said, defending Meg's question.

"This is Mike, and this is Adam," Brian said, a little tensely.

"Hi, Mike. Hi Adam, I'm Beth Bradford, and these are my brothers, Pete and Andy. These are my friends, Meg, Josh, and Paul Baker, and over here are our friends Dale and Diana Ganderson. I'm really sorry, Mike, for elbowing you in the stomach last night. Are you OK?" Beth made the introductions and her apology, smiling kindly at the boy she recognized as her victim the night before.

Mike smiled back at Beth and said, "Yeah, I'm alright now."

"You guys want to sit down?" asked Pete, and the BBGs took their places on the logs, with Brian, Adam, and Mike sitting near them.

"Nice guitars," commented Adam, looking at Dale's guitar sitting in its open case.

"Thanks. Do you play?" asked Dale.

Adam shook his head no.

"What kind of music were you playing?" asked Brian.

"Oh, just some stuff from church," answered Pete.

Brian laughed. "I know it was religious music, Pete, because I heard most of it while I was sitting up there. But in the few churches I've ever been in, I've never heard that kind of music. What's it called ?" he asked again.

"I don't know a name for it exactly. Contemporary worship, maybe ?" Pete said, and looked at Paul and Dale for confirmation.

"It's just off the tapes we get from church," said Dale.

"You really have that kind of music in your church?" asked Brian.

"Sure, but at church we have a full band, not just a bunch of amateur guitar players," said Dale.

Brian just shook his head. "Dale, you've got to be the weirdest son of a minister that I have ever met. And you hang out with the weirdest rich kids and the weirdest kids that have their names plastered on a street or building in every town in this county that I've ever seen. I just can't figure you out," he said.

The BBGs looked at each other in total confusion over Brian's knowledge of who they were. Brian grinned, and enjoyed watching their confusion.

"How do you know all that?" demanded Diana.

"Come on, first you expect me to show up by myself, and now you honestly think I'm going to come down here without checking up on you? You guys confuse the heck out of me! I hear you're so street smart, and you, Dale, are the only person ever to take me off guard like you did last night. That other group you were with last night told me some pretty impressive school tales, you know. But now I come down here, and I catch you singing Christian rock and roll and love songs! And you're all acting like you don't even know the kids who decked us last night. What is it with you?" Brian asked, clearly agitated over his inability to figure them out.

"Well, you're right about who we are, Brian. My dad's a pastor, Pete's dad is well, Peter Bradford, and Paul's dad is from the Baker family who helped settle this area before the revolutionary war," Dale agreed.

"And I guess Julia and Tim might know some of our worst horror stories from school," said Pete.

"And we were playing Christian rock," added Paul.

Brian shook his head. "That's what doesn't fit!" he exclaimed. "Miss Society debutante who can bring a guy to his knees with just an elbow, Miss Revolutionary war heroine who also snaps knee caps like a pro. Mr. Preacher, who gives me a bloody nose, and pretty near busts the thing. Then, a couple of hours later, you're all sitting around, acting like pious brothers and sisters. I heard you singing! I saw you, and you were definitely into it. But which act is fake? You didn't know I was up there listening to you, and you sure didn't have to act religious for the birds and the pine trees. I know, from hearing you, that this isn't the first time you've played and sung those songs. And I know my nose wasn't the first one you've ever cracked, either, Dale. So who are you?" Brian was definitely upset, and it showed in his voice, which was rising in tone and volume with each sentence.

The BBGs were silent for a minute, thinking about what Brian had said. Finally, Dale spoke in a gentle voice.

"You're right again, Brian. Yours isn't the first nose I've nearly broken. Nor are you the first to be elbowed, Mike, or the others the first to have their kneecaps snapped. I am really, really sorry about that," Dale said, sadly.

Brain threw up his hands. "Quit apologizing already! I deserved what you gave me! I'm trying to tell you that I'm impressed with what you all did, and how well you did it! I just don't see what that has to do with what the guys and I just saw here a few minutes ago. I can appreciate that you all have tough skins because of who you parents are and all. I know there are religious people out there, even tough, no nonsense religious people. But you can not be wimpy religious and street tough at the same time!" Brian exploded at the BBGs.

"Why not?" asked Meg innocently.

"Why not ?" Brian repeated, "Why not? Because the wimpy religious folks would have called security last night, or just left you hanging alone, Beth. You know, 'turn the other cheek' and all that. And I know that no street tough kid would be caught singing to an unseen entity, that's why!" Brian answered.

"You know, Brian, you're right again," Paul said, and then added, "religious wimps would have done that last night. But we follow a guy who blasted religious wimps and officials, and even wrecked the courtyard of a synagogue once. He wasn't afraid to stand up for a woman who was about to be beaten to death. I could never have any respect for somebody who would have left his sister or a friend in your clutches last night. But," Paul stopped speaking for a moment, then took a deep breath and continued. "But, I have the utmost respect for a man who could smash tables one day, cry for the death of a friend the next day, and who still takes the heat for me every day."

Brian and his friends were quiet, finally.

"Wrecked a synagogue? Are you talking about a skin-head or a Nazi?" Adam asked

"No, he was a Jew himself," Paul answered.

"A Jew? I thought you were doing Christian songs," said Brian.

"Well, actually, this Jew started a new religion." put in Pete.

"For real? A tough guy started a new religion?" Mike asked.

"For real. Well, actually, the Jews were already looking for someone like him, to fulfill all their prophecies, and their religious books all pointed to this one person as the man, but they couldn't see it," Pete said. "But he's a tough guy who knows how to love people and extend mercy." he added.

"To be honest," Dale said, "I don't know how he would have handled last night. I've been asking, but I haven't gotten an answer yet. I know he wouldn't have left Beth there with you unprotected, but violence isn't his trademark. Maybe tough isn't the right word. Strong is more like it."

"You've been asking? What did you do? Leave a message on his machine or something?" asked Brian.

Dale laughed. "Yeah, something like that," he said.

"Alright. So this guy, this Jew who started a new religion, he does Christian songs?" continued Brian.

"No, he doesn't do them, but he likes to hear them," Paul said.

"I can relate to that. I'm no musician, and I can't play an instrument or sing, but I like to listen to stuff," Adam said.

Pete smiled and picked up his guitar.

"But wait! If this guy is a Jew, and started another religion, and he's street tough and not a wimp, how do you guys know about him? Isn't your dad a minister, Dale? How did you find out about this guy?" Brian questioned.

"We met him personally once. Now we keep in touch by talking to him and reading his book," Beth said.

"What book? He wrote a book?" Brian asked.

"No, he didn't write it himself, exactly. He told people what to write, and they wrote it for him," Beth said.

"Lots of people do that. What's the book called?" asked Brian, who in spite of his tough exterior, was an avid reader.

"Here. Take this one. I always keep a spare," said Meg, taking a book out of her backpack.

"The Message?" Brian asked quizzically.

"Sure. It's a great book," said Dale.

"You mean this Jew is," started Brian.

"Jesus" finished Pete.

"You're joking!" Brian said

"Nope. Read it for yourself," Pete said.

"But, but, I've never met Christians who could pack a wallop like you!" Brian complained.

"Hey, Brian, it's not something we're proud of," Dale said.

"And it was something that Jesus took the heat for us on," added Pete.

"So you just get away with it?" asked Adam.

"Well, sort of. But think about it. Suppose that security guard last night pinned all the blame for everything you've ever done on Brian. Suppose Brian then had to pay all the fines, listen to all the lectures, spend all the time in jail that belonged to you. Could you stand there and watch him take the blame, not just last night, but every time you messed up? Like what if they kept hauling Brian out of jail to go to court every time you deserved it? How about if Brian never had anything to do with your stuff? What if he was sitting in jail, with sentence upon sentence being heaped on his head, and he was actually totally innocent? Would you or could you just sit by and keep on screwing up and going free?" Dale asked, passionately.

Adam was quiet for awhile. Finally, a whispered "whoa" escaped from his lips.

"So you really don't like to be tough?" asked Mike.

Dale laughed again. "Oh, I like it all right. I like it a lot. But knowing that Jesus is taking the blame every time I act tough like that, sort of takes a lot of the fun out of it," he said.

"Yeah, I guess it would. And you say the answers are all right in here?" asked Brian, holding his new Bible.

"The answers are in there, Brian. But the best part is that Jesus is my friend, and I can communicate with him every day, whenever I want, and I get answers from talking to him, too," Dale said.

"What do you mean, communicate?" asked Brian.

"Talk. I tell him everything. And I listen for his answers," said Dale.

"You're kidding," Brian said, doubtfully.

"Nope, I'm not," said Dale.

"How do you know when it's Him talking to you?" asked Adam.

"How do you know its Brian on the other end when the phone rings and you answer it?" asked Pete.

"I recognize Brian's voice," replied Adam.

"Well, there you go. We're trying to listen often enough so we can learn to recognize Jesus' voice, too," Pete said.

"You're really serious about this, aren't you?" asked Brian.

"You bet we are!" said Meg enthusiastically.

"And you still have fun?" asked Mike.

"Now, do I look like a stick in the mud to you?" giggled Beth.

Mike had to laugh at that thought, too.

"Definitely not!" he agreed.

Pete put down the guitar he had been playing softly. He set it in its case, and closed the lid.

"Anybody feel like a swim before we eat?" he asked.

"Sounds great! Maybe we can grab a bite to eat at the snack bar," suggested Meg.

"You game?" Dale asked Brian and his friends.

"Sure. Do you want to go now? We'd have to change first," said Brian.

"Well, we do have to get permission, and change, and take down our tents," said Pete.

"The guys and I will change, and come to your campsite. If you aren't done breaking camp, we'll help. Deal?" Brian asked.

"Deal!" agreed the BBGs, waving as they hurried down the path to their site.

The BBGs quickly changed into their swimsuits, and then began to take down the tents. Meg and Di rolled up sleeping bags and emptied air mattresses while Paul and Josh took down their tent. Pete helped Dale take down his tent, and Beth and Andy folded up poles and put them in the carrying bags. When Brian, Mike, and Adam arrived, all the teens took down the screen house, and packed it away. Then they walked to the pool, where they spent several hours swimming and playing in the water until Josh moaned that he was starved. The group got out of the pool and bought hamburgers, fries, and drinks, and then sat at the picnic tables to eat. When it was time to go home, the BBG's parents picked them up at the pool on their way out.

"Thanks for the swim, guys. I had a great time," Beth said sincerely to Brian and his friends.

"You're welcome," replied Brian.

"It's been fun," said Dale, shaking Brian's hand, and then Mike and Adam's.

"I hope we'll see you the next time we come," said Pete, also shaking hands.

"Don't show your face around here without looking us up," said Brian, grinning.

"You better be careful, Brian, or we may end up camping in your spot," laughed Paul, as he too shook hands all around.

"You'd be more than welcome. I think it's a double spot, anyway," Brian replied.

As the BBGs finished saying their good-byes, Beth impulsively gave Brian a hug. It surprised Brian so much that he jumped at first, but then gave Beth a quick hug back. When she left, Beth thought for sure that she had seen Brian's eyes soften just a little.

"I've got a feeling we're going to be getting a new brother or two or three," remarked Andy as he moved over in the van's seat to make room for Beth.

"I think you're right, Andy. I can feel it too," agreed Pete.

CHAPTER 5

Later that night, when the church service and the youth meetings were over, Carl asked Dave to speak with him for a few minutes in his office. After promising Carl that he would be honest in his replies, Dave listened with interest to Carl's camping story.

"You know the weirdest thing about this, Dave? After making mincemeat out of those bullies the night before, our guys witnessed the love and mercy of God to them this morning, with every bit of expertise they were supposed to have used to clobber them with last night!" Carl said

"And I bet it was received, too, wasn't it?" Dave laughed.

"Yes, it was. A good many seeds were planted between them," Carl answered, and then added, "but what I want to know, Dave, is how has their behavior been with you, in youth group? Are they belligerent? Bullies? Do they pick fights with the other kids? Do you look at them as a gang?"

Dave could see that Carl was genuinely concerned, and he thought carefully about what he was going to say before speaking.

"First of all, Carl, I don't think what they are now has much bearing on what they've been. The Lord's fire is still burning within them, and it's been over a month since they accepted Him. Of course, they're going to fall back into old habits and patterns occasionally, don't we all? Now if you would have asked me these questions 3 months ago, the answer might have been a lot different than what I'm saying tonight. Their behavior, as you know, hasn't always been the best in the past, and I've sensed the fight in all of the older boys, though I've never actually seen it in action. I can honestly say, though, that even back before the Lord, I don't believe they were ever a gang. They're a cohesive group that is very protective of each other, but that's it. Most of what people see as belligerent is simply the tough skin that comes with high profile families, and I think that they must get teased an awful lot at school just because of who they are. The belligerence is their front they put out there in order to cope. You know, Carl that I've called you every time I've had to deal with that belligerence. I don't tolerate that, and I've taken my cues from you as far as that goes. You've been a great role model to me, and I'm sure that my own, future kids will one day thank you for your input into my future parenting style," Dave said with sincerity.

Carl laughed and said, "Just don't tell them I taught you, OK? I don't want them to hate me."

Dave chuckled and continued. "What you have, in my opinion, is a great bunch of kids who are walking out their lives with the Lord. They have tremendous influence with the other kids in the youth group, and it's been great to see the turn around in the group just because of the attitude changes in your kids. I'm having the time of my life with them right now, so don't worry. If I see something that needs your attention, I'll bring it to your attention, just like I've always done. All right?" Dave finished, looking at Carl with a great deal of admiration and compassion.

Carl looked down at his desk, trying to thank God for the words he had just heard spoken from his trusted friend. His heart was about to burst, so instead of saying anything right away, he got up and walked around the desk to give Dave a hug.

"You're a good friend to all of us, Dave Smith," he said

The two men then walked out of the church together, and Carl waved as Dave drove out of the parking lot. Carl then walked slowly to his own home, and entered through the sliding glass doors off the kitchen. Dale was there, dishing up a bowl of ice cream when his father walked in.

"Well, Dad, what did Dave say? Are we trouble or what?" Dale asked, grinning and licking the ice cream scoop before throwing it in the sink.

Carl laughed, and said, "You, son, are lucky that Dave has that policy of calling me first before he acts on your disobedience. Fortunately for you, I didn't find out anything new. And no, he doesn't think you are trouble. He loves you, for whatever goofy reasons he has locked up in his brain."

"Maybe it's because we are just too adorable?" Dale whined like the girls did when they saw a new baby.

"I'm glad that you're not conceited, either," Carl laughed, as he patted Dale on the back and went up to bed.

On Sunday morning, the BBGs got one of the biggest surprises of their lives. As they stood in the lobby talking after Sunday School, Brian, Mike, Adam, and the two boys whose knees Meg and Di had kicked came into the church.

"Wow! This is a bit far for you guys, isn't it?" Dale asked, shaking everyone's hands.

"We had to see if what you were saying was true. We all got The Message, Meg, but we had to see if your church was any different than all the others," Brian explained.

"Well, come on in and see!" exclaimed Beth enthusiastically.

They introduced the boys to Dave, their parents and several friends before leading them to the BBGs regular seats. They took up 2 entire pews in the front of the church.

When the worship started, Brian just sat and stared at the band, listening. But finally, he too stood and began to participate along with his friends. Brian just kept shaking his head and saying, "It's true. It really is true. They have a full band and they play songs that sound like rock and roll."

The BBGs, however, were so full of excitement that they found it hard to concentrate on the worship. They didn't realize at that time that Brian and his 4 friends would only be the first of many that they would bring into the kingdom with them.

After a few announcements and the dismissal of the younger children, Carl stood to give the message. Brian and the other boys were hungry and ripe, and they listened intently to what he was saying. No one but Carl knew that the message given that day was not the one he had worked on throughout the week. Instead, he spoke from his heart to the boys' hearts, like a fisherman reeling in the catch. He had barely finished the ministry call when all 5 boys were standing in the front of the church. The BBGs surrounded them, answering the questions that the boys had and praying with them. Carl, Dave, Peter, and John stood near the back watching with teary eyes, and when the teens were done, the men greeted the new boys warmly.

"I guess I should apologize to you for treating Beth the way I did," Brian said to Peter. Peter smiled at Brian, and said, "You are completely forgiven, Brian." Then, in a soft voice, added, "but, don't let it happen again, OK?"

Brian smiled. "Not a chance. Not with these guys around, anyway," he said.

"Good. We'll keep it that way, then," Peter said, patting Brian on the back.

"These guys are going to stick around for youth group tonight, OK Dave?" asked Pete.

"You bet. Any friend of the BBGs is a friend of mine," Dave smiled.

The teens said good bye to their fathers and Dave, and then wandered over to the playground between the church and the Ganderson's home. They sat on the benches placed around the outside of the play area in silence for several minutes, letting the events of the morning sink in.

"What should we do for lunch?" Josh finally asked.

"I'm broke. I guess I get to eat with Mom and Dad," said Paul.

"The arcade wiped me out too," said Dale.

"Lunch at the snack bar did me in," agreed Pete.

Brian laughed. "Come on, Pete. Do you really want me to believe you are broke?" he asked.

Pete pretended to pout. "I earn my spending money," he objected.

"He does, just like the rest of us," Dale defended his friend. "The only favor we get is an account at the Pizza Place. We eat there Friday nights and Sunday nights," he added.

"I take back what I said, then. That's really impressive, Pete," Brian said sincerely.

"Well, Cook always has plenty for everyone, even if it is just burgers and hot dogs," Beth suggested, trying to get the attention off of her brother, who was supremely embarrassed by Brian's compliment.

"If that's an invitation, Beth, I'm getting my swimsuit and I'll be right over!" Paul said, getting up.

Beth smiled. "If you're questioning whether or not that was an invitation, I'd better hang around Mom some more and pick up some more social graces," she said, giggling.

"I think you're fine just as you are. Why don't you take your social graces and our guests over to your house and let your Cook know that there's an army coming. Maybe she'll even start up the grill for us. This boy is getting hungry!" Paul suggested, and then took off on a trot across the field to his home.

"Come on, guys, let's go," Pete agreed, motioning for Brian and his friends to join him and his brother and sister as they walked down the church's driveway.

A few moments later, the BBGs and their new friends were gathered around the Bradford's pool. The cook had started the gas grill, and left a tray of hamburgers and hot dogs ready for the teens to cook on the picnic table. As soon as Pete could get everyone's attention, he asked for numbers and choices, and then threw the correct items on the grill. Soon, the teens were enjoying their sandwiches. They also managed to polish off a bowl of potato salad, a bowl of coleslaw, a bag of chips, and a cake for dessert. They drank from the gallons of lemonade and ice tea that the cook had also left for them in a large cooler filled with ice.

After they ate, they returned the bowls and utensils to the kitchen, and then sat and relaxed on the chaise lounges around the pool. After a half hour had passed, Meg got up and slipped off her shorts and dove expertly into the pool. Di soon followed suit, and Beth, who had not changed yet, excused herself to go to her room and do that. Brian and his friends looked longingly at the inviting cool water in the pool, but said nothing.

Paul stood up, peeled off his shirt, and dropped a bag into Brian's lap. "Here's an extra suit of mine, and one of Josh's. Dale brought one, too. I think between Pete and Andy they can come up with enough for the rest of you, that is, if you want to join us," Paul said.

Brian's eyes lit up. "Thanks!" he exclaimed, and took the bag Paul put in his lap. Dale threw a bag at Mike, and Pete invited them all to join him and Andy in the house to change.

"Whoa. You really live here?" asked Mike, as the Bradford boys led them down a corridor to the main stairs.

"Yep. After my youngest brother, Micah, was born, Dad and Mom designed this house and had it built. The long halls are for Mom to hang her pictures on. She's a good painter and a great photographer, so most of these hangings are hers," Pete explained.

"And Dad loves the outdoors and the view, so they put the back of the house towards the view, and made most of the back walls on the first floor windows," added Andy.

"Wow," was all the other boys could say.

When they had changed and had made their way back to the pool, they found that Peter was there chatting to the other teens.

"Are you enjoying yourselves?" Peter asked Brian and his friends.

"Yes, thanks," Mike replied for all of them.

"Good. Now Pete, your mother and I are taking the kids to a matinee. The Gandersons are joining us. After the movie, Pastor Carl and Mr. Baker and I will be having a short meeting before the evening service, so Mom and the other kids will probably just stay across the road until the service starts. Since we're taking the sedan, Pete, you're welcome to take the van somewhere if you get tired of swimming. Just be sure to be back by the time church starts, OK?" Peter said.

"All right, Dad, and thanks for the van!" Pete said, already floating on a raft in the pool.

"Bye now," Peter said, waving as he walked back to the garage.

The teens swam for a while, and then Beth climbed out and sat on a lounge chair to dry off.

"Say, Pete, if you have the van, let's go for a ride!" she suggested.

"Yeah, let's!" agreed Diana.

"Well, considering we're broke, where are we going to go?" teased Pete.

"Oh, there's a lot of free places. Please, Pete?" pleaded Di.

"Well, I never could resist your pleas," Pete said, smiling broadly as he climbed out of the pool.

Dale glanced suspiciously at the two of them, but saw nothing on either of their faces to indicate something was going on between them. If there was something going on, Dale wanted to know about it. Not just because Di was his sister, but also because Dale felt a special feeling for Meg growing in his heart, and if Pete and Di were getting together, he was going to pursue his feelings for Meg a little harder.

"We could take a ride to the state park. I've got enough change rattling around to get one canoe," Paul suggested, as he got out of the pool and began to dry off.

"I think I do, too," said Josh.

"Well, that takes care of six of us," moaned Andy.

"How much are the canoes?" asked Brian.

"$2.00 an hour, " replied Pete.

"I've got five dollars," said Brian.

"Me, too," said Mike.

"Count me in," added Adam.

"Hey, we can go then! Come on everybody!" Beth said, jumping up.

"I'll have Cook make us some sandwiches and pack some chips and sodas. We can picnic while we're there," said Andy, dashing to the house.

"He's hungry again?" asked Mike

"He's never full," corrected Pete, laughing.

Everyone quickly got out of the pool, and dried off. The Bakers and the Gandersons went home to change, while Brian, his friends, and the Bradford's returned to the Bradford's house to do the same.

Several minutes later, Pete had the van, complete with Andy and Beth and their guests, along with sandwiches and drinks waiting in the church parking lot for the others to finish changing and climb aboard. As soon as everyone was present and seat belted in, Pete headed off to the state park, where they immediately rented 5 canoes. The boys sat in the front or the back of the canoes, manning the oars, while the girls were each placed in a middle seat.

"Follow us to a great picnic spot!" yelled Dale as they started out. The canoeists followed the placid shoreline until they came to a tiny cove. There they beached the canoes, and went in search of logs or rocks to sit on. They put their log and rock chairs into a circle and talked until finally Andy could not take it anymore, and went to his canoe for the sandwiches and sodas. As they finished eating, Brian made a comment about the sun, lowering on the horizon.

"Yikes! I bet it's getting late! What time is it?" asked Diana

Pete looked at his watch. "Gather up the trash, gang, and man the boats. We're going to have to paddle hard to get back in time for Youth Group!" he said, in a worried tone.

The teens hurried as fast as they could, but the wind had picked up, and the lake was a little choppier than it had been when they started out. This made the paddling harder for the boys.

"I think my arms are going to fall off," complained Andy as they returned the oars to the rental shack and hurried to the van.

Dale glanced at his watch. "Somebody else's arms are going to get a work out at this rate," he moaned.

Paul looked at his watch and winced. Pete drove as fast as he dared back to the church.

"Quick, girls! Go tell Dave that we're grabbing our guitars and we'll be right there. Paul, are you going to run home for your guitar, or are you playing the keys?" Dale asked.

"You kidding? I'm on my way to the ivories right now!" Paul said, running after the girls.

"Brian, just follow Paul and the girls, if you can. If they manage to ditch you between here and there, just wait in the lobby for us, OK?" Dale yelled over his shoulder, running to his back door.

Brian grinned at his friends and took off after the other BBGs, with his friends right behind him.

The group rushed, breathless, into the youth room. Dave was seated at a table and looked knowingly at his watch, and then at the BBGs and their friends.

"Sorry," mumbled Di.

"Pete and Dale are coming," added Beth.

Dave laughed at their red faces and labored breathing.

"You can join your committees for the summer retreat," he said, and then added, "Since we had no worship team to start with, we got right down to business matters. I'll give everyone 5 minutes longer to work on their tasks, and then we'll do announcements and worship. There will be plenty of time after that for a message and some volleyball."

Within several minutes, Dale and Pete plowed into the room. Dave laughed again.

"Welcome, fellows. We're working on our committees for the summer retreat for a few more minutes. Catch your breaths and get set up," he said.

A short time later, Paul was leading the youth into a time of worship, and then Brian and his friends listened intently to Dave's message. After that, the group headed outside for a volleyball game, and then came back in for a snack.

"Eat up quick, guys, so we can get to the Pizza Place for our ice cream," said Dale quietly.

"What's the rush, this time?" asked Adam, who was enjoying every minute of the busy and full lives the BBGs seemed to lead.

"If we're here when church is over, and our fathers manage to get back here before we get out, there won't be a trip to the Pizza Place," Pete answered.

"Why not?" asked Mike

"It's life in a fishbowl, Mike. If you're the Pastor's kids, or the elders' kids, you are not late for youth group or church. Unless, of course, it's your parents' fault," said Dale.

"And, of course, our parents are never late," put in Diana.

"Isn't that pretty harsh?" asked Brian. He lived in a home where the few rules were seldom enforced.

"That's the life of a fish in a bowl, Brian. We have to be better behaved than everyone else. Everybody talks about what we do and what we don't do, and everybody has an opinion on how our parents should raise us. Besides that, we're supposed to be setting the standard bar for behavior, here," sighed Paul.

"Man, that sounds rough," said Brian, sympathetically.

The 3 older boys laughed.

"Not really. We still know how to have fun, we just have to pay the piper when we're done!" said Pete with an impish grin.

"Come on, let's go get Andy and Josh and get out of here," urged Meg nervously.

As they walked through the door into the hallway, Dave stopped them and asked, "Leaving kind of early, aren't you?"

"These guys have a ways to go before they get home tonight. We don't want it to get too late," replied Dale.

Dave smiled, and looked directly at Dale. "Do you really believe your Dad is going to buy that?" he asked.

"Probably not, but what difference does it make whether we get grounded tonight or tomorrow?" asked Dale.

"That smells an awful lot like manipulation to me," Dave said doubtfully.

"Well, we've got to go! See you!" Dale said anxiously, when he saw Andy and Josh coming with Beth.

Dave shook his head as he watched the BBGs leave quickly through the lobby doors.

The teens hurried to the Pizza Place, ordered their snack, and finally relaxed when they sat down to eat their cold treat.

"Well, I will say you guys aren't boring," said Brian.

"That's something we never claimed to be," Josh said, laughing.

"But seriously, I never realized that being a Christian could be fun and exciting. I can even understand the adult's messages, here! It makes me want to go home and read some more, to see what you guys are talking about. This is the life," sighed Brian.

The BBGs grinned. It was still fresh in their minds how first Dale, then Pete and Paul, then the girls, and finally Andy and Josh had gotten caught up in the life. The teens finished eating, and then Brian looked at his watch.

"I hate to say this," he started sadly, "but we really do have to get going."

This caused a round of groans among the teenagers.

"Well, I guess all good things have to end some time," Pete said as the group cleaned their tables off.

The BBGs walked Brian and his friends to their van, gave hugs all around, and waved until they couldn't see the vehicle any more. It was beginning to get dark, and although there were fewer cars in the parking lot, Dale noticed that most of the lights in the church were still on.

"Well, I think I'll just leave my stuff over there tonight," Dale said

"Me, too," laughed Pete.

The teens wandered over to their tree house, climbed up and lit the lanterns that they kept in a plastic container there. They sat around on the pillows and cushions that were kept in another large wooden box, and talked about the excitement of having their first experience of leading strangers to the Lord. Suddenly, a voice floated up to them. Crowding around the railings, they could see that it was Dave.

"You guys still up there hiding?" Dave asked.

"Not hiding. Just delaying," said Paul.

Dave chuckled and said, "Your parents weren't real happy with your disappearing act tonight, that's for sure."

"They noticed?" asked Andy, with a grin that told Dave he was being sarcastic.

Dave laughed again. "You all are nut cases. Why don't you just go in there and face the music?" he suggested.

"Because I can face the music. It's my parents that I'm having trouble facing," grinned Dale.

"Coward," teased Pete.

"Well, I don't see you in there," complained Dale.

"I never said that I wasn't a coward, too," Pete laughed.

"Well, I expect that your dads will be locking up soon, then. I'll see you all Wednesday," said Dave, turning to leave.

"Coward," grinned Pete again, this time speaking to Dave.

"You bet I am. Especially when it comes down to your fathers practicing their back hand swings," Dave chuckled.

"Do you think that's going to happen?" asked Josh in a worried tone.

"Well, Josh, probably not if you'd all stuck around tonight and apologized for being late. But sneaking out quick to avoid your parents, and then not coming back in to get your stuff to continue to avoid the issue; I'd put my bets on Old Faithful," Dave said, this time speaking seriously.

"But Old Faithful is just for whenever we directly disobey what they have told us to do. We're not disobeying, we're just skirting the issue," said Josh.

"That's called manipulation, Josh, and I know that's a corporal offense," Dave said quietly, then added, "so, I'll see you on Wednesday." The BBGs had nothing to say about that, and just watched as Dave turned and walked to his car.

"Well, I think I better get going too, and get the van home. You two coming?" said Pete.

"Yep," answered Beth and Andy, climbing down from the tree house and heading for the parking lot.

"I'm going home, too," said Josh. "I'd rather meet Dad in his study at home than come face to face with that thing they keep in your Dad's desk drawer, Dale." he added.

Dale smiled at the younger boy. "That's right, you've never met Old Faithful, have you?" Dale asked.

Josh shook his head, no, and said, "And I'd like to keep it that way, if you don't mind".

Dale patted him on the back, and then Josh took the hand glider down to the ground. Paul and Meg followed him as Dale and Di used the ladder.

When Dale and Di walked into their kitchen, their brother Steve was putting the finishing touches on his ice cream sundae.

"Well, what's the verdict?" Steve asked

"What verdict?" asked Dale.

"Are you grounded?" asked Steve.

"No," said Dale tersely.

"Meet with something a little more unpleasant?" asked Steve.

"No, and I'm going to bed before Dad gets home," Dale answered, stomping up the steps.

"Whew. What happened?" asked Steve, as Di got a drink from the refrigerator.

"We haven't seen Dad yet. So do me a favor, and don't remind him when he comes in, OK?" Di answered.

"Oh, boy! Well, your secret's good with me, Di, but are you sure you want Dad simmering all night?" Steve asked.

Diana giggled. "Maybe a good night's rest will cool the pot instead of simmer it," she suggested.

Steve laughed. "Well good night then, enjoy it while you can," he said.

CHAPTER 6

The next morning, when no mention was made of the previous day's activities by any of the parents, Diana's wishful thinking seemed to be coming true. Dale's mood, however, had not cooled off, and he irritably snapped at his brother, Steve, more than once before breakfast.

"Why don't you just walk across the parking lot and talk to Dad? Why put yourself through this silly waiting and worrying game?" Steve finally asked Dale, as they put their cereal bowls in the dishwasher.

"When an opening comes up for the position of my conscience, I'll let you know, Steve. Until then, though, just leave me alone!" Dale snapped again.

Di, standing at the sink, turned and looked at Steve and shook her head. Steve grinned at her, which made Dale stomp noisily from the kitchen. He went into the garage to get the paint he needed to repaint the patio furniture.

After lunch, Beth called Diana. "Got all your work done?" she asked.

"For now," Di sighed.

"Well, then, do you want to go for a bike ride with Andy and me?" Beth asked.

"I've got to do something to get out of this mopey house," Diana agreed, and then added, "Isn't Pete coming?"

Beth giggled on the other end of the line. "No, your sweetie pie has a stale attitude," she replied.

Ordinarily, Diana would have scolded her friend for calling Pete her "sweetie pie," but today, she was more interested in what a stale attitude might be.

"What's a stale attitude?" Di asked Beth, after thinking about it for a moment and not figuring it out.

"As in lacking freshness, old, stale," Beth teased.

"What?" Di was still not getting it.

" It's a B.C. Attitude," explained Beth.

"B.C.? That's Before Christ, Oh! Now I get it! That's a good name for it. Dale is awfully stale here, too," giggled Di.

Beth laughed with her friend, and then said, "Well, if you're coming along, do you want to meet us at the foot of your driveway in 15 minutes?"

"Yep. Have you called the Bakers yet?" Di asked.

"I'm doing that now. See you in a few!" Beth said, and hung up.

As it turned out, it was only Meg and Josh who joined them from the Baker family. Apparently, Paul's attitude was no better than Dale or Pete's.

The group rode up to a nearby lake, and sat on the benches placed around the beautiful lake to rest after their ride. They stretched their legs out in front of them, and rested their heads on the back of the benches, silently wrapped in their own thoughts.

"Actually, I guess we're the wrong ones, not Dale, Pete or Paul," Beth said after a few moments.

"Huh?" asked Meg, breaking out of her own thoughts.

"I mean, I know it's their consciences that are bothering them," Beth started. When none of the other teens contradicted her, she tried to finish her thinking out loud.

"The way I figure it, if Dad's willing to overlook it, and not say anything about us being late, then who am I to bring it up?" she said.

"Yeah, but you know Dad's not just overlooking it. I don't know what he's doing, but I do know he's not just overlooking it," argued Andy.

"I don't get it, either," put in Josh. "Three months ago, they would have been down at the Pizza Place after church and dragging us out of there by force," he added.

"Three months ago, we wouldn't have had friends come to the Lord yesterday," Meg countered.

"That's true, but it doesn't explain why nothing's been said or what our Dads are up to now. This not knowing stuff is what's driving me crazy," said Di.

"Me, too," agreed Meg.

"It's not fair for them to drag it out like this, avoiding the subject all the time," complained Andy.

The others burst into laughter, and Andy looked confused.

"What?" he asked.

"Don't you see, Andy? That's exactly what we are doing! We're all dragging it out and avoiding the issue," said Beth.

"Yeah, but we do that a lot. Why would our dads being doing something so, so, juvenile?" asked Josh.

Beth rolled her eyes. "Who, besides our Moms, knows why our Dads do most of the things they do?" she asked.

The other teens nodded, silently thinking to themselves.

"But the bottom line is, that no matter what our fathers are doing or why, what we are doing is still wrong," said Josh.

"You're absolutely right," said Beth, sadly. "We are skirting the issue instead of facing it head on," she added.

"Come on, Josh, you know the girls will just get a lecture and get grounded. We guys have to face something a little stiffer, that is, if Dave knows what he's talking about. I, for one, am not anxious to meet my dad in his study," said Andy.

"Me neither," agreed Josh.

"So what's wrong with holding off as long as we can?" Andy pressed his point.

The pinched look on his face, however, told his friends that in spite of his words, he too, was uncomfortable sitting under the fingers of conscience and conviction.

"Shouldn't we at least wait for Pete, Paul, and Dale to come around before we say anything to our parents? Otherwise, it's going to look like we're snitching on the boys," said Di.

"Will it make a difference if we wait or not? I'm not sure I'm willing to go as long as those guys can go with these guilty feelings," Meg said.

"I don't know," said Beth.

The group lapsed into silence again and took the drinks out of their backpacks that they had brought along with them. After finishing the drinks without further discussion, the group got back on their bikes and rode home, arriving just in time for dinner.

"It's awfully quiet around here tonight," remarked John Baker, as his family sat around the dinner table.

"I'm really tired, Mom. Do you mind if I turn in after I get the dishes done? That bike ride really did me in this afternoon," said Meg quietly.

"Sure, Meg. Maybe a lukewarm bath and some bath salts will help," suggested Patti Baker.

"Great idea, Mom! Thanks!" said Meg, and got up to clear the table off.

"There's supposed to be a great meteor shower tonight. Want to grab a blanket and go take a look?" Josh asked Paul.

"Sure," replied Paul. The boys got up and helped their sister with the kitchen clean up.

As they disappeared into the kitchen, Patti grinned at her husband.

"This is sort of nice, this quiet and tip toeing around. How long can we stretch it out?" she asked.

John laughed heartily at his wife, and went into the family room to watch the news.

In the Ganderson household, Kristen kept up a steady stream of conversation around her family's dinner table. Finally, Carl seized the opportunity to ask Dale what he had done that day.

"I painted the patio furniture," Dale said sullenly.

"I see. And you, Di?" Carl asked his oldest daughter.

"Beth, Meg, Josh, Andy and I rode up to Silver Lake after lunch," said Diana.

"Just you guys? Where were the older boys?" asked Carl.

"They didn't want to come," mumbled Di.

"That's unusual," remarked her father, waiting for either Dale or Di to offer an explanation. Neither BBG said anything more, so Carl continued on his own.

"By the way, Dale," Carl said, "I brought the guitars back from the church for you. Can you make sure that Pete gets his?"

"Thanks, Dad. May I be excused? I'll run Pete's guitar over to him now," Dale asked.

"Go ahead, Dale," Carl nodded.

"Come on, Steve, help me with these dishes. I need to get to bed early tonight," said Diana, getting up.

"Kristen, take the plates in for Steve and Di, all right?" said Kelly Ganderson, getting up and following her husband to the family room.

Dale found Pete in his backyard, laying in a hammock.

"Brought your guitar back," Dale said simply, putting the case beside the tree that held the front of the hammock.

"Thanks, Dale. Did you run into the church today and get them?" Pete asked, rolling on his side to face Dale.

"No, Dad brought them with him when he came in for dinner," Dale answered.

"Are you OK?" asked Pete, sincerely.

"Nobody said a word," Dale replied.

"It's the same at our house," said Pete.

"Well, I guess I'll head back home," Dale said, then added, "enjoy the 'mock."

"Right. See you tomorrow," Pete waved at his friend, and then rolled back onto his back and closed his eyes.

Pete's parents were hosting a dinner party that night, and when he opened his eyes again, the pool, patio and garden lights were on. That meant that the guests and his parents had moved outside to enjoy the fresh air. Since the household help managed the entire affair, the Bradford children had been excused after supper. Beth and Andy were probably in their rooms, watching TV, or in the computer room playing games. Pete decided to go up to his own room and watch the newest video he had bought. By the time the dinner affair was over, Peter and Emma found all 3 teenagers fast asleep.

The next day, a heavy gloom seemed to settle on the BBG households. Diana waved to Meg as they hung up laundry in their yards together, and then waved to Andy as they appeared at the mailboxes at the same time. However, there were no afternoon phone calls or plans to get together after lunch. While the gloom made the younger BBGs tired and apathetic, it made Dale, Pete and Paul irritable. The older boys hardly spoke to anyone at all.

Late that afternoon, when Dale announced that he was going up to his room to read, Diana took a chance and slipped away to the church and her father's office.

"Dad?" she asked cautiously as she knocked on the open door.

"Wow, supper already?" asked Carl, starting to get up.

"No, not yet. Do you have a couple of minutes to talk?" Di asked timidly.

Carl sat back down. "Of course. Come in and close the door," he said.

Diana cringed inwardly. A closed door usually meant trouble. She couldn't continue in her present state of misery, though, so she bravely stepped into the office, closed the door and sat down in a chair her father placed in front of his desk for her.

"What's up, Di?" he asked, going back to sit in his own chair.

"I should be asking you that. What's my punishment? Please hurry up and tell me!" Diana said, closing her eyes tightly.

Carl laughed to himself at the sight of his daughter, sitting in the chair with her eyes closed and her hands gripping the chair arms tightly.

"Have you done something that needs to be punished?" Carl asked.

Diana opened one eye just long enough to say, "Come on, Dad! You know!" and then closed her eyes again tighter than before.

Carl got up and walked to the front of his desk. He sat on the edge of it, and loosened Diana's hands from the chair arms. He held them both in his large hands, and spoke as gently as he could.

"Diana? I can't punish you if you haven't done anything wrong, honey. The whole purpose of discipline is to get you to remember the consequences of your actions, so you don't keep doing the same wrong thing over and over," Carl said quietly.

Diana sat still, and didn't say a word.

"Diana? Please open your eyes, sweetheart," Carl said.

Diana slowly opened her eyes. She looked into her father's eyes and relaxed a little bit when she saw the love and compassion there.

"You came to talk to me, honey, remember?" Carl prompted when he felt her relax.

"What's this all about?" he added, when it looked as if she was having trouble getting started.

"We were late for youth group Sunday night. You knew that, Dad," Diana said, barely over a whisper.

Carl let go of her hands, smiling. "Yes, I did know that," he agreed.

"Well, then?" Diana pleaded.

"Well?" Carl asked.

"You always ground us or something for being late," Diana squirmed.

"Yes, that's true. And I did come looking for you guys after the service to ask you about it," Carl said, looking into Di's eyes.

She was so uncomfortable that she could no longer meet his eyes. "Brian had to get home," she mumbled.

Carl sat up straight and spoke firmly for the first time since Di had come into his office.

"Let me clue you into a little secret, sweetheart. Lying about what you've done or making excuses about it will only make it worse," he said.

"Well, he did!" said Diana insisted.

"That's funny, then, Diana, because I saw his car in the parking lot for quite awhile after church was over," Carl said, returning to the front of his desk, and taking his seat there.

Diana's eyes hit the floor. "We went for ice cream," she whispered.

"I know," Carl said, waiting for Diana to say more.

"Oh, Dad! Just ground me and get it over with!" Diana cried.

"That won't do your conscience any good, Di. Do you want to still feel this miserable after you're finished being grounded? What drove you to come to me this afternoon? If I slap a restriction on you, is that going to make all these uncomfortable feelings go away?" Carl asked.

Diana thought for a moment.

"This is about confessing our sins to each other, isn't it, Dad?" she said finally.

Carl sighed and whispered "Thank you" before he continued saying, "That's exactly what this is about, sweetie."

Diana smiled, and then said, "I feel better just thinking about doing that!"

Carl chuckled, then said, "I'm listening, Di".

"Oh, Dad! We knew we were late, and we knew you'd be looking for us after church, but we just wanted to spend more time with Brian! And then it got late, and we thought, well, the boys thought, it'd be better to face you at home instead of in here, with Old Faithful. Then none of you said anything more about it, and we all got so confused! Now Dale's a bear, and can't be lived with. He's hurting bad," Diana finished sadly.

Carl looked at his desk, thinking. Diana fidgeted nervously.

"You haven't seen Meg or Beth today, have you?" Carl finally asked.

"I waved at Meg when we were hanging up laundry," Diana replied sadly.

"Well, your mother tells me it's almost as if you've grounded yourselves," Carl said.

Di thought for a moment and then said, "Yes, I guess it is."

"Well then, Diana, I am confining you to the barracks until Youth Group tomorrow. No visits and no phone calls. Understood?" Carl said, as sternly as his smiling face would allow.

"I understand, and thanks, Dad!" Di said, getting up.

Carl stood up and gave his daughter a hug.

"And no more manipulating things so you can get the fun stuff in before you face the music. Do you hear me?" he said.

"OK, Dad!" Diana said lightly, as she walked out of the office and back across the parking lot to her home. Kelly Ganderson watched her daughter coming across the lot as she sat on a chair in the backyard patio. The look on Diana's face was enough to tell her mother that all was well again in Diana's world.

After dinner that evening, Diana did the dishes, and went back up to her room.

"What's she so cheerful about?" grumbled Dale as he and Steve took out the garbage.

"Seems that she and Dad had a talk and now she's grounded," Steve answered.

"Oh, that's great. Just great," Dale said, angrily. He expected a call to his father's den when he returned to the house, but no summons came at all throughout the entire evening. It just served to make Dale's anxiety and therefore, his misery, grow.

Over at the Bakers, while Di was speaking to her father, Josh and Meg talked together quietly as they made a salad for supper.

"I've got to talk to Dad," Meg sighed.

"Me, too. I just can't do this waiting game any longer," moaned Josh.

"What about Paul?" asked Meg.

Josh shrugged. "He's not getting any better, Meg. In fact, I think he's worse than he was yesterday. We're better off leaving him to his own devices," he answered.

"Do you think he's going to be mad at us if we do talk to Dad?" Meg asked.

"You bet he is. But what's easier to take, him or Dad?" Josh asked.

"I'll go with taking Paul's wrath upon myself," Meg said, grinning.

So, after supper, Josh helped Meg get the kitchen chores done as quickly as they could. Opportunity was presenting itself as they watched their parents make their way out to the patio with their evening coffee. Paul had taken his dishes into the kitchen, and then wordlessly disappeared back up to his room.

"Hurry up, Meg! We can talk to Dad as long as the bear hibernates!" Josh whispered.

Meg finished what she was doing, and the two walked outside to the patio.

"It's a beautiful evening, kids. Got any plans?" John Baker asked warmly.

"No," said Josh.

"Yes," said Meg at the same time.

They looked at each other and laughed.

"I mean we don't have plans to go out," Josh said.

"But we do have plans that will probably guarantee that we don't have plans to go out," Meg said.

This time it was their parents' turn to laugh.

"Now could we please have that in parentese?" John Baker chuckled.

Meg plopped herself into a chaise lounge.

"Oh, boy. I don't feel so good anymore," she moaned, looking at Josh.

"Are you sick, Meg?" Patti Baker asked, alarmed.

"Not exactly, Mom," sighed Meg.

"Well, what exactly do you mean then?" asked John.

"We, uh, Meg and I that is, we need to ask you something," Josh stumbled over his words.

"And what's that?" asked John, putting down his newspaper and giving his children his full attention.

"Well, not exactly ask you," Meg said.

"You're awfully full of not exactlys, Meg. What is this about? Meg, you go first," John said, looking at Meg.

"I guess we need to talk to you about Sunday night," Meg said, looking at the grass.

"And what about Sunday night?" asked John.

"Well, you know," said Meg, looking up in hopes of finding understanding in her father's eyes.

"Suppose you tell me," John answered instead.

"We were both late for youth group," blurted out Josh.

"And why was that, exactly?" John asked.

"We rented canoes at the park, and the water was a little choppier on our way back, and it just took longer," Josh said.

"That makes sense to me," John said.

Meg and Josh waited for their father to say more, wondering what their punishment was going to be. John, on the other hand, appeared to have finished discussing the topic, and picked his paper back up.

"So?" Josh asked finally.

"So?" John asked back.

"So are we grounded?" Meg asked

"Well, I'm sure that it was an accident that you were late," John said calmly.

Meg and Josh looked at each other in disbelief.

"That's it?" asked Meg.

"That's it," John said, smiling.

"You aren't angry with us?" asked Josh.

"Should I be?" his father asked back.

"Well, we did break the rules," stammered Meg.

"Yes, you said you were late for youth group," agreed John.

"And you usually ground us for that," Meg said.

"Meg, you sound as if you want me to punish you. I've told you that I believe it was an accident that you didn't get back on time. I'm sure you started out with good intentions, but you were just surprised at the choppiness of the waves. I can't call that intentional misconduct, kids. Unless you have more to add, I'm willing to overlook your lateness this once," John said.

Josh and Meg squirmed. Finally, Meg said, "There is more, Dad. We left youth group early so you wouldn't catch us before we could get to the ice cream place."

"And we've been avoiding you and the subject since then. Mostly because I was afraid," Josh stopped for a moment to push the sob back down in his throat.

"Afraid of what, Josh?" John Baker asked his son, as he leaned forward in his chair.

"Afraid of getting my name on Old Faithful," Josh admitted.

John laughed and got out of his chair to envelop his son in a big hug.

"So you were being manipulative to save your backside? Josh, look at me," John waited until Josh lifted his eyes to meet his father's. "I'm not interested in scaring you. I'm sorry you panicked. That's not what discipline is all about, son. Discipline is supposed to be helpful to you, not terrify you. It's supposed to get you to think about the consequences to your actions before you do something you might regret. Can you understand that?" John asked kindly.

Josh nodded.

"Now, you two, I'm not going to let manipulation slide. Megan, I've seen the punishment you've put on yourself, making yourself miserable. I'm just going to add a little bit to that. You're grounded until youth group tomorrow. Understand?" John spoke sternly to Meg.

"Yes, Dad," Meg said.

In spite of her father's stern face, she couldn't help the smile on her own face that came from being freed from her burden of guilt.

"Get to bed," John said, giving her a wink. Meg gave her father a quick hug, and her mother a peck on the cheek before running off to her room.

"Now, Joshua," John looked at his youngest child.

Josh cringed at the use of his full name.

"If you're going to run with the big boys, you should be ready for their punishment, don't you think?" John asked seriously.

Josh lowered his head. "I guess so," he said.

John gave him another hug. "Then stop being afraid of me! And I want you to be prepared to go to my work site tomorrow morning. You'll be putting in a full day with me," he added.

Josh beamed. "Thanks, Dad!" he said.

"Now get to bed," John told him.

Josh hurried to give his mother a hug and get inside. John and Patti exchanged smiles and went back to their newspapers and the cool evening breezes.

CHAPTER 7

At the Bradford residence, directly after lunch that same day, Beth walked out by the pool. She was restless, and even a phone call to a friend did not seem appealing. She was thinking about her father's upcoming trip to New York City. He would be leaving early the next morning, and not returning until dinnertime. If she was going to talk to him, it was going to have to be now. She paced back and forth in front of the pool, weighing her decision in her mind. If she spoke with her father today, it would put Andy and Pete in a bad predicament. If she didn't, however, she was looking at more days of guilty misery.

Peter Bradford sat in his office, looking out of the windows to the pool area. He could see Beth pacing back and forth, obviously weighed down about something.

"Give her courage," he prayed.

Finally, Beth sat down on a lounge chair. Her shoulders began to shake from the sobs that her father couldn't hear. He prayed harder for his oldest daughter, and suddenly, she dried her eyes with her arm, and started back for the house. Peter thanked the Lord for His help, and returned to his papers. When Beth knocked on his door moments later, he was ready for her. He gently asked Beth to come in, and kept the smile to himself as she planted herself in front of his desk. Beth took a deep breath and announced, "Dad, I need to apologize for being late on Sunday night. We went to the lake, and didn't know the waves were going to be so rough coming back. It took us longer to get back in the canoes than we planned. Then we slipped out of youth group early so you couldn't keep us from going to get ice cream. I know I've been avoiding you and the entire issue so I wouldn't get grounded. But I've decided that being grounded isn't nearly as bad as this miserable feeling of waiting for the boom to fall."

Peter almost laughed at her dry, mechanical way of confessing, but kept a straight face as he said, "Apology accepted, Beth. Go up to your room and stay there until I get back from the city tomorrow. I'll let the cook know that you will take your meals up there, and I'll speak to Mom about it, too. I understand that accidents will happen and that you didn't mean to be late. I'm also sure, though, that leaving youth group early was planned. That planning is also called manipulation, and that's something I won't tolerate. You know that, don't you?"

"Yes, Dad, and I am very sorry," Beth said, softly now, with all her defenses gone.

"I know you're sorry, honey. Now get along with you, and no phone calls, understand?" Peter said, standing up to give Beth a hug.

"Thanks, Dad," Beth smiled up at her father.

"I love you, Beth," Peter said, then chuckled out loud as Beth skipped down the long hallway.

Andy was in the family room at the end of the hall when Beth skipped by.

"Hey!" he called out, and Beth stopped momentarily.

"What are you up to?" Andy demanded.

"I am on my way to my room. To stay there until Dad gets home from the city tomorrow," Beth giggled.

"And that's good? It sounds like you're grounded to me," Andy said.

"I am, and believe me, it's never felt so good!" Beth laughed and went upstairs.

"She's either crazy or she's got something there," Andy said to himself. After thinking for a moment, he turned off the TV that he was watching and walked down the hall to his father's office.

"Dad?" Andy asked, knocking on the open door.

"Hi, Andy, come in," Peter Bradford smiled.

"Can I get in line for this miracle cure Beth found?" Andy asked.

"Of course you can. The doctor is in, so to speak," Peter said kindly.

"Well, I don't know what Beth told you, but I am really sorry about Sunday night. We were late, and then we tried to avoid you so you couldn't punish us while Brian was here. Sorry, Dad," Andy said contritely.

"I understand about not wanting to be reprimanded with Brian around. But why didn't you guys come in to the church to see us after he left? We waited quite a while in the church for you," Peter asked.

Andy blushed, which was something he rarely did.

"We, well, we figured it would be easier to face you here rather than over there," he said.

"And why is that?" Peter wondered aloud.

"It's called Old Faithful," mumbled Andy.

Peter had to let the laugh out at that remark, but then got serious and said, "I'm sorry, Andy, it's not funny to you. I'm glad Old Faithful is such a deterrent, but a deterrent is supposed to prevent you from doing things, not get you to find ways around the consequences after you've already done something wrong."

"Sorry, Dad," Andy repeated.

"Well, I'll tell you what I told Beth. I understand the accident that made you late. You probably would have been home free if you would have just come in and told us what happened before you went for ice cream. But this deviousness has to stop. No more manipulating. Understood?" Peter said.

"Yes, Dad," Andy said, humbly.

"You're grounded until tomorrow night. You are not to leave that room until I see you when I return from the city. Now skedaddle!" Peter said

"Wow! Thanks, Dad!" Andy said, leaving quickly.

"It's called undeserved mercy!" Peter called after him, chuckling.

That night, at supper, Pete looked at the two empty spots at the dinner table.

"That's funny," he thought, "I know Andy is in his room. I could hear the TV going, and I saw Beth going down the hall earlier, too." As much as his curiosity was piqued, Pete thought it was best not to mention the facts to his parents. It might lead to an embarrassing conversation. After his parents retired to the deck for their coffee, though, he cornered his brother Jon, and demanded, "What's with Andy?".

"I don't know," Jon said, "Maybe he's sick or something."

"I guess I better investigate," Pete said, going upstairs and knocking on Andy's door.

Andy called for him to come in. Pete opened the door and eyed the supper tray sitting on Andy's desk.

"You don't look sick," Pete commented.

"I'm not sick," Andy answered.

"Well, Jon and I thought that's why you weren't at dinner tonight," Pete said

Andy laughed. "No, I'm just grounded until youth group tomorrow," he said.

"Grounded? For what?" asked Pete.

"For our little prank on Sunday," replied Andy.

"You told?" Pete raised his voice, causing Beth to poke her head out of her bedroom door.

"Pete, you'd better keep it down, or you'll have Dad up here, too," she warned.

"Mom and Dad are outside, Beth. Anyway, Andy told Dad about Sunday!" Pete said, his voice only a little lower.

"Really? Good for you, Andy," said Beth.

"Are you crazy? Now Dad knows. What's going to happen to you and me?" Pete asked.

"I am going to be grounded until Youth group tomorrow night," Beth said.

Pete stood for a moment, letting those words sink in. "You too?" he finally asked.

Beth nodded. "I couldn't take the waiting any more. I was driving myself crazy," she said.

"It's a lot easier to live with yourself after you talk to Dad," Andy agreed.

"For you, maybe. As for me, I don't happen to be having a problem living with myself," Pete said angrily, going back down the hall to his room.

Beth smiled at Andy. "I still think we did the right thing," she said.

"Me, too," Andy smiled back.

When Peter Bradford returned from his train trip to New York City the next day, Pete went quickly up to his room before his father could spot him. After greeting Jon, Micah, and Suzi, Peter went up the stairs to his room. He showered, put on some casual clothes, and walked down the hall to Beth's room. He knocked on Beth's half opened door, and sighed a sigh of relief when he heard her cheerful "Come in!" answering his knock. It had been a long day, and he was not looking forward to any confrontations with his children.

When Beth saw her father enter the room, she jumped up and gave him a big hug. Peter held her tight and silently thanked the Lord for the gift of love from his daughter after a difficult day in the business world.

"How was New York?" Beth asked, pulling away from her father to look at his face.

"The same town it always is, honey. How are you?" Peter asked.

"I'm fine," Beth smiled.

"What did you find to do up here all day?" Peter asked.

"Oh, I read some books, played on my computer, slept late, nothing really special," Beth said.

"Well, sweetheart, let's go find Andy and get down to supper. I am hungry!" Peter said, putting his arm around Beth's shoulders. They walked across the hall to get Andy, and then walked down the steps to the dining room together.

Pete, meanwhile, fumed in his room. "Goody Goody two shoes," he grumbled to himself when he heard the cheerful voices of his sister, brother, and father.

"Sure, every thing's fine for them," he continued to himself as he threw himself on the bed, sulking.

As the rest of the family gathered for dinner, Peter noticed that his oldest son's chair was empty.

"Emma, dear, where's Pete tonight?" Peter asked his wife.

"I don't know, he hasn't left the house all day," Emma replied.

"He's in his room. I saw him laying on the bed when I came down," Jon offered.

"Oh, my! I hope he's not sick!" said Emma.

"I'll go check on him, dear. I'll be right back," Peter said, and disappeared up the stairs that were located outside the dining room. Steeling himself for his oldest son's anger, he knocked on the bedroom door. Pete grumbled a "Come in," but did not get up from his place on his bed. "You alright, Pete?" his father asked when he entered the room and saw Pete laying on his bed.

Pete looked at his father, seeing the day's weariness there in his face.

"I'm fine, Dad. I was just taking a little snooze. Is it supper time?" he said, deciding at that moment not to add more to his father's day.

"Yes, it is. And cook has a pot roast ready that I can smell from here. Let's go eat!" Peter said, thanking the Lord again for his son's sensitivity.

They walked down to the dining room and enjoyed their dinner. Shortly after they had finished eating, Pete got a phone call from Dale.

"Do you want to come over early and get a worship set together?" Dale asked.

"Sure. I'll be there in 15 minutes," Pete answered.

Pete and Paul arrived at the Ganderson's at exactly the same time. The boys sat with their guitars on the patio, planning the worship for the teens that evening.

As they were finishing up, Dave walked over from the church. "Hey, guys, how's it going?" he asked cheerfully.

"Fine," said Dale, curtly.

Dave chuckled, and said, "I can see from your faces that it is anything but fine. I'll see you in the youth room in a couple of minutes."

When the boys didn't reply, Dave headed inside the sliding glass doors to the kitchen, where Carl stood.

"They're miserable," Carl said, as he opened the door for Dave.

"Yes, they are. Is it because they've received their just desserts, or because they haven't?" Dave asked, grinning.

Just then, Diana flew into the kitchen. "Oh, hi Dave! Sorry to interrupt, but Dad, can I go over to the church now so I can return these books to the library?" she asked.

"Sure, honey," Carl said, and then when Diana had left, turned back to Dave. "To answer your question, Dave, one child has received their just desserts, the other hasn't. Can you tell which is which?" Carl chuckled.

"A split decision with that group? Will wonders never cease?" Dave laughed, shaking his head.

"Probably not in our lifetime, brother," Carl said, and the two men walked over to the church together.

At youth group that night, Dave learned a lesson that would remain with him for all the remaining years that he had BBGs with him. As hard as they tried, the BBGs were never able to lead worship when everyone's hearts weren't right before God. Tonight was the first time that the group had tried to lead worship when some of them had unresolved issues in their hearts, and the worship they managed to bring to the group fell miserably flat.

After their failed worship attempt, the boys sat in a moody silence as Dave gave the message for the evening. As the teens filed out for their weekly volleyball game, Dave stepped in front of the older boys who were purposely last in line.

"Any chance of an attitude adjustment?" Dave asked in a low voice.

"Like a snowball in hell," Dale said.

"Fine, Dale. But watch your language. I can still take you down if I need to," Dave answered, stepping aside. The boys passed angrily by, and joined their brothers' and sisters' team in the yard. Dave watched the game closely. Dale, Pete and Paul played more aggressively than he had seen in many month's time. Their fists slammed into the ball with such fury that Dave hoped the ball wouldn't pop. Just before the last game was over, Carl came out from the adult service.

"Early dismissal? Are you running for ice cream?" Dave teased his pastor.

"Sort of, without the ice cream run, though," answered Carl with a grin. "There's still some ministry going on in the sanctuary, but Mr. North was wondering if you'd mind if he came over to pray for these guys before they eat? He has a heart for youth," Carl added. Mr. North was the adults' guest speaker for the evening.

"These guys need all the prayer they can get," Dave said.

"The boys giving you a hard time?" Carl asked.

"Yes, but don't worry yet. I think the volleyball took a big chunk of their anger," Dave answered.

Just then, the other youth leader called, "Game point! This side wins," and pointed to the team opposite from the BBG's. Pete held the ball in his hands. He slammed it to the ground, making it bounce high and at a strange angle. It flew onto a nearby storage shed roof, and started rolling down the roof's steep incline. As it rolled, it picked up more speed, and headed straight for the screened window of the men's bathroom.

"Boom!" the ball hit the screen, and fell into the bathroom, leaving a large hole in the screening.

"Smooth move," whispered Dale, with the first hint of a smile anyone had seen in days.

"Easy for you to say," grumbled Pete, but with a smile growing on his face as well.

John Baker then joined the teens and adults standing outside, asking, "Who issued the invitation to play through the window of the bathroom?" He tossed the ball to Dave.

"Pete did that," Dave answered.

"That must have been some wild hit to get it to do that," John said.

"I didn't hit it in there. The shed roof sent it in there," said Pete.

"The shed roof?" John asked, with a puzzled expression on his face.

"It was a very unexpected result to a display of poor sportsmanship," Dave explained.

“Poor sportsmanship?” asked Peter Bradford, hearing the tail end of Dave’s comment as he came out to join his friends.

“Actually, I think it was incredible sportsmanship. I bet neither of us could have done that,” whispered Paul to Dale standing beside him. Dale laughed in response, then added in a low tone, “I think we better get out of here,” The men and teens were starting to head back inside.

“Pete!” said Paul, as loud as he dared, and when Pete turned to face him, Paul nodded towards the tree house. All 3 boys tried to nonchalantly move towards the tree house, but Dave was watching.

“Guys! Hurry up! Mr. North has asked to pray for the youth,” Dave said.

The boys looked at each other, their faces as dark as storm clouds.

“Oh, no! You’re not pulling the run off and hide routine tonight, fellows. Even if I did turn my back again, your dads would fly out of here so fast we’d think a sonic boom just hit us. Now get in here,” Dave said firmly.

Sullenly, the 3 boys went back into the building, and into the teen room. There, they joined into the circle the teens had formed, standing beside the girls. Diana looked at Dale’s sullen face.

“You can’t go on like this,” she whispered. “Please, please, talk to Dad,” she added.

Dale just gave her an angry look. Diana turned her face, hurt by her brother’s reaction.

Mr. North prayed for the group, and then approached the BBGs as they helped themselves to the snack.

“Thanks for praying for us,” Beth said kindly.

“Yes, thanks! We’ve heard a lot about you,” added Meg.

Mr. North smiled. “Girls,” he said slowly, “You’re very welcome. But I doubt that these young men will say the same thing when I’m done saying what I have to say to them.”

He immediately turned to the 3 older boys and said, “You 3 are a rebellious lot. But God has called you, and He is patient for you to come back to Him. This won’t be the only time you’ll run from Him, but it’ll be the farthest out you’ll go. Each time after this, your running will be shorter, and shorter, as your hearts draw nearer and nearer to Him. You are His now, and He will not let you go. Now my personal advice to you three is to stop playing this little game you’re playing, and confess whatever wrongdoing you need to confess to your parents. Like I said, God is not letting you go. Your lives will be miserable until you get your relationship back on track with Him. Okay?” Mr. North was serious, and the BBGs looked at each other, dumbfounded for a moment.

Dale crushed the cup he held in his hand, but his face was visibly paler than it had been.

“Stupid fishbowl” he said, and then threw his cup in the trash and headed for the door.

"Everybody talks around here," added Pete, glaring at Andy and Beth for a moment, and then following Dale.

"Just put the news in the bulletin," said Paul, as he angrily followed the other two.

"See, I told you that would happen," Mr. North said to Beth, grinning at her look of amazement as the boys stomped out of the room.

Just then, Carl, John, and Peter came up to the group.

"Hello, Mr. North. I'd like to introduce John Baker and Peter Bradford to you. They're my elders here. I know we haven't gotten a chance to talk with you yet, so I'm wondering, how long will you be in the area?" Carl asked.

Suddenly, a light bulb flashed in Diana's brain, and she realized something very important.

"Dad!" she said excitedly, "excuse me for interrupting, but do you mean that you haven't spoken to Mr. North at all?" she asked.

Carl looked at Diana, confused. "No, Di, we were introduced right before the service tonight. Mr. North's plane was delayed this afternoon, or he would have eaten dinner with us," he said.

"Then, all that stuff you said to the boys, you didn't already know?" Beth asked Mr. North.

Mr. North smiled at Beth. "No, dear. But now I understand the tall blonde's comment of 'stupid fishbowl'. That must have been your son, Carl," he said.

"A tall, blond boy hanging around these kids? Yes, that would be Dale," Carl replied, still confused.

"Come on, gang! We've got to go tell them!" said Meg, grabbing Di's hand, and motioning for the others to follow her out of the room.

They ran to the tree house, and clattered up the ladder.

"He didn't know you!" Di shouted, the first to reach the top.

"What are you shouting about?" asked Dale angrily.

"Mr. North, he had no idea of who you were!" added Meg, the next one up.

"Oh, come on, he knew exactly who we were," scoffed Paul.

"Well, he somehow knew exactly who you were, all right, but he had no idea whose sons you were," put in Beth.

"How do you know?" asked Pete.

"Because, Dad introduced himself to Mr. North right in front of us after you guys left. Mr. North was supposed to have supper with us tonight, Dale, but his plane was delayed. Dad's over there now, trying to set up another dinner date," Diana said.

"And he knew all that stuff about us without anyone telling him anything? And I'm supposed to believe that?" asked Dale angrily.

"But it's true! And he didn't know until just a second ago, that you were the PK!" exclaimed Meg.

"You're crazy! Everybody knows that," said Paul.

"Not if you just walk in the door to the church a few minutes before the service starts," Josh said quietly.

Maybe it was because Josh was the only one who wasn't shouting, but after he spoke, silence reigned for a few moments among the group.

"I'm going in," said Dale, finally. He used the hand glider and slid to the ground, the others following suit.

"Even if this is true, it doesn't make living in this fishbowl any easier. It just makes the bowl a little bigger. I hate it!" yelled Dale.

"Shhhhh . . . I don't want him to hear us. I don't want him telling me anything bad about myself," said Andy.

"Come on, let's just go get our guitars and get out of there," said Pete.

CHAPTER 8

The group walked back over to the church, and entered the Sunday School wing through a side door. They walked down the hall to the youth room hoping that it would be cleared out. To their dismay, Dave stood in the far corner talking to a group of teens. Worse yet, when he spotted them, he called, "Dale, Pete, Paul, I need to talk to you guys. Don't disappear again, please."

"Yeah, right, Dave," Dale muttered and picked up his guitar.

"You better wait!" said Meg fearfully, as Pete picked up his guitar as well.

"I've been waiting for 3 days now. If he wants me, he knows where to find me," said Paul, as the older boys started for the hall door, leaving the others gaping after them.

"Yo! Guys! I asked you to wait a few minutes!" Dave called after them. He excused himself from the other group of teens, and started after the boys. Before he could reach them, however, John, Peter, and Carl came out of the kitchen and stood in the hallway before their angry sons. The BBGs didn't know that after making dinner plans with Mr. North, their parents had returned to the kitchen for another cup of coffee. As the adults stood in the kitchen chatting and finishing their coffee, they could plainly hear Dave's two requests for the boys to wait, and they could also hear the sound of his hurried footsteps after the second request. The men now stood before the boys, blocking their way down the hall.

"Into the primary classroom, now, boys. Girls, you can go home with Andy and Josh," Carl said sternly, and then turned towards Dave, who had stopped in the doorway to the youth room.

"Dave, they'll be in here for you when you're finished in there," he added.

Dale then did what he later regretted very much. He shrugged his shoulders in an 'I don't care' manner, and walked as slowly as he could into the classroom. Carl watched his son for a moment, and then excused himself from his friends. He took Dale's arm and led him to a corner of the room. In a low voice, he said, "That reckless gesture, along with this attitude that's been hanging around for the last couple of days has just earned you a visit to my office when Dave gets through with you. If I were you, son, I'd start back peddling that attitude right now."

Dale wouldn't answer or look up. He just hung his head and sat down. Carl went back to the kitchen and rejoined his wife and friends with their coffee.

A few moments later, Dave walked into the room where the 3 boys sat.

"Hey, guys, I just wanted to know if beating the pulp out of the volleyball helped to get rid of some of that anger you're carrying," Dave asked sincerely.

"And why shouldn't we be angry?" demanded Pete.

"Whoa, Pete, back off, bud. I haven't done anything to you guys. I'm trying to help," Dave said.

"If you wanted to help, then why didn't you just let us go home? Why did you have to go and stop us?" demanded Paul.

"Did you really think that your dads were going to let this one slide? Pete, you've even got a broken screen to make amends for. Your dads aren't blind, you know. They can see you've totally lost it with your attitudes," Dave said, and then suddenly stopped. He looked at his hands for a few moments, and when he looked up again, the sadness in his eyes went right to the boys' hearts.

"What I wanted to help with, actually, I was hoping we wouldn't be having these conversations anymore. Maybe I should have just left you to your dad's designs, but I happened to have witnessed the Lord coming into your life, Dale, and then yours, Pete and Paul, through him. I just can't stand to see the old you come back out. I wanted to help you guys find the way back home. Maybe it was my own selfish motives all along, wanting something more for you guys. I'm sorry, fellows, for meddling, when my intentions were really to help," Dave said, and rose to leave. When he reached the parking lot outside, he noticed that his wife was not yet at their car, and he could see the remainder of the BBGs sitting around the Ganderson's picnic table. The light from an insect repellent candle played on their faces, and it looked as if they were praying. He decided to approach the teens, but was a little fearful of how they might view him at that moment. He held back until Andy raised his head and saw him.

"Dave!" Andy leaped from his seat, his actions and loud voice startling Dave for a moment. Andy rushed at Dave, not noticing the startled look on Dave's face and not seeing the look of fear flicker in his eyes momentarily. He wrapped his arms around Dave in a big bear hug, and said in a voice that was broken, "I'm afraid for them, Dave! Will they stop being the old Dale, Pete, and Paul? Will they come back?"

Dave relaxed and returned the embrace, saying, "I hope so, Andy," as gently as he could.

The teens made room for Dave to join them on the benches, and then looked toward the church. They saw the lights go off everywhere except for the light in Carl's office, and the lights in the rooms adjacent to his office.

"Dear Lord, please have mercy on the guys. Give Dad good judgment," prayed Di.

"Send your mercy to all of us," agreed Dave.

Meanwhile, in the church kitchen, Emma, Patti, and Kelly washed out the coffee pots and then headed home. Their husbands, however, waited in the kitchen for Dave to leave. When Dave poked his head into the kitchen and said good night, the men joined their sons in the Sunday School classroom. The men and boys sat silently for a few minutes, working to calm their emotions.

While he sat there in gloomy silence, Dale suddenly felt a twinge of something inside of him that he had only really ever felt once before. Carl had been watching his son stare unseeingly out the window. He saw Dale's face suddenly change for a moment. The rock hard look on Dale's face softened, the frown between his eyes disappeared., and his mouth, which was set in a tight line, relaxed.

Carl jumped at the opportunity. "Excuse us, gentlemen. Dale, can I see you in my office?" he asked.

Hearing his father's request made the frown and the tight jaw return to Dale's face, but the softness in his eyes remained. Without a word, or a glance at Pete or Paul, he got up and followed Carl down the hall. When he entered his father's office, he saw the plain, rectangular, wooden paddle they had nicknamed "Old Faithful" laying on his father's desk. A marker lay beside it.

"Go ahead and put another mark by your name, Dale," Carl said.

Dale picked up the marker and looked briefly at the names of his friends and siblings written on the paddle. He added another toggle mark to the row of marks next to his name, and noticed that the other marks had faded. He then realized that it had been a long time since he had last met Old Faithful in his father's office. Sighing, he closed the marker, put it back on the desk, and turned to his father.

"Sit down, Dale. I'm willing to be the first to listen," Carl instructed his son in a quiet voice as he made his way to his chair behind the desk.

Dale sat in a chair across from the desk, silently thinking. Finally, he said, "Aren't you the one who's supposed to be talking and bringing the charges?" he asked.

Carl noticed that the dark brooding had returned to Dale's eyes, and he shook his head.

"I will son, believe me, but first, I want to hear your explanation. Please, Dale?" he asked, with compassion in his voice.

The softness in Dale's eyes flickered back. He was confused. Why was his father being so polite? They both knew what the outcome to this meeting was going to be, and Dale could see no possible good coming out of prolonging the preliminaries. Suddenly, his eyes landed on a new picture hanging on his father's wall. It was a framed pencil drawing of a courtroom. A judge sat at the bench, and the artist's depiction of Jesus stood before the judge, an arm looped around a frightened looking man. Jesus stood pleading the sinner's case before His Father. A lump formed in Dale's throat at the picture, and the memories it invoked. Carl, who noticed that the picture had captured his son's attention, said, "Dave bought that picture for me, to remind me of the day that you accepted Jesus' defense for your life."

Dale nodded silently, unable to take his eyes off the picture to meet his father's gaze.

A knock sounded on the door, and Carl got up and silently handed Old Faithful and the marker to the father standing in the hall, who was hidden from Dale's view behind the door. After his father had seated himself again, Dale turned his attention back to the picture until he heard the familiar ring of Old Faithful coming from the secretary's office next door. It rang out again, and the sound of the second strike startled Dale. He looked at his father.

"Paul?" he whispered

"No, Pete," Carl answered.

"Dad?" asked Dale, shaking his head to rid his mind of the sounds he thought were better off forgotten.

"Yes, Dale?" Carl said kindly.

Just then, Old Faithful rang out again, and this time, Dale jumped up.

"Dad, you've got to make Mr. Bradford stop! I'll take it for Pete if I have to!" Dale said in a worried voice.

Carl got up and went to the door before Dale could get there.

"Take it easy, Dale. I'm sure that was Paul's turn. I wouldn't be so quick to volunteer myself, though, if I were you. Do you think my swing has gotten a little weak from not being used?" Carl asked, smiling.

"No, Dad, I'm sure your swing is just fine. Those guys are my best friends! Neither of them has done anything to deserve this! What have I done to deserve this, anyway?" Dale asked frantically.

"Sit back down, Dale, and let's talk about what we're doing here," Carl said, returning to his seat as Dale sat back down.

After a little knock, the door opened as they sat down. John Baker stepped in and put Old Faithful and the marker back on Carl's desk.

"Good night, Carl. Dale," John said, giving Carl a weary smile and turning to give Dale a nod.

"Everything OK?" Carl asked

"Mission accomplished," John answered.

"Good. See you Sunday," Carl said.

"Good night," John said again, and disappeared out the door.

"Now, Dale, what are we doing here tonight?" Carl started the conversation with his son again. The stormy look came back to Dale's face, and Carl sighed.

"If I have to stay up all night with you, Dale, I will. We can stay here for as long as it takes. I have some finishing touches to my message to work on. You just holler when you're ready to talk," Carl told his son, and then turned to his computer and began to type. Dale stood and walked over to a wall that was filled with pictures. Arranged on the wall in a wheel shape, were pictures of all 4 Ganderson children. Baby shots, formal portraits, and casual shots filled the wall. Many of them had been taken by Mrs. Bradford, who then had them framed and gave them as gifts to Carl and Kelly. Scattered in the hub of the wheel were pictures of the Community church. Beautiful shots at sunset, in the stark winter sky, in the bloom of spring, all of which were also taken by Emma Bradford. Carl and Kelly's favorite wedding picture hung in the very center of the scenic church photos. It showed only the backs of the bride and groom, but it showed the serene face of Carl's father, the pastor who presided over the wedding, with his hands on Carl and Kelly's shoulders, giving the final prayer and blessing before releasing them to the congregation as husband and wife. The photographer had wrapped the picture in a soft glow, and Dale could well understand why his father and mother loved the portrait as much as they did. It had an ethereal quality to it.

But Dale was not dwelling on that picture tonight. The picture that he found himself staring at was slightly to the right of the wedding picture, but still in the center of the wheel shape. It was of a black and white Bavarian scene, complete with snow topped mountains in the background, and a spire topped cathedral at their foot. In the center of the photograph were 3 men, dressed in white t-shirts and pants, standing in the middle of a small pond. Dale knew that this was a photograph of his father's baptism, taken when he was a young man stationed with the US military in Europe.

Dale's mind began to wander, thinking back to all the stories his father had told him about his military career. As Dale looked at that picture of the baptism, he realized that his father had never told him the story behind it. He knew his father's testimony by heart, but it always seemed to stop at the baptism part. Dale stepped closer to the picture. His father was in the middle, with a man holding each arm, heads bowed in prayer.

Taking his eyes reluctantly off of the baptism scene, Dale looked over to the section that held his pictures. He daydreamed momentarily about what other pictures would someday hang there. His high school graduation? His wedding? His baptism? Sighing, his eyes roamed back to his father's baptism picture. Would he ever get baptized?

"Oh, I meant to tell you, Dale, that we have plans to go to the Creation Festival up north with the Bradfords, Bakers, Smiths, and a few other couples at the end of this month," Carl said without looking up from his typing.

"What? Oh, Creation. OK, Dad," Dale said absently, then returned to his thoughts about baptism.

"Dad?" Dale asked after a few more moments.

"Yes, Dale?" Carl answered, this time looking up at his son.

"What do you have to do to be baptized?" Dale asked quietly.

"Believe," Carl said.

"What else?" Dale asked.

"Nothing. You're symbolically identifying with the death of Christ, and becoming a new creature in Him," Carl said, then added, "You mean you haven't been to enough baptisms to know that?"

Dale blushed. "Well, yeah, but I guess I never listened in terms of myself before," he said.

Carl laughed. "I think I understand," he said.

"Dad?" said Dale again, after a few more moments of quiet. "Yes, Dale?" Carl said patiently.

"Do you think Mr. North was right in what he told us?" Dale asked.

"What did he tell you?" asked Carl.

"That we, I mean, Pete, Paul, and I, were a rebellious lot," Dale said, looking at the floor.

"Well, as of 8:00 tonight, I'd say that was pretty accurate," said Carl.

"But he also said that this was the farthest we would travel away from the Lord. He said it wasn't the last time we'd run from Him, but each time after this, our coming back to Him would get shorter and shorter, because we'll be nearer to God, and the way home will be quicker. Do you think that's true?" Dale asked, sincerely.

"I hope it is, Dale, with all my heart," Carl answered quietly.

"He also said to stop playing this game and confess our wrongdoing to you," Dale said slowly.

"Sounds like very good advice to me," Carl agreed.

Dale sat back down, but continued his train of thought.

"But how did he know, Dad? How did he read us so exactly right?" he asked.

Carl stopped typing and turned his chair to face Dale.

"How did you know the right songs to play and the right things to say to Pete, Paul, Meg, and Brian?" Carl asked.

"Well, Dad, I just did. It was just like something that I knew, inside of me," Dale replied.

"I'd say that's exactly what Mr. North would tell you, too, Dale," Carl said.

"But, Dad, why would the Lord tell Mr. North anything about us? I mean, we know right from wrong, and we believe in Him already, we were just being rebellious, like Mr. North said," Dale wondered out loud.

"Dale, why would I care about what you've done? Why am I sitting here with you tonight?" Carl asked.

"Because I'm your son," Dale answered.

"And you're also a child of God, Dale. Don't you think God cares about you as much as I do? Is it that hard to picture God sending someone like Mr.

North to get your attention and point you in a better direction? Isn't that something a Father would do?" Carl pushed his point.

"Well, yes, I guess so," said Dale, trying to let that sink in. He got up and walked to the baptism picture again, turning his back on his father.

Carl smiled, shook his head, and went back to his typing.

Five minutes later, Dale turned around again.

"So, Dad. Let's get these charges cleared up so you can put Old Faithful away," he said, rocking back and forth on his heels.

Carl stopped typing again, and turned around to face Dale.

"I'm listening," he said.

"For what?" asked Dale.

"For you to talk to me," Carl replied.

"I've been talking!" Dale said irritably.

"When you're ready, son," Carl said calmly, going back to his typing.

Dale looked up at the ceiling. What did his father want? For him to calmly state his offenses and then calmly take the punishment for them? He had to be crazy! If that was what his father wanted, well, Dale would just say that he had nothing to say. Then they could both go home. After all, this whole meeting was his father's idea, and therefore it should be his father's responsibility to lead it. Why was he so cheerfully typing away at his sermon, and acting as if nothing was going on? Dale just didn't get this at all. The phone rang in the middle of Dale's thoughts, and Carl answered it. It was Kelly.

"Yes, dear, we're fine. We're just waiting for Dale to finish up business here, and we'll be home as soon as he does. Don't wait up for us, hon, just send the kids to bed and climb in yourself. I don't know how long this is going to take. I love you too, dear. Good night," Carl said, and hung up. Turning to Dale, he said, "Your mom worries about you, too, Dale, and loves you dearly."

Dale nodded, but then let his thoughts go back to his father's behavior.

"How can you do it?" Dale asked, finally.

"Do what?" Carl asked.

"Pretend like nothing is wrong, and be so polite and cheerful when you know the outcome of all this will end at my backside?" Dale asked

Carl looked at Dale's eyes. The hard sheen was back, this time with fire blazing behind it.

"The reason, Dale, that I can do this is because, unlike yourself, my conscience is clear before God tonight. I don't enjoy disciplining you or your brother and sisters. I do it because the Bible says that a father disciplines the child that he loves. And I do love you, in spite of any other crazy notion you might have rattling around up there in your brain," he said sternly.

"Then get it over with, and stop playing games with me!" Dale shouted.

"Sit down, son, and lower your voice to me," Carl said firmly.

Dale closed his mouth tight and sat, but his eyes still glowered at his father.

"I can't clear your conscience for you, Dale. I told Diana the same thing. If I just tan your hide tonight, you'll still be the same miserable goat you've been all week, only one with a tender backside as well. I'll wait for as long as you need, Dale, I've told you that already. But this is your responsibility," Carl said, looking straight into Dale's eyes.

Dale thought back to Mr. North's words. "Confess your wrongdoings to your parents," the man had instructed the boys. As Dale sat and angrily refused to bring that upon himself, he continued to survey his father's office. Across the room from the wall of photographs, Kristen's drawings peppered the wall. She was a good artist for a 7 year old. Mixed in with Kristen's art work was the cross stitch cartoon Diana had made for her father, and the shelf Steve had made in shop class the year before in school. Dale's eyes then abruptly landed on a single wooden frame, holding a typed piece of paper. Squinting to see it better, he realized that it was the poem he had written and printed out on the computer right after the eventful youth conference of a few months ago. He had given it to his father to read, but had never expected to find it framed and hanging on his father's wall. The poem expressing his feelings about personally meeting the Lord Jesus meant so much to him, that he sat quietly remembering the words. As he said them to himself, a funny feeling started in the pit of his stomach again. It was the same feeling that he had first felt at the conference, and then again just a bit ago in the Sunday school room. What was that feeling? It was getting stronger, and Dale was beginning to feel pretty bad, and a little afraid. The last time he felt like this, he had ended up in a small room with a man named Mark praying over him while he sobbed and sobbed. Dale did not want to repeat that scene in front of his father, so he tried to shake the feeling. He looked away from the poem, but his glance landed instead on the drawing of the courtroom. A huge lump began to form in his throat as he looked at the picture. Jesus was once again taking the blame for Dale's disobedience, and once again was going to have to act as an advocate with the Father for him. Dale realized then, that while Jesus was busy going before the Father for him, Dale himself did not even have the courage to admit his wrongdoings to his earthly father and accept a very temporal punishment.

While Dale wrestled with himself, Carl had finished typing and had turned his chair to watch his son. Suddenly, he was startled to see tears start streaming down Dale's face. Carl's heart lurched. Tears had not been seen from Dale's eyes in over 10 years. Certainly, Carl had seen the remnant of tears in the occasional red eyes and blotchy cheeks, but full blown sorrow was something new to him. Coming from this son, at first it frightened him.

"Dale! Are you OK?" he asked loudly.

"What?" Dale asked, and then realized himself that tears were falling down his cheeks.

"Ummm, no, Dad, I'm feeling kind of funny. No, not funny, bad. It's the same feeling that I got at the conference, but I don't know what it is, or how to get rid of it," Dale said sadly.

"What did you do at the conference to get rid of it?" asked Carl.

"Cried like a baby. For a long time," said Dale, with the first hint of a smile.

"What happened before you started to cry like a baby?" Carl asked, suddenly well aware of what his son was experiencing.

"Well, before that, I was just trying to tell God how sorry I was for . . . all . . . the . . . bad, rotten stuff I had done in my life up until that point," Dale said, as a light began to go on in his mind.

"It's called conviction," whispered Carl, as the sobs began to shake Dale's shoulders.

"Dad, I'm so sorry we were late last Sunday, it really wasn't our fault. The waves on the lake were really choppy, and we just couldn't make good time. And we wanted to hang out with Brian and his friends, so we just thought we'd delay your sentencing a little, and maybe try to get out of meeting with Old Faithful. Josh and Andy are really afraid, you know? But you never said anything to me, even after everyone else told except Paul and Pete and me. It was so hard to keep waiting and waiting for you to say something about it! I mean, I sure didn't want to bring it up in conversation, and then all of a sudden, the old me was back, and the attitude, and the negative thoughts about everybody, and then even worship fell flat tonight, and I felt like I had gone so far away, I'd never get back. I'm sorry, Dad, really, really, sorry," Dale choked through his sobs.

Carl tried to swallow the lump in his own throat. He was now not as willing to punish his son further, and he quickly considered doing nothing else except enveloping him in a hug. However, Carl knew the importance of consistency, and he knew that the ache in Dale's heart longed for an answer in tangible form. He desperately needed normalcy right now. What he did not need was for his father to pamper him and make him feel like a cry baby, or a weakling. So with great regret in his own heart, Carl finally said, "Dale, stand up and put your hands on my desk."

Dale stood and received his punishment, and then dropped to his knees in front of his chair, and poured out his heart to his heavenly Father. Tears began to form in Carl's eyes as well, and he stood behind his son, silently praying for him.

After a while, Dale stood up, wiped his eyes, and said to his father, "You're pretty smart, Dad, to know that's what I needed most."

"Thank you for thinking that way," Carl said, giving Dale a warm embrace that was returned by his son with equal measure.

"There's just one more thing to clear up, son," Carl said, after they had both wiped their eyes. He picked up Old Faithful to put it away, and laughed at

Dale as the boy took several steps back.

"I'm just putting this thing away, Dale," he chuckled, putting the paddle back into a drawer. Carl then went to stand in front of Dale.

"You know, there'd be one less mark for you on that thing if you would have just come to me and explained why you were late to begin with," he said firmly.

"I wish there'd be about 20 less marks," grumbled Dale.

Carl grinned and said, "I don't expect you to be perfect, nor do I necessarily expect tonight to be the last mark that will go on there."

"Well, I do," said Dale forcefully.

"Did you hear what I said a second ago?" asked Carl.

"Yes. You said that if we would have just explained why we were late on Sunday, there wouldn't have been a pow wow tonight. But, hey, Dad! What do you mean? I could have saved myself this little scene by just explaining what happened? Since when did any explanations change the course of things?" asked Dale in an angry tone once again.

Carl stepped back to his desk.

"Are you still carrying a sarcastic attitude, Dale?" he asked.

"No, but you tell me now that all this could have been avoided, and then you expect me not to be a little upset? These last few days have been a little bit less than fun, you know? And it certainly isn't fun to have my backside meet with that thing you have in your drawer. What would it have cost you to tell me all this in the first place?" Dale asked, his anger rising.

Carl sat down and opened the desk drawer again. "It sounds as if Old Faithful's work is not done yet. Your attitude could sure use a little tweaking," he said, looking intently at Dale.

Dale sighed, and walked back to his father's desk. He put his hands flat on the surface and said, "I'm sorry, Dad. I don't like this attitude any more than you do. If it can be whacked out of me, I'm willing."

Carl closed the drawer, and walked over to Dale. He put his hands on his shoulders and prayed for him, instead.

"Lord, I thank you for my son. I thank you for residing in him, and for the gifts you've given him. I thank you for his willingness to deal with his old self, and I ask you to give him the desires of his heart, and the grace to deal with old attitudes and feelings," Carl prayed, and then embraced Dale again.

"All I wanted to do, Dale, is to let you know that since I've seen your life change, I can ease up on the law a little bit. I know you didn't intentionally come in late on Sunday, because I know that your heart wants to be here. Your desire to be here and hear Dave's message is no longer because you're afraid of meeting up with Old Faithful if you don't show up. In other words, it is no longer just me making you show up, you come willingly because it has become your own desire. Can you see the difference I'm trying to point out?"

Carl asked.

Dale nodded. "Yeah, Dad. I just hope I deserve that trust," he said.

"You've already proved that to me," Carl said warmly.

"Thanks, Dad," Dale said quietly.

Together, the father and son turned off the remaining lights, locked the last door, and walked across the empty parking lot, with Carl's arm looped around Dale's shoulders.

Diana and Kristen's room overlooked the parking lot, and Diana had been sitting on the window seat watching and praying. When she saw the lights in the church go off, she looked hard in the dim light of the parking lot to be able to see her father and brother come out of the building. When she finally spotted them, she looked intently at Dale's face. She couldn't be sure, but his expression seemed to have lost its hardness, and he seemed peaceful. When she heard the back door open, she waited quietly in the hall for her father's footsteps.

"Dad?" she whispered when she saw him.

"Yes, Di? Why are you still up, honey?" Carl asked

"Is Dale, is he OK?" she asked.

"He's fine," Carl said, opening his arms to give her an embrace.

"I was so worried!" Di said, clinging to him.

Carl smoothed her hair. "We were all worried, honey. But remember that God does not give up on us that easily. He loves Dale, and the rest of you hoodlums dearly," he said.

"Thanks, Dad! " Di whispered and hurried back into her room so that Dale wouldn't see her in the hall.

Carl smiled as he watched Di retreat, and then went into his own room. Kelly was sitting in bed reading, but she put her book down and got up to give him an embrace as soon as he came in the door. Carl held his wife, and allowed his emotions to drain from him while he was wrapped in her love and acceptance.

Finally, Kelly pulled herself away just far enough so that she could see Carl's face. "Tough night?" she asked.

Carl smiled weakly. "Kelly, we've raised an awesome son. I just hope I make it through the next couple of years until we can set him free," he said.

"Ah, sweetheart, but by then you will have 2 more waiting for their turn in the final mold," she teased.

Carl tickled his wife in the side. "Stop encouraging me!" he teased.

Laughing, they both called it a day, and slept soundly for the first time in several days.

CHAPTER 9

The next day, the BBGs met at the Bradford's pool for lunch and a swim.

"Man, I'm glad you're back," Andy said to Pete, Paul, and Dale.

"Yeah, it makes me wonder how any of us put up with you before Jesus straightened you out," agreed Josh.

"You didn't have to put up with us, you weren't any different than we were!" said Pete, splashing both the younger boys.

"Well, I'll tell you what!" said Dale, "I'm a lot smarter now than I was a couple of days ago. Did you guys get the story that all we had to do was explain why we were late on Sunday, and everything would have been fine?" he asked.

"Yes, I heard that," said Paul, with a little regret.

"Me, too. Sure made me mad though," said Pete.

"Oh, man, I was so mad, Dad even got Old Faithful back out again," Dale said.

"Twice?" asked Pete, looking meaningfully at Dale.

Dale laughed, understanding exactly what Pete was saying.

"No, I said I was a lot smarter now. I jumped off that mad high horse, and hit the humble pie mighty quick," he said.

"Well, at least we've learned something and it's all over now," said Meg thankfully.

"It's not quite all over for me," Dale said, sadly.

"What do you mean? Are you grounded, too?" asked Beth.

"Do I look grounded?" asked Dale, spreading his arms .

"Well, no, but that minor detail hasn't stopped you from swimming before, especially if your parents weren't home," Beth said, defensively.

Dale smiled warmly at Beth, and gave her a quick hug.

"I'm sorry for that sarcastic remark, Beth. You're right. I might still be here even if I was grounded. A couple of months ago, that is," he said.

Beth smiled back to show she forgave him, and then asked, "So why isn't it over?"

"I need to apologize to Dave. I just don't think I'm going to be able to live with myself otherwise," Dale said, sadly.

"I think you're right, Dale. Can I come along?" Pete asked.

"Count me in," added Paul.

"I was going to run over after supper," said Dale. The boys arranged to meet at the Ganderson's after dinner, and then went back to their swimming. Shortly before the time when the families would normally sit down to eat, all of the BBGs went home and took showers. Dale called Dave and Anne's home and asked if the boys could visit for a few minutes that evening. Dave answered the phone, and told Dale that a visit was welcome, and then suggested that they bring the whole gang for dessert.

Dale relayed this message to Diana, who promptly called the Bradford's. Beth excitedly agreed, and then called the Bakers.

Soon after they had all finished supper, Pete pulled his family's large van into the Ganderson's driveway, and all the BBGs piled in. Carl had walked over to the van with Di and Dale, and peeked in the window at the teens sitting there.

"You guys and gals all OK?" he asked sincerely.

"Sure, Dad," "Yes, Pastor Carl," was cheerfully called out to him. Carl smiled, patted the car, and waved as Pete pulled out of the driveway and headed towards Dave and Anne's home.

When they arrived at the Smith's home, Dave answered the door before they had a chance to knock.

"Come on in, kids!" he said enthusiastically, and when they had all gathered in the living room, he added, "Dale, did you and Pete and Paul want to talk to me in private, or should we all just sit in here?"

"The living room's fine, Dave. We don't keep secrets in this group. At least, we shouldn't," said Dale, looking right at Diana.

"What? I didn't keep a secret from anyone!" Diana said, surprised.

"Well, somebody went clean with Dad and didn't clue me in beforehand!" Dale said.

"We all did. But you and Paul and Pete didn't want any part of it," said Meg, in her friend's behalf.

"You could have at least warned us," put in Paul.

"Are you kidding? We couldn't say hello to you without being bitten or barked at," said Josh.

Dave cleared his throat, and the teens immediately stopped bickering among themselves.

"The living room is fine," Dale repeated.

When they had all greeted Anne, and were seated on the couches and chairs in the living room, Dave said, "So what's this all about, fellows?"

"I wanted to apologize for being so obnoxious and for using BC language with you again. I'm sorry, Dave. I'll try my best to not let it happen again," Dale said.

"Your apology is accepted, Dale. I forgive you," Dave said kindly.

"I'd like to apologize for being so angry and mouthy with you last night, too, Dave. I know how difficult we used to be, and I never want to put you through that again," said Paul.

"Thanks, Paul," said Dave warmly.

"And I'd like to apologize for my outburst and my attitude, too. And the broken screen in the bathroom," said Pete.

"You're forgiven, too, Pete. Just for the record, how will the screen be replaced?" Dave asked, grinning.

Pete looked at the floor for a moment, and then said quietly, "That screen cost me plenty. There should be a workman there to repair it tomorrow."

"I'm sorry, Pete. I shouldn't have brought it up," Dave said sincerely.

"Oh, Pete, what did Dad say?" Beth asked.

"It's not what he said that hurt," grinned Pete, and then added, "The worst part is that for the next 2 weeks, my spending money is nil. Which means that I won't be going anywhere until then."

"That's OK, Pete, we just charge the pizza and the ice cream anyway," Beth said comfortingly.

"Not for the next 2 weeks, we won't," Pete corrected her.

"What do you mean?" asked Andy.

"Just what I said, Andy, we can't charge anything to the pizza place for 2 weeks," said Pete, his cheeks flushing from embarrassment.

"But Beth and I and the rest of us didn't break that screen!" Andy said angrily.

"I know, and I'm sorry, gang. I thought the punishment was a bit harsh, myself, and like I said, those opinions cost me plenty last night. I tried to get you guys out of it, honest!" Pete said sadly, his eyes focused on the carpet.

Dale suddenly remembered hearing Old Faithful ring out twice in Peter Bradford's hands, and said "That's OK, Pete. We'll be fine for 2 weeks. We'll just bum our treats off of our other friends, like Dave and Anne. See, they offered us ice cream sundaes before they even knew we couldn't get them at the pizza place."

"And anyone who gives Pete a hard time can meet up with Old Faithful and then tell us it's unfair. Right?" Paul added, looking at the others as if to challenge them.

Although it had been many, many years since the girls had put marks beside their names on the paddle, Josh and Andy remained the only two BBGs who did not have their names on it at all.

"Hey, speaking of ice cream, Anne, are we ready for sundaes?" Dave asked, in an attempt to lighten the atmosphere a little.

Anne nodded. "Just come into the kitchen, everyone. I'll be right back with the ice cream," she said, hurrying to the basement steps to get the ice cream from the large freezer that was kept down there.

As the group enjoyed their treat, talk centered around the upcoming Creation Festival. Finally, as they got ready to leave, Dave gave each teen a hug and said, "I sure do like this new group of teens that are coming to Youth group nowadays. And I'm also sure glad the old kids are gone."

The BBGs laughed, said their good byes and hurried home. Everyone was tired, so instead of doing anything else, they just went home and climbed into bed.

The next day, Andy approached his father in his office while Pete took Micah and Jon to the library.

"Dad?" Andy asked, knocking on the door.

"Yes, Andy?" Peter said, putting aside his paperwork.

"Ummm, do you think we could talk about Pete's punishment?" Andy asked.

"Sure, Andy, sit down," Peter said amiably.

Andy sat across from his father's desk.

"Go ahead, Andy," said Peter after Andy had seated himself.

"Well, don't you think it's, well, I mean, see, the rest of us didn't break that bathroom screen, and I mean, it just doesn't seem fair that we can't go to the Pizza Place just because of Pete's poor attitude and dumb actions," Andy stammered.

"You're right, Andy. Pete broke the screen on his own, and it isn't fair that you can't go to the Pizza Place because of him. But I never said you couldn't go. I don't even mind if Pete goes. What I said was that Pete won't have any spending money given to him for the next 2 weeks, and there will be no charging our account at the Pizza Place during that time. I don't have any objections to the rest of you going, or even if you want to pool your resources and treat Pete there," Peter explained.

"Well, that sounds a little better, but Dad, why are you punishing all of us?" Andy asked.

"Because the actions of a single person often affect the rest of the group, especially a group as tight as the BBGs are," Peter said.

"But we tried to get Pete to talk to you, Dad," Andy insisted.

"I don't doubt that you did, Andy, and I'm not asking you to be responsible for Pete. I'm only trying to make the point that what Pete did, from trying to manipulate his way out of the consequences to his own misdeeds, all the way to his attitude and his anger that ended up breaking a screen at the church, it all affected you. His grumpy moods affected our family and the youth group. I'm trying to show Pete and the rest of you that what you do is not just your problem. It can snowball like it did this time and touch many other lives. It's part of being a responsible person. A responsible person can look forward and see the bigger picture around them," Peter said.

"Yeah, so thanks a lot, Pete," grumbled Andy.

"Would you care to take the punishment that Pete took?" Peter asked firmly.

"Why should I?" asked Andy.

"Because you don't seem to think Pete's been punished enough," Peter said.

“I didn’t say that. I’m just upset that he had to drag all the rest of us into what he had coming anyway,” Andy said.

“What he had coming? Andy, I’m surprised at you! Maybe I should take back the undeserved mercy I handed out to you on this same matter,” Peter said.

Andy thought for a moment.

“Well, I guess it might have seemed unfair to Pete that Beth and I were just grounded for a day, and he ended up on the wrong side of Old Faithful,” Andy conceded.

Peter smiled. “I bet that thought crossed his mind,” he agreed.

“But Beth and I did talk to you sooner,” Andy said, and added, “and it wasn’t our fault that Pete didn’t do the same.”

“All right, Andy, I’ll lay it on the line here. You, Pete, Beth, and the little ones are all individuals. I do try to treat you as such. I was proud of you and Beth for coming to me when you did, and so I let the punishment slide a little bit. Beth should have been grounded for a week, and you should have met with my friend, the strap, here. But you guys lucked out this time, because I want to encourage you to come to me when you’ve messed up. Pete took a little convincing to get him to confess his wrongdoings, and because of that, I came down harder on him. Then when I told him about my Pizza Place decision, he fought for you guys to be able to go there free of charge as normal, knowing full well what that argument and attitude was going to cost him. If you think you’d be willing to take the punishment you deserved, like Pete did, I’ll be willing to reinstate the Pizza Place privilege,” Peter said.

“You mean, me take a strapping just so everyone can go have pizza and ice cream for free?” Andy asked, incredulous.

“Not just for that, Andy, but so that everyone will get what’s coming to them, and so we’re sure to be fair about this,” Peter said.

“But that’s crazy! That’s suicidal!” Andy exclaimed.

“But its fair, Andy,” Peter said.

“You can’t punish me twice for one simple little thing!” Andy said.

“Why not?” asked Peter.

“Because that’s not fair!” Andy said.

“Not fair to whom? You?” Peter asked.

“No, Yes, it’s not fair for me to take 2 punishments, especially for something I didn’t even do!” Andy said, getting a little worried at where his conversation might be taking him.

Peter smiled at Andy’s anxiousness.

“It’s Ok, Andy. I’m not trying to make you do something you don’t want to do. I’m just trying to show you that even though Pete didn’t do what you wanted him to do and when you wanted him to do it, he ended up doing the right thing. And he took your corporal punishment on himself by trying to stand up for your privilege of going for pizza and ice cream. Let me clue you into something, Andy, that apparently, Pete didn't tell you. My decision on the Pizza Place was made before the shredded screen. It's not a punishment for that screen. Pete's spending money will take care of that. It was meant as a lesson to all you BBGs to watch your actions, and consider how they will affect the rest of you. My attempt at teaching you guys that lesson infuriated Pete, and he understood what was coming to him if he argued with me against it. He was willing to take what should have been yours in the first place in order to try to protect you. So instead of blaming him, your attitude should be one of gratitude that he was thinking of you instead of himself," Peter said.

Andy thought quietly for a moment.

"Andy?" Peter said quietly.

"Yes, Dad?" Andy replied, looking at his father.

"If you're still undecided, can I throw in one more thing for you to think about?" Peter asked.

"Sure, Dad," Andy said, listening intently.

"I see you were not so willing to take the punishment for the others when you were given the opportunity to do so a few minutes ago," Peter said, gently.

Andy's face clouded. "You're right, Dad," he said, thinking hard.

"So be gentle with your brother, son. He paid a pretty high price," Peter said.

"OK," Andy said, and left his father's office, still in deep thought.

Andy walked into the family room, still wrapped in his thoughts. "We have to talk," Andy finally said to the girls as he sank into the soft pillows on the couch.

"What's wrong?" asked Diana, who was working with Beth and Meg on some BBG scrapbooks.

Andy explained what his father had just told him.

"Oh, man! Poor Pete!" said Beth.

"We ought to do something special for him," agreed Meg.

"Let's pitch in and take him out to eat," suggested Diana.

"Somewhere he really likes to go," added Meg.

"Like where?" asked Andy.

"Like that new steak house in Camp Hill?" said Beth.

"Yikes! How much does that place cost?" asked Diana.

"We were just there last month. I think the dinners were like $15 to $20. If we all pay for ourselves, and add a few bucks to pay for Pete, we should be able to do it," said Meg.

"So we'd all need about $20 or $25 dollars?" asked Beth.

"I've got that much," said Diana, not mentioning that she was saving her money for a new bathing suit.

"Me, too," said Beth, mentally putting away the new portable CD player she was hoping to buy.

"I have my birthday money left," put in Meg.

"I think I may even have $30!" said Andy.

"Go call Josh and Paul, would you, Andy? Maybe we can even go tonight, instead of trying to get a pizza. I'll go home now and make a dessert, and I'll tell Dale. I'm pretty sure he hasn't spent his lawn care money yet this week," said Diana, excitedly heading for the door.

Andy went for the phone. Meg went to look at the movie channel guide.

"Look!" she called excitedly, "Here's that new Mickey Peters' movie we've been wanting to see!"

Beth hurried over to look. "And it's on at 9:00! That's perfect, Meg! Let's see if we can make it a surprise sleep over!" she gushed.

Meg laughed. "It's going to be a surprise, alright," she giggled, and then left to do her chores and get ready to go.

When Pete got home with the younger boys, Beth met him in the hall.

"We're going out to dinner," she happily announced.

Pete looked closely at her, and noticed that she was dressed in a cute sun dress and nice sandals.

"We're going out to dinner with Mom and Dad on a Friday night?" Pete asked.

"Not with Mom and Dad, silly. With the BBGs," Beth said.

"Count me out, then. I'm broke," Pete said, with a sad sigh.

Beth could see that her brother's feelings were hurt by what he thought were his friends'

inconsiderate actions.

"Suit yourself," she said, and went to answer the doorbell. It was Dale and Diana, who were also dressed nicely.

"He's falling for it!" Beth whispered.

Diana smiled and slipped into the family room to put her dessert on the large coffee table. Pete looked over the balcony at them briefly before disappearing down the hall to his room, shaking his head sadly.

Paul, Meg, and Josh arrived next. Meg deposited sodas, chips, and salsa in the family room, while Paul and Dale went upstairs to Pete's room.

They found him flipping through the channels of his TV, while laying on his bed. Paul went to Pete's closet, and took out a nice polo shirt and a good pair of pants. He put them on Pete's chair and said, "Come on, Pete. Get dressed."

"What for? I told you guys several times that I don't have any spending money. I am broke," Pete said, irritated.

"Just get dressed and come on. We're all going and we need you to drive the van," Dale said.

"Yeah, you need me to drive. But I can drive in my t-shirt and shorts," Pete said, standing up to turn off the TV.

"Come on, Pete. Don't be a sourpuss. We'll even bring you a doggie bag hand-out," Paul said, grinning.

"Oh, you're too funny," Pete said, but took off his shirt and put on the one that Paul held out to him.

He grumpily changed his pants and followed Paul and Dale down the steps to the dining room, where his parents and 3 younger siblings were eating.

"Is it OK if I drive these guys to," Pete started, then realized that he didn't even know where they were going. He looked over at Beth.

"The Revere Tavern," she said sweetly.

She couldn't help the smile that played on her face at Pete's reaction to that news, so she turned her head. Pete looked at his parents for their answer.

"Is it OK?" he asked again.

Peter nodded his assent. Beth had already filled her parents in on the BBG's plans, and Peter had thought that it was a wonderful idea. He made sure that they had plenty of money to cover their meals, along with some extra to leave as a generous tip.

When they were all in the van, Dale, who sat beside Pete in the front, suggested that they stop at the church's property that they had nicknamed, 'the acreage'. It was a partially wooded area, with a pond for baptisms, and several sports fields. Pete didn't say a word in response, but instead drove to a parking area on the property and turned off the engine. Dale looked back at the others, and mouthed the numbers, 1,2,3, and then suddenly everyone yelled, "surprise!"

Pete had no idea what was going on. He looked around, confused.

"What's going on?" he asked.

"Drive to the Revere Tavern, Mr. Bradford. These are your friends, and this is your friendly appreciation dinner!" Dale said, gleefully.

"What? What do you mean?" Pete asked.

"We heard about what you took on our behalf, Pete. We just want to thank you for standing up for us," Diana said quietly.

Pete's face flamed.

"What? Who?" he stammered.

"I talked to Dad while you were out with Jon and Micah. I was pretty angry about losing our pizza privileges. But you made it sound like it was all your fault. Dad straightened me out on a few points," Andy said.

"Yeah, like Dad had already decided to take our pizza away before you did the screen thing," said Beth.

"And that you didn't think it was fair, so you stood up for us, even when you knew what was going to happen if you did," Paul said.

"We wanted to say thank you, Pete, so this is our way of doing it. You're in store for the best steak dinner you've ever had, on us!" Dale said.

"You mean, I'm not just driving? I get to come inside and eat with you guys?" asked Pete.

"You get to eat inside until you can't eat any more!" agreed Meg.

"You're serious? But isn't that place kind of pricey?" asked Pete.

"We're dressed for it," said Beth.

"And prepared for it!" giggled Diana.

Pete just put his head back on the headrest.

"Man, I have to apologize to you all. I had some pretty nasty thoughts going through my head about you guys. I am really, really sorry," Pete said, sincerely.

Diana, sitting behind him, patted his shoulder.

"You're forgiven, but let's go! I'm hungry!" she said.

Pete drove to the restaurant, where the girls had called in a reservation. When they got out of the car, Pete hugged the girls and gave hearty handshakes to the guys. Diana was the last in line for a hug, and Pete just casually left his arm around her shoulder as they walked across the parking lot. No one seemed to notice it, but Dale smiled to himself at the sight. He knew that his sister was beginning to have feelings toward Pete.

"Save room for my 'mud pie'," Diana said as they were finishing their meal in the restaurant.

"Your mud pie? This has got to be a mistake. I must be in heaven!" said Pete with a grin.

"And a Mickey Peters flick on at 9:00," added Beth.

Pete just rolled his eyes.

"For this treatment, I can almost say that what I went through was worth it," he sighed.

CHAPTER 10

They finished up their dinners, and then Pete drove them home. Since it was only 8:00, Andy suggested a flood light swim. He flipped the switch for the floodlights in the pool as he passed the box in the hallway, and the teens hurried upstairs to change into their suits. Each BBG kept a spare suit at the mansion, just for spontaneous times like this.

They swam for a while, and then sat in the chaise lounges wrapped in their towels and gazing at the stars. Finally, Beth complained that she was cold. She and the other girls excused themselves and went inside to shower and change back into their clothes.

"Why don't you take the kid's guest room, Meg, and Di, do you want to use a room on the 3rd floor? That way, we'll all be done at the same time, more or less," Beth suggested.

"Sure. Any of the rooms being used right now?" Di asked.

Beth had to think, which made the other girls giggle.

"Nope, nobody's here this weekend. Take any one you want, Di," Beth said.

The girls walked down the long hall, through the reception room, and then climbed the stairs to the 2nd floor.

"Meet you back downstairs!" Beth said, as the girls got their clothes from her room and continued down the hall to the guest rooms. As they passed the bedrooms, they could hear Beth's sister Suzi, giggling in her room with a friend. Micah's door was open, but he wasn't there.

"Whew!" said Meg as they crossed over the second floor's large open middle room with the grand staircase. "I don't know how Mr. and Mrs. Bradford keep track of who is in and who isn't. This place is huge!" she said.

Diana smiled and waved as Meg slipped into the children's guest room. For as long as she had known the Bradfords, there were never any kids in the children's guest room. She and the rest of the BBGs always bunked in their friend's room with them. Pete even had a roll away bed stored in his closet for the times when he had Dale and Paul over. Diana climbed up one more set of stairs, turned the corner, and walked down to the last guest room on the right. Going in, she locked the door, and began to daydream as she got ready for her shower.

Pete will probably own this mansion someday, she began thinking. The lucky girl who was chosen for his wife would then be the lady of the house. Diana turned on the shower and stepped in. What if she was the lucky girl? She remembered how nice it felt to have Pete's arm around her shoulders as they walked across the parking lot of the restaurant that evening.

"I wonder if it meant anything?" she thought and then chided herself for seeing more than there was to a simple act of friendship. She quickly finished her shower, dried her hair, and gathered her wet things together. She put them down the laundry chute, and then decided to take the elevator downstairs.

The elevator dropped her off outside the dining room, and she looked out the windows as she made her way down the hall to the family room. The pool area was now dark, so she guessed the boys were also upstairs taking showers.

When she reached the family room, she realized that she was the first one there. She turned on the TV, and then went over to the table to cut up her mud pie. The cook had conveniently left a knife, paper plates, forks, and cups for the kids. Diana cut the cake, put the knife on a napkin, and then turned around to go sit down on one of the comfortable couches. She jumped as she saw Pete, standing by the couch, watching her. She gasped, and that made Pete jump. Laughing, they both said 'sorry' at the same time.

"I guess I was in dreamland, Di," Pete apologized.

"Me, too. Your house can be so quiet," Di said.

"Only when we aren't entertaining," sighed Pete, as he sat down.

Diana sat on the other couch, facing the TV. Pete grinned.

"I did take my shower, so it can't be the smell," he said.

"What?" asked Di, a confused look on her face.

"If I don't smell bad, why are you sitting over there?" Pete asked.

Diana giggled. "Oh. Gee, I don't know," she said.

Pete got up and came over to sit beside her.

"I guess I'll have to fix it myself, then," he grinned.

Diana had no chance to respond, because at that moment Beth came in, followed by Meg. Apparently, neither girl found anything odd in Pete and Di sitting together on the couch, because the expressions on their faces didn't even change. The 4 other boys came in right after Beth and Meg, and whatever might have been beginning between Pete and Di ended with everyone's laughter and joking.

Peter and Emma Bradford stopped in on their way to bed to say good night to the teenagers.

"Beth, do you have clean towels for your guests?" Emma asked.

"Yes, Mom," Beth said.

"Did you tell the cook what you're having for breakfast?" Emma persisted.

"Oh, Mom, I didn't! Don't you think she can just throw in some extra eggs or pancakes?" Beth asked.

"Beth, a single guest is one thing, dear, but when you add 5 of your friends, plus Jon and Suzi's guests, it becomes a little more than just throwing in some extra eggs or pancakes," Emma said.

"What should I do?" Beth moaned.

"Leave a note in the kitchen for her, dear, with an apology for not telling her sooner," Emma said, smiling as her daughter got up slowly and trudged to the door.

"We'll go with you!" said Meg, jumping up, and motioning for Di to follow her.

The 3 girls raced down the hallway. Emma sighed and shook her head. The boys laughed, and finally Emma had to smile, too.

"Pete? How was your dinner?" she asked.

"Oh, Mom, it was great!" Pete said enthusiastically.

"Are your guests taken care of?" Emma asked.

"Guests? What guests? All I see are a couple of extra brothers," teased Pete.

"Well, they are like sons to your father and I, too, dear, but they still require clean beds and toiletries. Can I depend on your ability to be a congenial host?" Emma said warmly.

"Sure, Mom. All the way," Pete said.

"Good. Well, we'll leave you to your host and hostessing, then. Now remember, Beth, your sister has a guest, too. Try to keep the noise down to a bearable level on both sides of that bathroom, OK?" Peter Bradford said, looking at Beth as she and Meg and Di dashed back into the room.

"No problem, Dad. I never hear Suzi anyway, so I figure she can't hear us either," Beth replied, giving a little hop and jumping into an overstuffed chair.

Emma frowned. "Elizabeth Bradford! That had to be the most unladylike entrance I've ever seen! Please tell me you can do better!" she said with a smile in her eyes.

Beth sighed.

"Come on, ladies. Let's do this over again," she said, motioning for Meg and Di to follow her. They giggled and got up.

"But you have to make Pete and Andy do their part, too," Beth said, as she looked at her brothers, who were sprawled on the floor.

Emma and Peter smiled, nodded their agreement to Beth's request at Pete and Andy, and then stepped all the way into the room so they could get a good view of what was going to take place.

"What are we doing?" asked Meg in the hall.

"Learning some high society poise," Beth answered.

Di grinned, remembering her daydream in the shower. If it were ever going to come true, she was going to need all the training she could get in upper class etiquette.

"Just follow me," Beth instructed. "Make your face into this ridiculous half smile," she added, making her face into a blank expression with just a hint of a smile.

Di and Meg tried to copy her.

"Good enough. Now come on," Beth said, walking slowly to the doorway where she paused. When Pete and Andy saw the girls standing in the doorway, they quickly jumped to their feet. The other boys followed suit, enjoying the game. Beth entered the room, using tiny ladylike steps, her gaze still fixed on an invisible spot on the far wall. Meg and Di did their best to follow her.

"Good evening, Mr. Bradford, sir," she said, with a little curtsy to her father.

"Good evening, Mother. You're looking especially lovely tonight in your jeans and cashmere sweater set," she continued.

Both of her parents were trying to stifle their chuckles, so they just nodded at her. It took Beth a little while to get all the way into the room with her tiny steps, but eventually, she reached Pete. Paul, Dale and Josh were mesmerized at the quick, cool change in their friend Beth.

"Good evening, Peter, Andrew," Beth said, giving a nod to each of her brothers. "May I present my friends, Miss Megan Baker, and Miss Diana Ganderson?" Beth said regally.

Meg tried her best to act regal as well, and offered Pete and Andy her hand. They nodded and shook it gently once. When it was Di's turn, she blushed fiery red in front of Pete. What silly mind games was she playing? Pete was just a good friend who cared about her like another sister, she scolded herself. But still, she couldn't stop the blushing. She offered her hand to Pete, and he took it gently and kissed the back of it.

"It's marvelous to see you again, Miss Ganderson," Pete said in a clipped, stuffy tone.

"May I present our friends, the misters Paul and Joshua Baker? And of course, we have the honor of your brother's presence as well," Pete finished, looking at Dale.

Diana nodded as ladylike as she could to Paul, Josh, and Dale.

"Please sit down, ladies. We were about to watch a movie that I hope meets with your approval," Andy cut in, motioning the girls to the couch.

"May I get you ladies some refreshment? We have a delicious dessert, and some drinks," Pete continued.

Beth said, in her same quiet, unemotional tone, "That would be so comforting, thank you."

The girls seated themselves on the couch, legs neatly crossed at the ankles to await their dessert. Pete asked his parents if they would care to join the teens in a "bit of dessert", but they had politely refused, so the boys served the girls and then themselves. They perched on the chairs, trying to balance their food and drink on their laps.

"With your permission, Miss Ganderson, I'll start the movie," Pete smiled sedately at Di. When she nodded demurely, Pete hit the remote.

Finally, Peter Bradford could bear it no more. He burst into gales of laughter, Emma joining him. The teens, pretending to be hurt at first, finally dissolved into giggles themselves.

"Emma, dear, you are a wonderful mother to be able to instill these social graces into these ruffians. I'm proud of them, too. Thank goodness they know when they need to behave that way, and when they can just be normal. I don't think I could take large doses of this behavior," Peter laughed.

Emma beamed at her husband's praise.

"Thanks kids, for showing me how dependable you can be. I now know that you won't mortally embarrass me in a true social function," she smiled.

"Sure, Mom," said Beth, flinging her legs over the side of her comfortable easy chair.

Peter and Emma laughed again, and then said good night and went to their room.

"You are just too much, Elizabeth Bradford," teased Meg.

"I truly am, aren't I?" Beth pretended to put on her airs again.

Pete threw a pillow at her.

"Watch the movie, Princess," he said.

Beth turned with another pillow to throw back, but then thought better of it. She focused her attention instead on the beginning of the movie.

When the movie was over, the tired teens took their things to the kitchen, and headed upstairs and fell asleep immediately.

The next morning, the cook served the teenagers outside on the large deck. There was a platter of steaming pancakes, a hot tray of scrambled eggs, and another hot tray with slices of fried bacon. The food was placed on a picnic table, along with a container of juice, a container of milk, and a fresh fruit salad.

"Yummmmy!" said Meg, as she finished eating.

"Yeah, I'm sure glad that you left that note for the cook so she made extra for us," Paul said to Beth, who was seated beside him.

"Me, too. But I think I better get going. I told Dad that I'd help him air out the camper again, and repair the one window screen on it," Dale said, getting up.

"When are we leaving?" asked Meg.

"Right now. Come on, sis," Paul teased, getting up with Dale.

"I meant, when are we leaving for the Creation festival?" Meg repeated, throwing a napkin at Paul. She then got up and stacked her plates on the cart the cook had left for that purpose.

"I think Dad said Tuesday," Dale answered her, and threw away the napkin that Meg had thrown at Paul.

"Well, I guess that means that the working class members of the BBGs will have to get working. We have lots to do before then," Josh said, grinning.

"Hey, we have to prepare, too, you know," said Andy, taking Josh's jibe.

"Really? Like how?" asked Josh.

"Well, like ordering the food," Andy said

"Decisions, decisions," laughed Josh.

"And we have to pack our clothes," said Beth.

"Oh, I feel badly for you," whined Meg.

"Alright, you two, knock it off. You know we all benefit from the Bradford's generosity," Paul said to his siblings.

"Pete and Di might have undeclared feelings towards each other," Paul thought to himself, remembering several times in the past few days that he had seen the two of them together, "but I'm kind of partial to a Miss Elizabeth Bradford."

"See you tomorrow, and thanks again!" Diana said, breaking into Paul's thoughts.

The BBGs who did not live in the mansion headed to their own homes. Tomorrow at church, each of them would be handed a bag of neatly folded, clean laundry from last night. No one ever figured out how the maids and the laundress knew who belonged to what clothing, but the BBGs were grateful for the work being done.

CHAPTER 11

Tuesday morning dawned bright and clear. The parking lot of the church buzzed with activity as families gathered to go to the festival together. After much hilarity, and a final prayer for safe keeping, the small caravan of campers and cars pulled out. When they arrived at the festival site, the teens once again helped to set up camp, and then set out to explore the grounds. Since the festival did not officially start until Wednesday, the place was not crowded. At the headquarters building, Dale found a brochure listing the times of the activities, and several pictures of the grounds. His eyes fell on the picture of a pond and the description of the baptismal time scheduled for later in the week. He studied it carefully, then seemed to get lost in a daydream. Paul, who was talking to Beth, finally looked over Dale's shoulder to see what had captured his attention so completely.

"What are you looking at, Dale?" Paul asked, when he couldn't see anything but the picture of the pond on the page.

"There's a pond here for baptisms," Dale said.

"Yep," Paul agreed, waiting for more, but Dale didn't say anything else.

"There's a pond at the acreage for that, too," said Pete.

"I know, but I've got a funny feeling," Dale said, his words trailing off again.

Suddenly, he was back in the present, and said, "Come on! I see an ice cream place that's open already! Let's go! Pete, I'll treat you!" and he set off on a light jog, the others scrambling to keep up with him.

After eating their treat, they wandered over to the book tent, and then took a quick hike up the mountain, and came back down to their campsite in time for supper. Later that evening, Peter Bradford built a campfire in front of his motor home, and the whole church group gathered around it with their folding chairs for some worship time.

The next day, the BBGs watched in awe as the festival site grew by leaps and bounds. A steady stream of campers and cars poured into the site, and the sounds of mallets pounding tent stakes into the ground beat out a soothing rhythm. Early that evening, the smells of supper cooking over hundreds of open campfires made the BBGs mouths water for their own supper. After everything was cleaned up, the Community church families took tarps and blankets and went to the natural amphitheater at the foot of the mountain to hear the evening worship and message.

The following day, Emma and Kelly took Micah, Kristen, and Suzi to a special children's tent. Jon and Steve found a middle school meeting tent, and the others put down their tarps and blankets in front of the main stage for more worship and speakers. After lunch, the BBGs discovered that a popular teen speaker was speaking in a smaller amphitheater set in the woods. They hurried over to the designated meeting place, and spread their blankets in the shade of the trees. They listened intently to the man who was speaking for the next 40 minutes. They were so intent on the man's message that they didn't notice that Dave and Anne had also slipped in several rows behind them to hear the message.

When the speaker finished, everyone except the BBGs left the amphitheater. Dave and Anne realized that the teens were still seated on their blankets, busy scribbling last minute notes. They smiled at each other and waited for the BBGs at the bottom of the hill.

"See, Dave? You're not the only one who can't seem to fill those kids up," Anne said, giving her husband a hug. Dave chuckled and nodded back.

As the speaker packed up his Bible and his notes, he too noticed that the BBGs hadn't left. Since he wasn't scheduled to speak anywhere else that afternoon, he decided to introduce himself to the teens and try to get some feedback from them.

"Hi," he said, and then chuckled as every BBG head looked up at once.

"Oh, Mr. Towers! Hello!" Beth said in a surprised voice.

Dave and Anne watched to see how the teens would react to meeting a nationally known speaker. The Bradford children had some experience with meeting celebrities, but for the most part, the others did not.

"We really enjoyed your message," Dale said, going back to his notes.

"I'm glad. It's hard to tell sometimes," Mr. Towers said.

He sat quietly while the BBGs hurried to finish their writing, and when they had put their pens and notebooks back into their packs, he asked, "Do you guys have a minute or two right now to spare?"

The BBGs looked at each other in surprise, and then Pete looked at his watch.

"Actually, we've got a couple of hours," he said.

"Would you mind talking with me, then? I have a funny feeling about you guys, and I'd like to get to know you a little better," Mr. Towers said.

He had been hard pressed not to stare at the little group during his message. His gaze kept returning to their interested and eager faces. In his past experience, an unwavering interest in a set of individuals within a group usually meant that God had something specifically for them. Justin Towers just didn't know yet what that something was.

The BBGs looked at each other again, this time in amazement.

"Do you mean us?" Josh asked.

Mr. Towers laughed. "Yes, you," he said.

"Well, sure, I mean, I don't know what you want to know about us, but we'd be happy to talk to you," Paul said, looking at the others, who nodded their heads in agreement.

"Are you here with an adult?" Mr. Towers asked.

"Is this bad news?" asked Andy, a little suspiciously.

Justin Towers laughed again.

"No, not at all. But generally, I like to have a responsible adult with me when I talk to kids. It gives me a peace of mind," he said.

Dave and Anne had been listening to the conversation, and decided to walk up to where the BBGs were sitting.

"Hi, I'm Dave Smith, and this is my wife, Anne. We're the youth leaders for these guys, and we can go along with you, if you'd like," Dave said, putting his hand out for Justin to shake.

"What do you guys think?" Justin asked the BBGs.

"That's fine with us," Dale said, and then added, "Did you guys hear Mr. Towers' message?"

Dave smiled, and said, "Yep. We were right here all along."

"How about coming down to the speakers' quarters then? There's a big room with lots of comfy couches there," Justin suggested.

The BBGs nodded and followed the adults to the large hotel style building. Once inside, Justin offered them all sodas or iced tea, and they settled themselves in a circle of couches and easy chairs. Justin looked at all of them for a moment, and then settled on Dale's face.

"So, tell me about yourself," he said, looking deeply into Dale's warm, brown eyes.

Dale squirmed. "What do you want to know?" he asked.

"Let's start with your name, and tell me what you like to do," Justin said, with an encouraging smile.

"Well, my name is Dale Ganderson. I have a brother and 2 sisters, one of them is Diana, here," Dale started, putting an arm around Diana, who was seated on one side of him.

"Well, Dale, what's your favorite thing to do?" Justin asked.

"Well, pretty much just hang out with these guys. We do lots of things together, go swimming, hiking, to the movies, stuff like that," Dale said, looking at the other BBGs for help.

"Do you live close to each other?" Justin asked.

"Yes, we all live next door or across the street from each other," Dale answered.

"You've known each other for a long time, then?" Justin asked.

"Most of our lives," Dale admitted.

"What's the best thing that's ever happened to you?" Justin asked, looking into Dale's eyes again.

This time, Dale didn't hesitate.

"When Pete and Paul and I went with Dave and Anne to a youth conference about 3 months ago," Dale started.

"Just 3 months?" mumbled Justin to himself.

"It was at the end of April," Dale said, and then continued, "Anyway, while we were there, we met the best Friend anyone has ever had. I think Dave would agree that He changed our lives forever in the span of a couple of hours, huh, Dave?"

Justin looked at Dave and said, "Well, is that a fair assessment?"

Dave laughed and said, "Totally"

"How did your life change?" Justin asked Dale.

"That's really hard to explain," Dale said, and thought for a moment. Then he continued. "See, Di and I are PK's. We've always been in church. At least, our bodies were in church. I knew all the doctrinal stuff, and even prayed sometimes, but," Dale looked down at the floor, suddenly embarrassed.

"But real life with Dale or Di wasn't exactly the picture of a real believer, was it?" Dave finished for him.

Dale nodded, but his eyes stayed focused on the carpet. Justin then got up, and went to sit in an empty chair on Dale's other side. He put his arm around Dale's shoulders and said, "It's all right, Dale. What's the past is over and done with. You are a new creature in Him, and that much at least is obvious to me. When we're baptized, it's like being born again, given a whole new chance to start over. You'll get to the point where you won't be embarrassed to talk about your past anymore, because that old Dale Ganderson no longer exists. It'll be like talking about somebody you used to know. Right?" he said, kindly.

Dale looked up and smiled. "You're right!" he said.

"Would you come to the pond for my baptism tonight?" Dale added excitedly.

Dale could now fit the pieces of the last few weeks together. Although he had never doubted that God was involved in other people's lives, it still amazed him that God would be willing to orchestrate the events of his life as well. Suddenly, the memory of Dale's inability to take his eyes off of his father's baptism picture a few nights ago, and the memory of how the picture of the pond on the festival brochure had captured his mind as well, all made sense now.

Justin could see wheels turning in Dale's mind, and he very sincerely said, "I wouldn't miss it for the world."

"And Dave? Will you come into the water with me and Dad?" Dale asked.

"I'd be honored to do that," Dave answered.

"Hey! Before you all run off, could I hear something about the rest of you?" Justin asked as the teens seemed to get caught up in the idea of a baptism, and appeared to be ready to end the interview.

The teens laughed at their mistake, and settled back down on their chairs.

Each one then gave Justin their name, a little information about their families, and how they had come to meet the Lord Jesus.

When the teens were finished talking, Justin looked at Dave and Anne.

"So you've been in on this since the beginning?" he asked.

Dave laughed.

"The beginning? Well, yes, and no. We've only been youth leaders at their church for three years. But we have been in on the beginning of their walk with the Lord," he said.

"I'd like to pray for these guys, if you'll join me," Justin said.

Dave and Anne moved closer to the circle of teens. Justin prayed in such an amazing way that the teenagers all had tears running down their cheeks.

"Do you guys play any instruments?" Justin finally asked.

The boys all nodded.

"I thought so," Justin mumbled, and then blessed their playing and their worship.

In just two short years, the BBGs would again stand in that room at a Creation festival. They would be there as the worship band for a different popular festival speaker, but they would remember clearly what had happened there this day, and the blessing Justin was now bestowing upon them. For the present, though, nothing other than the knowledge that they had just been touched by the hand of God seemed to matter.

Finally, Justin prayed for Dave and Anne with more astonishing accuracy, and when he was finished, everyone sat on the couches and chairs, exhausted and quiet.

Justin looked at them with deep appreciation, and asked, "You OK?"

It was a spontaneous and unanimous answer. "Yeah," they said together and then everyone laughed.

"Well, then, Dave and Anne, can I pick your brains a little further, maybe over some ice cream?" he asked.

"Our pleasure," replied Anne.

"We'll either be at the ice cream place or at our campsite, guys. Just let us know what time the baptism is," Dave said, as the BBGs headed out the door.

"Baptisms," corrected Pete. "I'm in too."

The other BBGs gave each other knowing glances.

"So are the rest of us," Meg said.

"Cool. We'll be there," Justin said, waving.

"Well, I guess we'd better find Dad and fill him in," said Dale, as they left the building.

"Gosh, I hope he can do it!" said Diana.

"Come on, Di, what else could he possibly be doing tonight, out here in the middle of nowhere?" asked Dale.

Diana giggled as she thought about what she had said. .

"No board meetings out here around the camp fire," said Pete.

"You're right. I guess I just worried out of habit," Diana said.

"It's OK, Di. Somebody has to be the responsible one in this crew," Beth said, giving Di a quick hug.

"Thanks," Di said warmly.

"Yeah, and notice that Beth used the word, 'crew' and not 'gang'?" teased Pete.

Beth made a face at him, which made the others laugh.

The teens found their parents enjoying some iced tea in the large screen house. The younger children were either in the Bradford's motor home using a generator to watch a video, or between the tents, throwing a Frisbee.

"Wow. The lost children have returned," chuckled John Baker.

"You'll never believe what we just did!" exclaimed Meg.

"It was so cool!" agreed Beth.

"Well, if we will never believe it, why don't you tell us anyway. A little fiction right about now would be nice," Peter Bradford laughed.

"We went to hear Justin Towers after lunch," started Pete.

"And then he asked us if we'd come to the speaker's hotel and talk to him," said Andy.

"And Dave and Anne were there, too, so they offered to come with us," put in Beth.

"Otherwise, we'd have had to find you guys," said Pete.

"And anyway, we answered some questions and then he prayed for us and, man! I thought I was going to burst into a zillion tiny pieces if he didn't stop praying when he did," said Dale.

"That's for sure. I think Dave and Anne were pretty blasted, too," agreed Diana.

"Well, that does sound like an amazing afternoon. I'm rather fond of Justin Towers' messages myself," Carl said, shaking his head in confusion over what had really happened to make all the teens so animated.

"But that's not all, Dad. We all wondered, I mean, when we talked to Justin, it all seemed to fall into place for me, we all wondered if maybe you would baptize us tonight?" Dale asked.

The adults' mouths fell open, and then shut in wide smiles. Emma put her hand on Peter's arm.

"Oh, Peter, it's what we've been praying for!" she whispered.

The adults could scarcely believe their ears. Just three short months ago, they were in the midst of a teen age nightmare. Now these same teens were asking to be baptized.

"Dad? Will you do it, Dad? You said the only requirement was to believe and accept what Jesus did on the cross, and who He is, and we all do now," Dale said, getting anxious at the seeming lack of response.

"Dave and Anne will help," said Diana.

"And Justin agreed to come too," added Josh.

"Of course, I'll do it. It's just sort of a shock," Carl said, grinning from ear to ear.

Paul laughed at that statement.

"You mean you never thought this day would come for us?" he asked, pretending to pout.

"Well, never is a pretty strong word," Carl said.

"Let's just say we had our prayers and our fears," said John Baker.

"Especially just last week," agreed Peter.

"From the looks on your faces, I'd say the kids just asked you the million dollar question," said Dave as he came into the screen house, followed by Anne and Justin.

"We're really still in shock," said Carl.

"Hello, I'm Justin Towers," Justin said, as he extended his hand to Carl, who had gotten out of his seat to meet the newcomer.

"Carl Ganderson, Dale and Diana's father. This is my wife, Kelly," Carl said.

John got up next and introduced himself and Patti, and finally Peter introduced himself and Emma.

"So what time is the pond open?" asked Dave.

Carl looked at his watch. "This seems to be the best time, right now. Kids, go get your swimsuits on. Mr. Towers, I'm sure we can rustle up enough extra food for you if you'll be our guest for a celebration dinner afterward," he said.

Justin readily accepted, asking the adults to call him by his first name.

Meg and Di ran into their pop up campers to get their swimsuits, and then followed Beth into her parents' bedroom in their motor home to change. Pete and Andy followed Dale to his tent, while Paul and Josh changed in their own tent. Soon, Carl and Dave had also changed into a pair of shorts and t-shirts. The teens all wore t-shirts with their swimming suits. Knowing that their mothers had cameras in hand, they were certain that they didn't want such a momentous picture to feature them in their bathing suits.

When they reached the pond, Carl said, "Let's go from oldest to youngest. Pete, that means you're first. Come on into the water."

Carl and Dave walked until they were about waist deep in the pond water. Pete stood between them.

"Pete, do you renounce all your sins, and will you make every effort to walk away from them now?" Carl asked.

"Yes, I will," Pete answered.

"Do you believe that Jesus is the son of God, and that he died and rose again, for you? Do you accept His work on the cross on your behalf?" Carl asked.

"Yes," Pete replied.

Carl looked at Dave, who laid his hands on Pete's head and prayed. Then the two men put Pete under, and Kelly snapped the picture as he came up. Pete stood nearby as Paul came into the water at Carl's invitation. Dale, Meg, Diana, Beth, Andy, and Josh followed. After the baptisms were complete, the wet, dripping teenagers stood in the pond for a few moments in a group hug. Carl and Dave stood to the side this time, but were soon drawn into the hug by the teens. More pictures followed, and then teens and wet adults went to the shower truck for showers, and the dry adults went to prepare a feast at the campsite. After a delicious dinner, the group gathered their jackets and blankets and went back to the amphitheater for the evening concert and speaker. It was a tired, but very happy group that returned late that night and fell into an easy, relaxing sleep.

CHAPTER 12

The next morning, Pete was the first to wake up. Tapping Andy on the shoulder to wake him up, the two brothers slipped out of the motor home and went to the Ganderson's tent. Pete unzipped the tent flap and gently tapped Dale's foot until he woke up. Meanwhile, Andy had gone to the Baker's tent and managed to rouse them.

"Want to hike to the top of the mountain before breakfast?" Pete asked.

"Well, before the second breakfast, you mean. If I'm hiking up a mountain, I'm going to take some of these donuts and a juice bottle along," Dale said, grabbing a snack from the screen house.

The other boys also grabbed donuts and juice, and then Dale wrote a short message on the chalkboard that hung on the crossbars of the screen house, telling the adults where they had gone.

About a half hour later, the boys reached the top of the large, rocky but forested hill that formed the edge of the natural amphitheater.

"Wow, would you look at that view!" exclaimed Paul.

The others just nodded as they looked over the little valley below.

"Spectacular, isn't it?" asked a voice behind them.

The boys jumped and turned at the same time to see Justin Towers behind them.

"Gosh, how did you find us up here?" asked Pete.

Justin laughed. "I didn't find you. You found me. I was sitting over there against that rock, praying," he said.

The boys glanced over to the rock that he was pointing at, and saw a small blanket, a thermos of coffee, and a Bible.

"Yikes. Sorry for the interruption," said Dale.

"That's quite all right. How are you guys, anyway?" Justin asked.

Somehow, when Justin asked that simple question, the boys felt like he was looking directly into their hearts.

"I feel a little different than I did yesterday somehow," Dale said.

Justin smiled. "Different? How?" he asked.

"Oh, I don't know exactly. Maybe a little lighter?" Dale said with a grin.

Justin chuckled, and the boys looked out over the valley again. They could see smoke rising from some of the campsites, signaling that breakfast was underway in many of the family's sites.

"We should be going," said Paul, reluctantly.

"Would you join us?" Pete asked Justin.

Justin smiled. "Well, maybe for some coffee," he answered.

As the group walked down the hill, Justin talked about his wife and two small sons. The boys laughed at the stories he told them.

"Sometimes, it's not so funny to me as a Dad," Justin said, smiling.

"Yeah, yeah, but to us, it's hysterical," chuckled Andy.

When they got back to their campsite, the BBGs' families were already seated around the picnic tables and eating. Carl stood up, looked at Dale, and tapped his watch.

"Something wrong, Dad?" asked Dale.

"Seems to me that you could have left a message. That's what this chalkboard is for," he said, as he pointed at the board. Carl then noticed Justin Towers coming into the screen house behind the boys. He extended his hand in greeting to Justin, and said, "Sit down, Justin. There are plenty of flapjacks to go around."

"Thanks, could I bum some coffee off of you too?" Justin asked, giving Patti his thermos.

"Of course," Patti smiled.

Emma quickly filled a plate with pancakes and bacon and brought it over to Justin, while the boys filled their own plates at the camp stoves, and then sat down to eat as well.

Micah Bradford and Kristen Ganderson sat quietly, waiting to see what would happen next. They had gotten up shortly after the boys, and since none of the other adults were up yet, they had used the chalkboard to play a few games of tic tac toe to amuse themselves until the adults got up to make breakfast. They were too young to be able to read the message written in cursive on the chalkboard, and they had no idea that Dale had written it that very morning. They did know, however, that they were in for a scolding if anyone found out that they had erased anything on that board. They nervously ate their pancakes and waited to see if the subject would be brought up again.

When the boys and Justin had taken their fill of pancakes, Carl rose, and said to Dale, "Come on, Dale, let's take a walk."

Dale's mind lurched back to the chalkboard question.

"Sure, Dad, but hey, we did leave a message for you guys. We hiked up the mountain to see the sun rise over the valley," Dale said, putting his breakfast things away.

Carl looked at the chalkboard. It was empty.

"Anybody see a message written up here?" he asked.

Micah and Kristen slipped out of their seats unnoticed and went into the Bradford's motor home. Everyone else seated around the tables shook their heads, no.

"I saw Dale write the message," said Pete.

"So did I," agreed Paul.

"It must have gotten erased somehow," said Josh.

"Somehow, by somebody," thought Andy out loud, looking at the people still seated around the tables. There was no question that the girls or their mothers had erased the message, so the deed had to have been done by one of the BBGs' younger siblings.

Steve, Jon, and Suzi sat together, looking confused, their eyes going from fathers to older brothers and back again. Andy mentally dismissed them, and then looked around for Micah and Kristen.

"Where are those two?" asked Andy, completely unaware that no one else knew what he was thinking.

"Who?" asked Peter.

"Micah and Kristen," Andy replied, and then called them.

They poked their heads out of the motor home door.

"Did you see something written on the chalkboard this morning, Micah?" Peter asked.

Micah hesitated, the only evidence that Pete needed to accuse his youngest sibling.

"You did, didn't you? What happened to it, squirt?" Pete asked, irritation showing in his voice.

"Pete, give him a chance," Peter said sternly, looking at his oldest son.

"In fact, why don't all of you hit the bathrooms and get cleaned up. We'll discuss this when you get back," Peter added.

"That's a good idea. Get going, guys," John agreed.

"I don't know what there is to discuss," grumbled Pete, as he started for the motor home to get his shower bag.

Micah flinched as Pete walked by him, and the action made Pete stop and look at his brother in astonishment. Suddenly, memories of the many times that Pete had cuffed the little boy for somehow getting him in trouble rose up in his mind. Pete's heart broke for the little boy, and he stooped down to look him in the face.

"Oh, come on, bud. Don't be afraid of me. I'm making you a promise right now, and that's that I will do my best to control my temper and never swat you again. All right?" he whispered to Micah. Micah grinned and gave his brother a warm hug.

"Really?" he whispered back.

"Pinkie promise, buddy," Pete said chuckling.

As Pete opened the door of the motor home, Kristen scampered out, and ran over to Dale. Wrapping her arms around him, she whispered, "I'm sorry."

Dale kissed the top of her head.

"Don't worry about me, sweetie. But you had better start worrying about you," he said, smiling down at her.

"Oh yeah," she giggled.

Carl took her arm, and gently led her to their pop up camper.

"Go get cleaned up, Dale," he said, giving him a wink.

When all the boys had left, Peter took Micah aside as well, reminding him of the importance of the chalkboard, and telling him that there would be consequences if any message ever happened to be erased again.

By the time the boys got back, the campsite was calm again. Kristen and Micah were playing 'go fish' at the table, and the older girls sat in the camp chairs, reading their Bibles. Steve, Jon, and Suzi were inside the motor home watching a video, and the adults were sitting around the tables in the screen house lingering over the morning's last cup of coffee.

The next few days of the festival went quickly. On the last morning, Justin again joined the BBGs and their families for breakfast. They were all enjoying the last of the donuts, pastries, and coffee.

"Hi everyone!" he called cheerfully.

"Good morning!" Carl said, getting up and getting the coffee pot off the camp stove so he could refill Justin's thermos.

"Thanks. Say, boys, how are you? When I left you the last time, things were a little bumpy," Justin said, grinning at Dale, Pete, and Paul.

Pete shook his head to clear it. How did Justin always manage to bypass all the polite pleasantries and get straight to their hearts every time?

Micah and Kristen suddenly found something very interesting to look at on the ground.

"Oh, we're OK. The pint size members of our group bravely admitted their mistake," Pete said, putting an arm around Micah's shoulders.

"Bravely? For real?" asked Micah, looking up and beaming.

"For real, Micah," assured Peter.

"Was I brave, too, Dale?" asked Kristen.

"You too, little bug," Dale said, grinning at his sister.

"Guess we're important then, huh?" Micah said to Kristen.

"Yep," Kristen agreed so hard that her pigtails bounced.

"Silly, you're always important!" said Diana, squeezing her little sister.

"Say, Carl, I was wondering, is there was any chance that my family and I could visit you next month?" Justin asked.

"You're always welcome, Justin. Do you want a Sunday morning service, the Sunday evening service, or the mid week services? Maybe all 3?" Carl asked.

Justin laughed. "I wasn't thinking at all about taking any service at all. I was just looking for a place to get refreshed myself," he said.

Carl laughed too. "Sorry," he said, "that would work too, I suppose. Although I would enjoy hearing you speak."

"All right. We'll compromise. I'll take a Sunday evening service if I can hang out on a Wednesday night and a Sunday morning service. Is that fair?" Justin suggested.

Carl laughed again. "You don't have to do anything, Justin, really. Your suggestion fits perfectly, though, if you wouldn't mind doing it."

"Great!" said Justin. "I should be up that way in about 2 weeks. Do you have motels you can recommend in your area?" he asked.

"No need for a motel, Justin. We have several guest rooms. We'd love to have you," Peter spoke up.

Justin smiled. "With 6 kids? You have guest rooms?" he asked.

"The 3rd floor is yours," Emma agreed.

"I have 2 small boys," Justin hedged.

"I have two porta-cribs if you need them," Emma replied.

"They're not that small, but thank you. The floor in our room is fine, but I know my wife will worry that our boys will be too rambunctious for your home," Justin said.

Peter laughed. "Nonsense! We won't even know that they're around. We have a pool, a playground, and a room full of toys and gadgets. Now we won't take no for an answer," he insisted.

Justin looked doubtful, but finally agreed to stay with the Bradfords.

"He's in for a real surprise," whispered Meg to Diana.

"You said it!" giggled Di back.

The Community church group left the festival shortly after saying good by to Justin and arrived back at home in time for the evening church service. There was no youth group that night, so the teens sat in the adult service with Dave and Anne.

The next day, all the teens spent the day helping their parents to clean the campers, catch up on the garden work, and do the laundry chores. They had no time to meet until after supper, when they gathered in the Baker's family room with bowls of ice cream.

CHAPTER 13

So what's on our agenda this week?" asked Paul, as they sat in the family room eating their dessert.

"Did you hear about that free concert at the park Thursday night?" asked Meg.

"Yes! I'd like to go to that, too!" said Beth.

"It starts at 7:00," put in Di.

"I'll see if I can get the van that night," said Pete.

"I'd also like to go to the mall and get some stuff," said Di

"The ever present blond mall groupie," teased Dale.

"I want to check out the new worship CD myself. How about tomorrow?" Pete asked, smiling at Di.

Diana blushed.

"Is anyone else invited?" teased Beth.

Pete threw his napkin at his sister, and everyone laughed. Before saying good night, they all agreed to go to the mall the next afternoon.

Promptly at 2:00, the next day, Pete pulled his family's van into the church parking lot. Carl was walking back to his office in the church after his lunch break, and decided to greet the teens before they left.

"Hi, Pete, Beth, Andy. Where's the bus headed this afternoon?" Carl asked before the other kids arrived.

"To the mall," Pete said, smiling as he saw the Gandersons and the Bakers sprinting across their yards.

"Didn't you guys spend all your money on treats at the festival?" Carl asked with a mischievous grin.

Pete laughed. "Begging your pardon, sir, but all my spending money is invested in a new bathroom screen. I am dead broke until Sunday," he said.

Carl chuckled and asked, "Then why are you going to the mall?"

"Because Diana wants to," teased Beth.

Pete's face flamed. "Be quiet." he growled, and then said, "I'm the only driver of a vehicle big enough, anyway."

Andy howled from the seat directly behind Pete. "Diana's not that big, Pete. She's not even chubby," he laughed.

Pete thought about what he had said, and then amended his statement. "Big enough to fit all of us at one time goof ball," he said.

He couldn't help but laugh at his brother's joke, though, and Carl, Beth, and Andy joined in.

"Besides, I'm allowed to have friends," Pete said after he stopped chuckling.

Carl reached in and patted him on the shoulder.

"You're OK, Pete. Just take care to drive safely and protect that friend of yours," Carl said.

Pete nodded. "Her and everyone else in the van," he said.

At the mall, Pete listened to the sample worship CD in the store.

"I can't wait until next week when I can buy this," he said wistfully.

It didn't take Diana long to find what she needed, and the others soon finished looking and window shopping as well. Pete then headed the van toward home, and the BBGs were soon swimming in the Bradford's pool.

On Thursday evening, the group enjoyed the free concert in the park, and on Sunday afternoon they returned to the mall so Pete could buy his worship CD.

When they arrived at the mall, the teens split up into several groups, and each group went a separate direction. They agreed to meet at the food court in one hour.

Pete, Paul, and Dale headed straight for the music store.

"Ah, money in the pocket is a very good thing," Pete sighed, as he purchased his longed for CD.

The girls went to look for sales on summer clothes. Josh and Andy decided to walk the mall, stopping only when something caught their eye in a store. They were leaving a store where they had stopped to look at a new skateboard when they spotted a girl they knew from school sitting on a bench in the middle of the mall.

"Hi, Cindy!" said Josh.

The girl looked up. "Oh, hi, Josh, Andy," she said.

Since she was sitting in the middle of the bench, the boys sat on either side of her.

"How's your summer going?" asked Andy.

"Umm, it's going OK." Cindy said, and was going to say more when tears filled her eyes instead.

Josh looked over her head at Andy with an alarmed look.

"Can we help?" asked Josh gently.

Cindy looked at him, brushing the tears away quickly.

"I don't know what you could do," she said sadly.

"We can listen," suggested Andy.

"You'll think it's too bizarre. I don't even know what to think," Cindy said.

Josh and Andy slouched down on the bench to get comfortable.

"Try us," Andy said.

"Well, I went to Utah earlier this summer," started Cindy.

"Cool," said Josh.

"Well, it might have been cool, but this time I was cleaning out my grandmother's house. She died earlier this year, and her estate is being settled now," Cindy said.

"Oh, I'm sorry," said Josh.

"Thanks," sighed Cindy, and then continued.

"I was looking through some old boxes by myself up in her attic, and I came across some baby things. You know, pictures and stuff."

"Belonging to you?" asked Andy.

"I thought so, I mean the face looked like me, but, the name on the back of the picture was totally different," Cindy said.

"Was it a relative who looks like you?" asked Josh.

"I've never heard these names before," Cindy said.

"Well, I guess that is a little weird," Andy agreed, not seeing Cindy's problem at all.

"Well, it gets worse," Cindy said. "I also found pictures of my mom holding me, and standing with someone, but the other person has been cut out of the picture," she added.

"Hmmmm?" asked Josh.

"And then I saw pictures of a little girl with my name on the back, but my hair is a different color! Like I was blond as a 2 year old, and then suddenly became a black haired 3 year old. It was totally, totally bizarre," Cindy said.

"But how did you know the blond 2 year old was you?" asked Andy.

"Well, I didn't at first. I only linked them together when I found the picture of me and my mom with the other person cut off," Cindy said.

"What about the names? Were there names on the backs of the pictures? Maybe your mom was holding another baby," asked Josh.

"There were names on the backs, and the one with the person ripped off has a third person's name on it, but it's crossed out. I couldn't read it. My mom's name is the same, but the baby's name is 'Barbie'," said Cindy.

"Then it must have been a different baby," said Andy.

"But then there's also birthday pictures, and a first birthday party, with 'Barbie' written on the back, and my mom standing there with the cake, and the date on the back of the picture. It's my birth date," Cindy said.

"Wow. That is a mystery. Have you asked your mom about it?" asked Josh.

Cindy giggled. "Now that answer is even more bizarre," she said, and then continued.

"My mom claims that she had a twin sister, who had a daughter my age. They are both supposed to have died in a fire. Now will you please tell me what parent would name both their twin daughters 'Melissa'?" she said.

"Both named Melissa?" asked Josh, confused.

"Yes. The woman who looks like my mom on all the pictures is called Melissa. We have pictures of Melissa and Barbie, and we have pictures of

Melissa and Cindy," Cindy said.

"Well, then it must have been your mom holding your cousin," suggested Andy.

Cindy sighed. "I suppose that could be true, and maybe I did have a cousin that looked exactly like me. It doesn't matter what the name on the back of the pictures is, the little girls always look the same. The only difference is that I had black hair when I was 3 years old. All the pictures of this 'Barbie' stop before her 2nd birthday. She might have died right about then, but that only makes me wonder why my own baby pictures aren't in this mix, then. I mean, why wasn't my mom ever holding me in any of the pictures, and where was my Dad before I was 3? For that matter, where are the pictures of my first birthday?" Cindy wondered.

"Oh you know how it is with old pictures, Cindy. The ones up in the attic were probably doubles, or ones that your grandmother didn't need," Josh said.

"I could believe you guys except for one other thing," Cindy said, pulling out a faded, creased piece of light cardboard.

"I also found this," Cindy said, handing the paper to Josh, almost as if she was afraid to touch it.

Andy walked over and leaned over Josh's shoulder. The paper was an old 'have you seen this child' advertisement. The picture of the child and the man who was supposed to have seen her last was faded, but the words underneath were readable. They said, "Barbara Jeanette Beslinger, age 19 months, possible family abduction from Linsburg, Michigan". Andy and Josh's mouths fell open.

"Cindy?" they both said at the same time.

"I think that's me," Cindy whispered.

Andy went back and sat down, speechless.

"That's not the worst of it" Cindy said.

"There's more?" asked Josh.

"The picture of the man, there, that's, it looks like, I mean it could be," Cindy was stumbling over her words, and the tears were forming in her eyes again.

"Who?" asked Andy quietly.

"It looks like my father! This man who is supposed to have abducted this baby, he looks just like my Dad! His name isn't the same, but it looks like him!" Cindy gushed the words out so quickly that it took a moment for them to sink into Josh and Andy's mind.

"And," Cindy went on, "for about 2 years now, this man who claims to be my father has been," she took a deep breath so she could continue, "has been difficult to be around when my mom's not in the house."

"Has he hurt you?" demanded Josh.

"He's slapped me around a couple of times, if I don't do what he's asking me to do. But I'm afraid of what will happen if I'm around when my mom goes out for a couple of hours. He's threatened me. So far, I've managed to get to a girlfriend's house before Mom leaves," Cindy said tearfully.

"Don't you have brothers and sisters?" asked Andy.

"Yes, my brother is 10, and my sister is 8," replied Cindy.

"Has he ever threatened them?" Andy asked.

"No, not that I know of," said Cindy.

"Have you tried to talk to your mom about what happens when she goes out?" asked Josh.

"Yes, but she insists that I'm blowing the whole thing out of proportion. She says Dad only does that because he is trying to help me grow up to be a responsible adult, and I'm just being rebellious. I don't know. Maybe I am crazy and imagining all of this," Cindy sighed.

"Well, at the very least, you deserve logical answers to your questions and someone who takes your fears seriously," Josh said.

Cindy glanced up and a look of fear came over her face.

"Oh-oh, here whoever he is comes now, and he doesn't look happy," Cindy whispered.

Josh and Andy got up to leave, but the man Cindy was talking about reached them before they could move away from the bench. When he arrived at the bench and saw Andy and Josh with Cindy, his face changed from a frown into a smile, and he put his hand out to shake Josh and Andy's hands.

"Hi guys. I'm Tim Rathers, Cindy's dad," he said.

Josh and Andy both shook his hand and introduced themselves.

"Well, Cindy, your mom wanted us home 5 minutes ago. We better hurry. Nice meeting you, Josh and Andy," Mr. Rathers said cheerfully, putting his hand on Cindy's back and leading her down the mall.

"Sure, Dad," Cindy said, and turned to press the faded piece of cardboard into Andy's hand.

The 2 boys stood for a moment, looking after the man and their friend.

"Whew! What was that?" asked Josh, letting his breath out in a whoosh.

"Will you look at this picture?" Andy said, showing Josh the paper he had in his hand.

"That really is Mr. Rathers, only with a little longer hair, and no mustache," breathed Josh.

"Do you think he kidnapped Cindy's look alike cousin?" asked Andy.

"I don't know. Cindy seems to think that this little girl is her," Josh said, jabbing his finger at the little girl's picture.

"Then do you think her father kidnapped her?" asked Andy.

"Well, the card doesn't list the man as her father. If they thought her father kidnapped her, don't you think they would say that?" countered Josh.

"Well, it does say 'family abduction'," replied Andy, reading the card again.

"But Cindy has pictures of her mother. She's sure that part of her life is real. So if this man kidnapped Cindy and took her to her mother, that would make it a family abduction," said Josh.

"And then changed his name and married her mother?" Andy speculated.

Both boys fell silent then, trying to process what had just happened. Finally, Josh looked at his watch.

"We've got to meet the others. Come on, let's go and talk to them about this," he said.

The boys hurried to the food court, and told the story to the others as they ate their snack.

"Let me see that piece of paper!" said Beth, and she and the other girls looked at it intently.

"Do you think this is Cindy?" asked Meg.

"I don't know. But I know for sure that poor girl is mixed up, big time," Josh answered.

"Poor thing," said Di.

"Well, the poor BBGs have to get home or miss the evening service again. I don't think I want to press my luck on that one," said Pete.

The teens laughed, and then threw their trash away and hurried out to the parking lot.

In the van, Pete brought up the subject of Cindy again.

"So the guy in this photo, the one who they think kidnapped that little girl, he looks like Cindy's dad?" Pete asked.

"Yep," answered Andy.

"Well, OK, I'm clear on that. But I don't understand the connection with Cindy. Run that part by me again," said Pete.

"Look at it this way," Andy started. "What are the chances of a husband and wife giving birth to a set of identical twin daughters, and naming them both Melissa?"

"I've heard of doing flip flops with the names, like Melissa Anne and Anne Melissa" said Beth.

"All right, then what are the chances of those twins having baby girls on the same day of the same year?" asked Andy.

Pete scoffed. "Come on, Andy, I don't think you can stretch the truth that far," he said.

"Well, that's what Cindy's mom wants her to believe. She wants her to believe that she had a twin sister, who had a daughter on the exact same day that Cindy was born," Andy said.

"Well, Cindy's mom just said that her twin sister had a daughter Cindy's age," put in Josh.

"Then why did they always have Cindy's birth date on the other girl's birthday pictures?" asked Andy.

"You got me," admitted Josh.

The BBGs thought quietly the rest of the way home, trying to come up with a logical explanation.

As soon as Andy walked into the door of his house, a maid brought him a cordless phone.

"Hello?" he said.

"Andy, it's Cindy Rathers. I just wanted to ask you to please, please don't tell anyone about this, OK?" Cindy sounded panicky on the phone.

"Don't worry, Cindy. It'll stay between you, me, Josh, and our brothers and sisters. We already told them while we were at the food court in the mall," Andy said.

Cindy gasped. "Oh, man! Are you sure that's OK?" she asked.

Andy laughed. "Of course, I'm sure! If you need a friend to talk to, don't be afraid to call again, all right?" he said.

"Thanks, Andy," Cindy said, and hung up.

At youth group, the BBGs brought the other teens into a heady worship time, but the high was not to last. Trouble was brewing, and it had Cindy's name all over it.

Justin Towers, his wife and his two sons arrived at the Ganderson's home on Tuesday. After eating supper with the Gandersons, the Towers family was taken over to the Bradford home. Justin and his family settled themselves on the 3rd floor of the mansion, with every bit of shock that Meg and Diana had predicted.

Shortly after midnight that night, Andy turned the light off in his room and fell into bed. The phone rang a moment later, and Andy turned the light back on to answer it. It was the Bradford's teen line, with a panicky young woman on the other end.

"Andy? Thank goodness you answered! It's me, Cindy. I'm at a pay phone at the mini-mart. My mom left earlier this evening, and the friend that I thought I could stay with had to go visit her grandmother or something. Anyway, I don't have anywhere to go. I can't go home at this hour!" Cindy cried.

"Why not?" Andy asked.

"Because, my mom isn't there! She's spending the night in Delaware so she can go to a business meeting tomorrow morning!" Cindy explained.

"Cindy, how did you get to the mini-mart?" Andy asked.

"The way I always get around, with my bike. It has a light," Cindy answered.

"All right, stay right there. I'll get Pete and we'll come pick you up with the van," Andy said.

"Oh Andy, no! Pete will have to ask permission to drive the van, won't he? I can't risk getting adults involved!" Cindy was becoming hysterical.

"Ok, Ok, Calm down, Cindy. Josh and I will bike over to where you are and bring you back here. You can pretend you're staying with Beth or something," Andy suggested, and then continued forming his plan out loud.

"It'll be about a half hour, though, until we get there. Be careful, OK?" Andy finished.

"I will," Cindy answered.

As soon as Andy hung up, he jumped back into his clothes, and went downstairs to the garage. Getting out his bike, he pedaled silently over to the Baker's home.

Standing under Josh's window, Andy noticed with relief that the night was cool enough for the Bakers to have their windows open instead of the air conditioning on. Andy picked up a handful of tree bark mulch, and threw several pieces at Josh's window pane above his screen. At the same time, he hooted loudly like an owl. On the third try, a light came on in Josh's room.

"Andy?" Josh asked, sleepily, peering out his window screen.

"Josh, come down!" whispered Andy as loud as he dared.

Josh got dressed and met Andy on the porch.

"What's up?" Josh asked.

Andy explained, and Josh went to get his bike immediately. They rode quickly to the mini-mart, where Cindy sat on the curb, away from the lights of the gas pumps. When she saw them, she jumped up and hugged both of them.

"You guys are life savers!" she exclaimed.

"Where's your bike? We need to get home, quick, before someone notices we're gone," Andy said.

"Over here," Cindy said, as she wheeled her bike into the lit area where the boys were standing.

"Oh, no!" said Josh, dismayed, as he looked at Cindy's front tire. It was definitely flat.

"Oh-oh," Cindy said, looking at Josh and Andy with a scared look on her face.

"The air pumps are over here," sighed Andy, walking over to the other side of the building.

"Air costs a quarter. I'll get some more change," Cindy offered.

Josh left his bike leaning against the dark side of the building and took Cindy's bike over to the air machine. In a few moments, Cindy had the extra change, and Andy began to put the air into her tire.

"I hope this holds until we get home," he muttered.

After the tire was full, the 3 teenagers returned to where the boys had left their bikes. Josh gasped when he saw the empty spot where his bike had stood.

"What's the matter now?" asked Andy, as he retrieved his bike from where he had parked it.

"My bike. It's not there anymore," Josh cried in alarm, pointing to where he had left it.

The group searched around the whole building, but the bike was no where to be seen.

"Somebody ripped off my bike!" said Josh angrily.

"This is a dream, just a very bad dream," moaned Andy.

"Now what do we do?" cried Cindy, close to hysterics once more.

"Now we have to call Pete. He has his own set of van keys. Maybe he can sneak out to come get us. There's no way I am going to walk all the way home at this time of night," Andy said decisively.

"Do you have another quarter?" Andy then asked Cindy. She dug in her pocket and found one. Andy took it and walked to the public phone to dial the Bradford's teen number.

Thankfully, Pete had heard the phone ring when Cindy called, and then had heard Andy leave. He picked up the phone on the first ring.

"Andy?" he asked into the phone.

"How did you know it was me?" Andy asked.

"I heard you leave. Where are you?" Pete asked.

"At the mini-mart. Josh just had his bike stolen. Can you come get us in the van?" Andy asked.

"Who is 'us'?" Pete asked.

"Me, Josh, and Cindy," Andy answered.

Pete sighed. "All right. I'll be there in 10 minutes," he said.

When Pete arrived at the mini mart, the boys loaded the two remaining bikes into the van. Then Pete opened the door for Cindy and Josh and Andy to climb in.

"Drop my bike off at Josh's," Andy said, when they were on their way home.

"Why?" Pete asked.

"They're just about the same. Don't you think Josh's Dad will think something's wrong if there are only 2 bikes in their rack?" Andy said.

Pete shook his head. "And our father?" he asked.

"We'll put Cindy's in our rack. With 6 bikes, I doubt that Mom or Dad count them or even look at them very often," Andy said.

Pete had to agree with that logic, so he dropped Andy's bike off with Josh at the Baker's. When they got home, Andy put Cindy's bike in the bike racks in their garage, and finally climbed the stairs back up to bed. Pete had shown Cindy to the children's guest room for the night, and was waiting for Andy in his room.

When Andy arrived in his room, Pete said, "I hope there's a good explanation to this, but I don't want to hear it tonight. Will you fill me in tomorrow?"

"As much as I can," Andy agreed.

The boys then both went to bed and fell asleep quickly.

CHAPTER 14

The next morning, Beth was surprised to see Cindy in the hall.

"Are you Beth? I was just sort of waiting for somebody to wake up," Cindy explained. "I'm kind of lost."

Beth laughed. "Yes, I'm Beth. I'm not sure that I know you, though. Did you come with Mr. Towers?" she asked.

"I'm Cindy Rathers. Andy's friend?" Cindy prompted Beth, hoping that she would recognize the name.

"Oh, yes! I recognize your name. Are you looking for Andy?" Beth said, wondering what Cindy was doing there before 8:00 in the morning.

"Well, no, not exactly. I guess, that is, Andy said we could say I was staying with you," Cindy said.

"Oh-kay," Beth drawled, thinking and trying to piece things together.

Cindy sighed and said, "I came last night, around midnight. I slept in that room over there."

Beth looked to where Cindy was pointing. Apparently, someone had put Cindy up in the children's guest room.

"Well, welcome, then. Is there anything I can get you now?" Beth asked.

"This isn't going to work," muttered Cindy.

"What?" asked Beth, not understanding Cindy's words.

"I mean, you don't know who I am or what I'm doing here. Your parents are going to wonder the same thing. I should just leave now before anyone else sees me," Cindy said sadly.

Beth almost had to agree with Cindy. If the girl left now, the only people who would know she had even been there would be Beth and . . . suddenly Beth realized that she didn't even know who brought Cindy to their house. Since it was obvious that Cindy didn't really want to leave, Beth put on her friendliest face and put her arm around Cindy's shoulder.

"Don't be silly. My Mom and Dad welcome all my friends. They don't have to know when you arrived," Beth assured her.

Cindy looked relieved.

"Come on, let's go down to the kitchen and grab some breakfast. I'm hungry, and the boys can sleep a long time," Beth said.

"Sounds great," Cindy answered, and followed Beth downstairs.

As they walked along the hallway to the kitchen, Cindy marveled at the view outside the windows and at Mrs. Bradford's framed photography hanging on the wall.

"Did you bring a bathing suit? We can go swimming later if you'd like," Beth said.

Cindy grew quiet, and her eyes clouded up with tears.

"I'm sorry, are you afraid of water?" Beth asked.

"No," Cindy stammered. "It's just that I didn't bring my bathing suit. I didn't bring any clothes," she said, a tear falling down her cheek.

Beth stopped and stared at Cindy for a moment.

"Come on, let's grab some OJ and some coffee cake and sit out by the swing set. I am really confused," Beth said, grabbing Cindy's arm and hurrying her to the kitchen.

Once they were seated outside with their breakfast, Beth looked intently at Cindy.

"All right. Give me the story," she said.

Cindy told her about her mother's business trip, and her midnight ride to the mini-mart to call Andy. She told Beth about Josh's bike, and about Pete coming to pick them all up in the van.

"Are you going home sometime today?" Beth asked.

Tears flooded Cindy's eyes again. "Not if I can help it," she whispered.

Beth sighed. "Would you like to stay with us for another night, until your mom gets home from her business trip?" she offered.

Cindy looked down at her clothes. "I would," she said, "but I don't think you guys are going to be able to put up with me for another 48 hours in these clothes. Maybe if I just jumped into the pool, clothes and all, I would smell a little fresher."

Beth laughed. "No, don't do that. I have huge amounts of clothes from last summer just sitting in the basement. Let's go get some for you, and we'll throw in a bathing suit as well," she said.

Cindy began to look a little more hopeful, so the girls finished their meal and hurried down to the basement.

Beth opened a large wardrobe, and began pulling out shorts, shirts, and a bathing suit. Then she walked over to another wardrobe, and pulled out a wicker basket with her name on it. Inside the basket were bags of unopened underwear and socks. Beth added to the pile in Cindy's arms, and then closed the wardrobe.

"Come on, let's get these things upstairs and into the dresser in your room," Beth suggested, leading the way.

"While you're getting settled, I'm going to go see if Andy is awake," Beth said, leaving Cindy in the guest room and walking down the hall to Andy's room.

She knocked on the door. There was no answer, so Beth peeked into the room. Andy's sleeping form was still in his bed.

"Yeah, right, sleepyhead. You snooze on while I tend to the problems you've created," Beth said as she shut the door again.

She returned to the guest room and reported that Andy still slept.

“I need to take my shower,” Beth said. “If you want to take a shower too, you can use the bathroom in this room. There should be towels and soap in there,” she added.

“Thanks. Are you sure your Mom won’t notice that I’m wearing your clothes?” asked Cindy.

“Not a chance if you’re wearing shorts and T-shirts. If you wear one of my gowns, she might wonder if I had one similar to it. But clothes to hang out in, never,” Beth assured her.

“Okay. Can we both shower at the same time?” Cindy asked.

“Sure, no problem. I’ll see you back here in a half hour,” Beth said and went back to her own room to shower and dress.

When Mr. And Mrs. Bradford ate breakfast with the Towers family later that morning, the teenage Bradfords were no where to be found.

“It’s not unusual for them to be out and about when Emma and I sit down to eat,” said Peter to Justin, as he looked at the three empty chairs around the table. “Still, it’s not like them to be so impolite when we have guests,” he added.

Justin chuckled. “We’re going to be here for a few days, Peter, so don’t worry about it. I know teenagers lead busy lives,” he said.

As they ate, Justin thanked the Bradfords once again for their hospitality.

“You really weren’t kidding when you said we wouldn’t put you out by staying here, were you?” he said.

Peter laughed. “No, we weren’t. Please, make yourself at home here. Boys, tell me again how old you are,” he asked, looking at Justin’s sons.

“I’m 8,” said the bigger one.

“I’m 6,” said the other.

“Well, then, our Micah is 7 years old, and I’m sure that you’ll find plenty to do with him. We do have a few rules, though, and the biggest is that you can not go anywhere near the pool without an adult or one of the big kids with you. Everything else is yours for the using, Okay?” Peter said, looking directly at the small boys.

“I already played with Micah this morning. He’s got the coolest stuff!” the older boy nodded and said.

“Good. Now, Justin and Lori, the fence around the pool is 7 feet high, and the gate has a keypad entry on it. The code is Christmas day, 12–25. Please feel free to swim whenever you want to,” Peter said, turning to look at Justin and his wife.

Justin had opened his mouth to thank Peter again, when Micah excitedly spoke up.

“Daddy, can we be excused? I want to show these guys my trains and my Lego city and my,” Micah began, but was interrupted by his father, who said,

"And go ahead. Have fun!"

Justin shook his head at the eager boys tearing down the hall. When he looked back at Peter and Emma to see if the excited children bothered them, both Bradfords were quietly sipping their tea as if there was nothing unusual about three small boys flying through the house.

The teen age Bradfords did make an appearance at the lunch table. Beth introduced Cindy to her parents and to the Towers. Cindy was relieved that neither Peter nor Emma seemed to think another guest in the house was unusual. After everyone had finished eating, the BBG's and Cindy met at the tree house.

Cindy was introduced to the BBG's that she didn't know, and then Josh and Andy told the others the tale of their late night adventure.

"You had better call the police to report your bike being stolen," Paul said to Josh.

"Oh, no! Please don't do that!" cried Cindy.

"Cindy, we're going to have to at some point. I can't keep using Andy's bike," said Josh.

"But maybe, could you wait until I call this Beslinger man and see if I can get this straightened out?" Cindy asked.

"Is that what you want to do?" asked Beth.

"Yes," Cindy said.

"Then come on. We'll do it from our house," said Andy, climbing down from the tree house.

The BBGs went upstairs to the children's computer room and library, and shut the door firmly behind them.

"Wow, 3 computers?" asked Cindy, looking at the neat computer desks lined up against one wall.

"We need all of them with the homework from 6 kids," said Pete.

Andy found a Linsburg, Michigan, phone directory on the computer, and found a listing for a Charles Beslinger. He wrote the number down and handed it to Cindy.

"You can try now, but he might be at work. There's a time zone difference," said Andy.

"They're an hour behind us, I think," added Meg.

"That puts it at 3:15 there," said Dale.

"I may lose my nerve. I better try now," said Cindy, picking up the phone.

She jumped when a man answered the phone, and Andy switched to speaker phone mode. Every teen sat on the edge of their chairs.

"Mr. Beslinger?" Cindy said nervously.

"Yes?" he answered.

"Ummm, my name is Cindy Rathers and I," Cindy started to say.

“I’m not interested in buying anything,” Mr. Beslinger said in a firm voice.

“Oh, no sir, I’m not selling anything. I just wondered,” Cindy held her breath for a moment, and then rushed on, “did you ever have a daughter named Barbara Jeanette?”

There was silence on the other end of the line.

“Is this some sort of prank?” Mr. Beslinger growled.

“No, No! You see, my mom is Melissa Rathers. I mean, she was Melissa Porter before she got married to Tim Rathers. Were you ever married to a Melissa Porter?” Cindy asked, stumbling over her words.

“My ex-wife’s maiden name was Lynn Evans,” Mr. Beslinger said sadly.

Cindy’s face fell, and the disappointment seeped into her voice.

“Her name was Lynn Evans? I wonder who this card belongs too, then,” Cindy wondered out loud.

“I’m not following you. What card?” Mr. Beslinger asked.

“I found this missing child card in my grandmother’s attic. It lists your name as the parent from whom the child was taken. For a minute, I thought that maybe I was the child on the card,” Cindy explained.

Again there was silence on the other side.

“You found a card with my name and Barbie’s picture on it in your grandmother’s attic?” asked Charles in a much gentler tone.

“Yes. You know, one of those missing children cards that come in the mail every Friday,” Cindy said.

“Where does your grandmother live?” asked Charles.

“She’s lived in Utah for as long as I can remember,” Cindy said.

“Utah? No, I don’t think Lynn’s parents would have moved there,” Charles said.

“I’m terribly sorry to have bothered you, then, Mr. Beslinger. I must be mistaken,” Cindy said, sadly.

“What made you think that the baby on the missing children’s card was you? It must be very faded by now,” Charles asked, quietly.

“Well, there’s this huge mix up in my family over who’s who in the pictures we took out of my grandmother’s attic. There aren’t any baby pictures with my name on the back. The pictures that have my mom in them, though, always say, “Melissa and Barbie”. My pictures don’t start until I was over 2 years old. And anyway, the man on the missing child picture sort of resembles my Dad,” Cindy finished.

There was a long silence on the phone. Finally Mr. Beslinger asked Cindy how old she was.

“I was 14 just 2 weeks ago, on the 10th,” Cindy said.

“June 10th?” the man’s voice was barely over a whisper, now.

“Yes, June 10th,” repeated Cindy.

"Is there anything else on those pictures that seems odd to you?" asked Mr. Beslinger.

"Well, some of the pictures have my mom holding a baby that looks like me, and she's standing beside someone, but they've been cut out of the picture," Cindy said.

"Cindy, can I have a phone number where I can reach you? I want to check into this story a little more. I hope this isn't some sort of cruel prank, though, because I can have you charged with harassment if it is. Understand?" Mr. Beslinger said.

"I understand, it wasn't easy for me to call, either, you know," Cindy answered, and then gave the man the Bradford's teen phone number.

The BBGs sat in the library, playing computer games for about 20 minutes until the phone rang again. Cindy answered it.

"Is this Cindy Rathers?" the voice on the other end asked.

"Yes," Cindy said, breathlessly.

"It's Charles Beslinger. I've found out some interesting information," he said.

Cindy sat in a chair because her wobbly knees didn't seem capable of supporting her any longer if she remained standing.

"What did you find?" she asked.

The man on the other end began to tell a story of a lovely wife and beautiful daughter. They seemed to be very happy until the baby daughter turned a year old. Shortly after the baby's first birthday, the wife apparently found someone new to love while searching on a singles matchmaking internet service. The person she began corresponding with thought that she was a single woman, living with her parents.

The wife took a trip to Texas to meet the internet friend. She told everyone at home, however, that she was going to help the victims of a recent hurricane. Upon her return from Texas, she unexpectedly filed for divorce and moved out of their home, leaving the little girl behind. The mother gave sole custody of her daughter to the father, making the divorce go through quickly. The woman then moved to Texas to remarry. There had been no word from her since.

As the father adjusted to the life of a single parent of a baby girl, they both seemed happy and content. One day, however, a stranger appeared at the back gate of Charles' home. Charles was outside, watching his little girl play in her sandbox. The stranger said that he needed help with directions, and then engaged Charles in a conversation for some time. Finally, Charles slipped out of the gated yard, locking the gate behind him, and went to the front yard to point out the direction to go. The stranger finally seemed to understand the directions, and thanked Charles. He got back into his car and drove off. Charles hurried back to the back yard, only to find out that his little baby girl was gone!

In the long search that followed, Charles found the matchmaking site his wife had frequented on the internet. It came as no surprise to him that the stranger who had asked him for directions wasn't really a stranger. The stranger was his ex-wife's new husband, staring out at Charles from the computer monitor.

The police detectives realized that the man had purposely distracted Charles just long enough for Melissa to grab the baby from the yard. They figured that Melissa had then walked quickly to an arranged site several blocks down where she and the baby were picked up by the husband.

"Oh, I am so sorry," Cindy said, sniffling into the phone.

"I don't know what to make of this, Cindy. You say that the picture of the abductor on the missing child's card looks like your father?" Charles asked again.

"Yes, he does. But my mother's name is Melissa. Her maiden name was Porter You said your wife's name was Lynn Evans. It can't be the same people," Cindy said.

Mr. Beslinger sighed loudly.

"My wife's full maiden name was Melissa Lynn Porter Evans. The only people who ever called her Melissa were her parents," Charles said.

Cindy gripped the edge of her chair.

"Cindy?" Charles asked, "There's one other thing you should know. Your birthday is the same day as my Barbie's."

This news brought a choking sob from Cindy, and she could barely acknowledge his words.

"I hope you understand that I am positive that the man who came to my house that day was the man whom my ex-wife married. I've seen several photos of him. How sure are you that the picture on the card matches your dad?" Charles asked.

"Really sure." whispered Cindy.

"Before I called you back, I spoke to my brother, who is also my attorney. Would it be possible for the two of us to meet with you? I don't mean meet with you alone. I would prefer a public place, and if possible, could you bring an adult with you?"

"That's going to be a problem. Mom doesn't know I'm doing this. If she sees you or finds out, what I've done, she'll kill me!" Cindy said.

"I didn't mean that the adult had to be either of your parents, Cindy. In our case, it would probably be better if it was a different adult. Is there someone else you trust, that would be willing to come along with you?" Mr. Beslinger asked.

"I don't think so. The only people who know about this are my friends who live at this phone number," Cindy hedged.

"All right, then, let's make the meeting at the airport. I'll call you back when I get my reservations and give you the flight numbers and times. You and your friends can come to the airport, and we'll meet as soon as I get off the plane. If this is for real, my brother will know how to handle it from there. If we've both made a mistake, my brother and I will just catch the next plane headed back out for Detroit. Does that sound okay?" Mr. Beslinger asked.

Cindy looked at her friends. They nodded, so she agreed.

"Where should I call to give you the flight information?" Mr. Beslinger asked.

"Just use this number. I'm not going home if I can help it," Cindy said.

The BBGs looked at each other frantically behind Cindy's back. They hadn't discussed this part at all.

"Well, then, I'm looking forward to meeting you and your friends," Charles said gently.

"Me, too," Cindy said and hung up.

"Whew," she said as soon as she hung up the phone, and slumped back into her chair.

"You said it," Pete agreed.

The teens talked for awhile about the phone call and what it could all mean, but none of the BBGs brought up Cindy's comment about staying at the Bradford's home indefinitely.

Finally, Meg stood up and stretched.

"I've got clothes to get in. I'll see you guys at Youth group," she said.

"We better go, too. See you all in a few!" said Paul, as he and Josh followed Meg out of the room.

Shortly after the Bakers left, Dale and Diana went home, and then the Bradford teens got ready for supper.

When everyone was seated around the table, Justin looked at the BBGs and said, "You guys were sure scarce this afternoon."

"Sorry. We sort of had some pressing business to take care of," Beth said.

Justin caught the evasiveness in her voice, but decided not to press her any further on it.

"You two guys having fun?" asked Pete, trying to get the attention away from him and his brother and sister. He sat between Justin's 2 sons, and looked at them expectantly.

"Yes! Lots!" they exclaimed.

"Good. Carry on, men," Pete said jokingly.

The conversation then turned to general topics, and Cindy and her teen hosts and hostess sighed with relief.

Shortly after supper, the Bradford family and their guests made their way over to the church. Since Justin was bringing a message to the youth, Dave and the middle school youth leader combined both groups in the Sr. High youth room. The BBGs led worship, and although it wasn't up to their normal excellence, Justin was still impressed.

"Hey, they're not bad," he said to Dave, in the middle of the set.

"Well, usually they're excellent," Dave answered, and then added, "I wonder if something is up again."

"What do you mean?" asked Justin.

Dave explained, but then said, "I can't imagine that they're up to something again so soon, though. Maybe it's just because Cindy is here."

Justin smiled. "She's another mystery, Dave. I don't know when she arrived at the Bradford's home. I went to bed around midnight last night, and she wasn't there before that. The first I saw of her was at lunchtime," he said.

"Pete must have gone to get her this morning, then," Dave suggested.

"That could be, but I don't think so. I heard the maid tell Emma this morning that there was someone staying in the children's guest room. I know Emma was shocked to hear that. She asked the maid twice if she was sure it wasn't the little boys playing in there. The maid sort of looked at her funny, and said that it was definitely not little boys," Justin said.

Dave chuckled. "Emma and Peter can't keep up with the BBG's comings and goings, but it generally doesn't include someone they've never seen before," he said.

At the end of worship, Justin got up and began to talk to the kids on honesty. He spoke at length about being honest with themselves as well as with other people. Justin noticed that Andy and Josh looked uncomfortably at each other throughout his message, and he reminded himself to say something to Dave about it later that night.

As soon as he stepped outside on his way to play volleyball after the message, Dale suddenly stopped in his tracks. He stared across the field to the Baker's driveway, where a police car had just pulled in.

"Hey, what's up?" the boy who was walking behind Dale said, as he bumped into Dale's back.

"What? Oh, sorry Dan. I shouldn't have stopped so suddenly," Dale said, absently.

The rest of the group walked around Dale and continued toward the volleyball court. The BBGs, however, followed Dale's gaze and then stood rooted to the spot as they too, spotted the police cruiser in the Baker's driveway. They could also see Carl and John walking toward the Baker's home.

"What do you think they want?" asked Josh nervously.

"I've got to hide!" whispered Cindy.

"Why? Why would the police being at Josh's house have anything to do with you?" asked Andy.

"I don't know. My dad doesn't even know where I stayed last night. Maybe he has the police out looking for me," Cindy said in a nervous voice.

"Your Dad doesn't even know my last name, Cindy. We just met him at the mall last week. There's no way that the police are looking for you at my house," Josh insisted.

"Besides that, Cindy, you can't just disappear like that," Pete said.

"Sure I can. I do it a lot," Cindy said.

Pete groaned.

Suddenly, Josh grabbed Andy's arm.

"That's what this is about! Look! They've found my bike!" Josh said, as they watched a policeman finish pulling Josh's bike from the trunk of the police cruiser.

"Wow. Good thing we have them registered," said Andy.

Paul clapped his hand over Josh's shoulder.

"Ummm, I wouldn't be too happy to see that bike there, kiddo. You sort of neglected to tell Dad that yours was stolen, and that you now have Andy's bike in your rack," he said.

Josh began to look nervous. "It just happened last night. I wasn't up when Dad went to work this morning, and besides, Andy's bike has been in our garage before. He could have just left it in there," he said.

Paul laughed. "I don't know, Josh. I think you are standing on shaky ground."

"Put me on the shaky ground list too then," said Pete in a worried tone. "Remember that I'm the one who hauled these guys home in the middle of the night because of that stolen bike. And it all happened after my license had expired for the day, by the way," he added with a sigh.

"It's all my fault," said Cindy.

"We all should have said something before this," Pete said.

"But, you can't say anything now! I mean, please, Josh, please, don't bring my name into this," Cindy pleaded.

"Your name's already involved," Josh said, as he watched his father open the garage door. The policemen entered the garage after John and Carl had gone in.

"You guys playing ball?" Dave called around the corner of the building at them.

When none of them answered, he took one look at their worried faces, and then followed their gaze to the Baker's driveway.

"Whoa. Anything wrong, Paul?" he asked.

"Josh's bike was stolen last night," Paul said.

"That's too bad. Did the police find it?" Dave asked.

"Yes," Josh said, with a forlorn face.

"Do you want to go home?" Dave asked kindly.

"Not unless I have to," Josh answered nervously.

Dave looked confused at Josh's answers for a moment.

"Well, let's play ball, then," he finally said.

They had just started the game when Kelly Ganderson came out to the volleyball court to find them.

"Pastor Carl just called, Josh. You need to go home," she said quietly.

Josh sighed, and walked off the volleyball field.

"Promise me you won't tell on me!" Cindy whispered as he passed her.

Josh looked at her frightened face. "I promise," he said, sadly.

"Please, Lord, work this out," prayed Meg as she watched Josh jog across the field that separated their home from the church.

"Yes, Dad?" Josh asked as he went to stand in front of his father.

"Joshua, these policemen need to talk to you," John said.

"Yes, sir?" Josh replied, speaking to the policemen.

"You're Joshua Baker?" asked one of the officers.

"Yes, sir, I am," Josh answered.

"I'm Officer Landon, son," the policeman said, reaching out to shake Josh's hand.

Josh shook hands, and then looked at Officer Landon to continue.

"Is this your bike?" the officer asked, bringing Josh's bike over to him.

"I believe so, yes," Josh said.

"And the almost identical bike in the garage here belongs to Andrew Bradford?" the officer continued.

"Yes, sir," Josh said, secretly wondering if his father knew all along that it was Andy's bike in the rack.

"Is there a reason why his bike is in your garage?" the policeman asked.

"Well, I didn't steal it!" Josh said, a little defensive.

"What's the reason, Joshua?" John Baker asked.

Josh squirmed.

"The truth, son," John spoke again.

Josh looked at his father's face. He saw compassion there, so he continued.

"Andy and I put his bike there so you wouldn't realize that mine was stolen," Josh admitted.

John smiled at Josh's admission.

"That's the first thing I've heard so far that makes sense," he said.

"Mr. Baker, this bike was used to vandalize the elementary school early this morning. Your son was spotted at a convenience store on this bike around the same time," Officer Landon said.

John frowned at that information, and turned to Josh.

"Can you explain this?" he asked.

"Yes, Dad. I was at the convenience store. That's where my bike was stolen! I left it leaning against the wall for a few minutes while I uh, helped someone, and when I came back to get it, it was gone!" Josh said emphatically.

"Who were you helping? Did you walk home after you finished helping this person? After you realized your bike was stolen, I mean," the officer asked.

"I was helping someone put air in their bike tires. Andy was there with me," Josh said.

"Why did you and your friend Andy decide to bike to a convenience store at 1:00 in the morning, Josh?" the policeman asked.

"I told you. We were helping someone. We didn't vandalize the school," Josh said.

"How did you and Andy get home then?" the officer asked again.

"We got a ride from someone," Josh said quietly.

"But you're not going to tell me who you were helping, or who brought you home, are you?" the officer asked, looking intently at Josh.

"No," said Josh.

Mr. Baker's mouth dropped open at Josh's answer.

The officer sighed, and pulled out a citation book.

"Mr. Baker, I'm issuing you a $25.00 citation for your son breaking curfew. Is this friend Andy the same Andrew Bradford that owns this other bike?" he asked.

Josh nodded, and the policeman continued.

"Mr. Bradford will be getting a citation, too, then. Mr. Baker, your son's story sounds plausible, but without the names of the other people involved, we can't finish the investigation or clear his name as a possible suspect in the vandalism. He was seen near the school at the time of the incident, and his bike has flecks of the same paint that was used by the vandal. Do you plan to be around town for the next few days?" the officer said.

"We don't have any plans to go away for several weeks," said Mr. Baker.

The officer nodded, and then said, "Luke, go get Andy's bike out of the garage and let's take a look at that one, too. Mr. Baker, could you get me the Bradford's phone number so I can call and ask them to come and claim this bike?" the lead officer asked, as he put his citation book back into his pocket.

Carl offered to call the church and have Andy and Peter sent over. When the officer agreed, Carl used his cell phone to call over to the church. In a few minutes, Peter and Andy were standing in the drive with the others. The officers took Andy and his father aside and asked Andy the same questions that they had asked Josh. Josh watched the officer get out his citation book and hand a citation to Peter. After that, the officers said good night and left. Andy and Josh stood miserably, looking at the pavement in the Baker's driveway. Their fathers studied their faces, trying to read what was going through their minds.

"I'm sorry," choked Josh, finally. He looked up at his father, and then at

Andy and finally at Peter.

"I'm sorry, too," said John, and then said, "Why don't we all go into the den and sit down to talk about this?"

Peter nodded, and he and John and Carl walked into the house as the two boys followed slowly behind.

When they were all seated in the den, John said, "Joshua, I know it's not like you to go traipsing about the county on a bike in the middle of the night. Why did you do something like that?"

Josh shrugged and said, "I just needed to."

Andy spoke up then, "He went because I asked him to."

"Well, then the question falls to you, Andrew. Why?" Peter asked.

"We needed to," Andy replied.

"Did you vandalize the school?" asked John seriously.

"No, Dad, honest!" cried Josh with such alarm in his voice that his father knew immediately that Josh was not the one who committed that mischief.

"Then tell me why you were at this store, who you were with, and how you got home," John insisted.

"I'm sorry. I just can't," Josh said, his eyes hitting the floor.

"Joshua, you're on the fast track to meeting up with my persuasive measures," John warned his son.

"I'll take the strapping, Dad, but I can't tell you the answers to your questions just yet," Josh said quietly.

"Go to your room, son. I don't want to see you until you're ready to tell me what this is about," John said in an angry tone.

Josh winced. He hated to make his father angry. It seemed to tear at his insides on the rare occasions that it happened.

Peter dismissed Andy as well, with similar instructions. After the boys left, the men looked at each other, their anger slowly turning into smiles.

"I would have never believed it about Josh," said John, giving up his anger for a grin.

"I admit, this is my first juvenile citation," agreed Peter, grinning as well.

"They're covering up for somebody," said John in a thoughtful voice.

"I don't doubt that. But who is it?" asked Peter.

"I'll ask my BBG members. I can't imagine that they aren't part of this somehow," Carl said, getting up to leave.

"Check on Josh, will you, Carl? I was awfully hard on him a minute ago, and I know he's running scared. I'm going to stay down here and think and pray for a little bit longer," John said, suddenly looking very tired.

CHAPTER 15

Peter rose with Carl, and after shaking hands with everyone, also said good night. Carl walked up the stairs to Josh's room before he went home, and knocked on the door.

"Come in," Josh said, and then when he saw who was entering, said, "Oh, hi, Pastor Carl."

Carl walked over to Josh's desk, and leaned against it.

"This isn't like you, Josh. Would it be easier to talk to me, I mean, as your Pastor?" Carl said kindly.

Josh thought for a second, and then said, "It's easy enough to talk. I just can't."

"Are you protecting somebody? Covering up for them?" Carl asked.

Josh looked at Carl's eyes, and the concern there made his own fill with tears.

"I really, really blew it with Dad, didn't I? I've never seen him so mad at me. I hope when this is all over, he'll forgive me," Josh said, and let his tears fall. Carl walked over and embraced him.

"Your Dad loves you very much, Josh, and he's already forgiven you. He's worried right now because this is so serious. You don't need a police record, bud," Carl said.

"There isn't anything I can do!" Josh cried.

"You could let us help you. We all know you and Andy didn't vandalize the school. We just need to prove it. Do you know who did the vandalism? Are you protecting them?" asked Carl.

"No, I don't know anything about the school!" Josh said, louder than he needed to.

"OK, Josh. It will be OK," Carl said, patting him on the back before leaving the room.

Carl walked back downstairs and poked his head into John's den. John sat, with his head resting on his arms at his desk, praying. He looked up at the sound of Carl's gentle knock, hopeful that Carl had good news. But Carl just shook his head, and said, "Nothing, John, I'm sorry."

"Thanks for trying, Carl," John said, smiling at his friend.

Shortly after he arrived home, Carl's family came back from church. Carl asked Dale and Diana to join him on the patio. Dale and Di nervously took seats across the picnic table from their father.

"What do you guys know about Josh's bike being stolen?" asked Carl.

"Just what he told us. That it was stolen," Dale said, and Diana nodded her agreement.

"The police found it?" asked Dale.

"Yes, they did. Do you know where?" Carl asked.

"No, where, Dad?" Dale asked.

"About a quarter of a mile from the South Elementary school," Carl said, looking at both of his children to see if the name registered with them. They looked blankly back at him, so he continued. "The school was vandalized with paint last night."

"Wow," both Dale and Diana said together.

"And there are specks of that paint on Josh's bike tire," Carl added.

"Whoa! Do you mean someone stole Josh's bike and used it to vandalize the school?" asked Dale.

"Yes, that's right. Josh and Andy are in deep trouble with the law right now," Carl answered.

"But Dad! Josh and Andy didn't do it!" cried Di.

"I know that. But the police don't. Josh and Andy were spotted at the convenience store close to the school shortly before the vandals hit. We need witnesses to prove that Josh and Andy came home, and didn't go to the school from there. Do either of you have any idea of why Andy needed to go to a convenience store at that hour of night? Do you know how they got home on one bike?" Carl asked seriously.

Dale and Di said nothing, so Carl continued. "Do you know who they are protecting?" he asked.

Dale and Diana sat silently and thought. Apparently, Pete was not yet tied into this mess, and they were unwilling to be the first to drag him into it. They also were not willing to lie to their father, so the best thing they could come up with right now would be to keep quiet. Carl understood this tactic perfectly. His children's silence indicated that they knew the answers to at least some of the questions he had raised.

He shook his head, and said, "Josh and Andy need friends right now."

"Will they go to jail?" asked Di, tears forming in her eyes.

"That's not likely on a first offense for vandalism, Di. It would more likely be a police record and a high fine for their fathers to pay. The worst part would be the police record. Nobody needs one of those," Carl said seriously.

"Good night, Dad. Sorry we couldn't help," Dale said, pulling Diana back towards the house with him.

"Couldn't or wouldn't, Dale?" Carl asked, looking at their faces.

Dale looked at his father for a moment, but then allowed Diana to pull him toward the house.

At the Bradford home, Pete, Beth, and Cindy headed directly for Andy's room after church.

"Well?" whispered Cindy.

"Well, your secret is still safe for now. But we have big trouble. Whoever stole Josh's bike vandalized the South Elementary school with it. There's paint on the tires to prove it. The vandals also left a receipt from the mini-mart near Josh's bike when they dumped it, so the police traced the bike there. The clerk at the convenience store described me and Josh, and then told the police all about how we were there with our bikes around the time the school was hit. They looked up the registration for Josh's bike and got his name and address. Now we are suspects in this stupid case. We need a witness to say that we came right home from the mini-mart," Andy said.

"Oh, no!" Beth cried.

"You mean, you haven't told anyone that it was me who picked you up?" Pete asked.

"Dad already has a $25.00 fine for one kid breaking curfew. Do you think I wanted to add another Bradford kid, driving illegally on a Cinderella license on top of it?" Andy asked.

"Yikes. Did they really hit Dad with a curfew fine?" asked Pete.

"Yes, they really did," said Andy, and then added, "and there's going to be a whole lot more going on if Josh and I get charged with vandalism and end up with a police record, or whatever they do to kids who do that kind of stuff."

"We've got to tell." said Beth firmly.

"No, not yet!" said Cindy.

"Dad doesn't need any more embarrassing fines, and I could lose my license until I'm 18, or later if they decide to charge me with the vandalism, too," said Pete.

"Besides, we can't let Andy and Josh take all the blame!" cried Beth.

The teens all looked at each other, with none of them knowing what to do next.

"Come on, let's just go to bed. Maybe we'll come up with something by tomorrow," Pete suggested.

The next morning, all the BBGs except Josh and Andy were joined in the tree house by Cindy. They discussed the dire situation that they found themselves in.

"I'm not going to stand by and let Josh and Andy get charged for something they didn't do," said Diana.

"Me, either," said Beth, with Meg shaking her head in agreement.

"Will it help if I came forward?" asked Pete.

"Or will it just make it worse?" asked Dale.

The little group could not come up with any solutions, so they broke up and went home. After supper that evening, they again gathered in the tree house.

"How's Josh?" Dale asked Meg and Paul.

"Still in his room and still not talking," said Meg.

"And your Dad?" asked Di.

"He seemed OK at supper. He took Josh's dinner up to him, and they both ate up there," said Paul.

"How's it going at your house?" Dale then asked Pete.

"The same," said Pete, and then jumped as Diana gasped and pointed to the Baker's driveway.

"Do you think that they're going to take Josh away now?" she cried, looking through the tree's leaves at the police cruiser that was once again parked in the Baker's drive.

"Not if I can help it. Come on!" Paul called, taking the hand glider down to the ground.

"You stay here," Pete said to Cindy, as the tree house quickly emptied.

Cindy nodded, a frightened look on her face telling Pete she would stay put.

The BBGs burst into the Baker's family room just as Peter Bradford, Justin Towers, and Carl Ganderson arrived. A police officer was in the process of putting a video tape into the Baker's VCR.

"What's happened?" asked Peter.

"I'm afraid we have some new complications," said the officer, as he started the tape.

"This is the security video cam of the area around the gas pumps at the mini-mart around the time the school was vandalized," he continued.

Everyone watched as Josh, Andy, and Cindy came into view, walking to the air pump and pumping air into a bicycle tire.

"Why, that's Cindy!" Peter exclaimed in astonishment.

"When was the last time you saw this girl?" asked the officer.

"At dinner this evening. She's a guest in my home," Peter said.

"Not anymore. Get Cindy out of here, now," whispered Pete to Beth, as they stood in the rear of the crowd watching the TV.

"But where?" asked Beth.

"It doesn't matter. Just away from here. Give her Meg's bike and give her directions to someplace so she can leave right now. She has no time to lose!" Pete urged.

"Meg, come here," Beth whispered, and the girls slipped out of the house, unnoticed.

"Call Mrs. Griffith. Tell her I'm bringing a friend who needs a place to stay for a few days. She'll understand!" Beth said, once they were outside on the porch.

"Got it," said Meg, as Beth raced to the garage, hopped on Meg's bike, and rode to the tree house.

Mrs. Griffith was an elderly woman from their church who had been a foster parent for many years. All the BBGs knew that she used to care specifically for teens in a crisis situation. Right now, Beth couldn't think of a bigger crisis than the one they were in.

"I'll be delighted to help," Mrs. Griffith said, when Meg told her the story about Cindy.

Beth had sent Cindy down the road on Meg's bike with specific directions to Mrs. Griffith's home. Beth then ran to her garage and took out Cindy's bike. She pedaled hard and caught up to the girl. Together they knocked on Mrs. Griffith's door, and after getting Cindy somewhat settled with the elderly woman, Beth hopped on Meg's bike and hurried back to the Bakers. Meg was sitting on the patio, waiting in the waning light for her friend to return.

"Everything settled?" asked Meg.

"Yes," Beth was breathless from her ride, and was silent as she put Meg's bike away.

"What happened here?" she finally asked, coming back to sit on the picnic bench with Meg.

"Oh, Beth! This has got to be the worst!" cried Meg.

"Tell me!" insisted Beth.

"Well, the police said that originally, they weren't even going to look at the security video cam tapes because they were sure the clerk could ID Josh and Andy. If no other suspects turned up and the police decided to charge Josh and Andy, all they would need would be her visual confirmation. Then, early today, they got a call from Cindy's parents, saying that she's been gone for 2 days, and none of her friends have seen her," said Meg.

"Except for a couple of unknown, brand new friends," mumbled Beth.

"Well, the first thing the police did after that, was to go to the mini mart near Cindy's house and put up a flyer about her. The clerk that was working this morning very happily told the officers that Cindy used to come to the mini mart often, and even sometimes came late at night. So the police took the last few days' tapes back to the station with them to watch, and bingo. There Cindy is with Josh, Andy, and Pete. On the night that the school was vandalized," Meg said.

"Well, it does prove that Josh and Andy were helping someone, just like they said," said Beth, not getting the whole point Meg was trying to make.

"Yes, and it also proves that Pete was the one who brought them home," Meg said again.

"What?" asked Beth, in a raised voice.

"Yep. Your van is clearly on the tape. License plate and all," Meg said.

"But how could they tell it was Pete? Can the video cam see the driver in the car?" asked Beth.

"Pete got out of the van to help load the bikes. There's no doubt it was him," said Meg.

"Oh, boy. What happened next?" asked Beth.

"Well, the officer asked if anyone knew who the boy driving the van was.

Since it was so obvious, Pete stepped right up and admitted that it was him. Then the police asked Pete how old he was," Meg said.

"They thought that he was 18, and that he wasn't driving on a Cinderella license?" asked Beth, hopefully.

"He's lucky he's not 18. If he was, he might have been charged with kidnapping," Meg said seriously.

"Just because he was caught on tape helping load Cindy's bike into the van, they're going to call that kidnapping?" Beth asked.

Meg sighed. "It's obvious on the tapes that Cindy is distraught. It doesn't really look like she wanted to go with Pete in the van that night," she said.

"What about Pete's license?" whispered Beth, changing topics and scrunching her face up to try to soften the blow.

"Actually, you don't have to make that face. That's the only positive part to the story. Now Josh and Andy have their 2 witnesses. If the police catch the real vandals, then the tape proves that Pete was really out on a 'good Samaritan' run to rescue Josh and Andy. His license will be fine, in that case. If they don't find the vandals, though, Pete can kiss his license good by until he's 21, because then he'll be implicated in the crime with Josh and Andy," Meg said.

"They just have to find the vandals. Or something," sighed Beth, and then added, "I guess I better get home."

"God Speed, friend," Meg said, smiling.

When Beth arrived home, Peter was sitting in an easy chair in the reception area waiting for her.

"Hi Dad," Beth said slowly.

"Sit down, Elizabeth," Peter Bradford said, nodding toward the chair next to him.

Beth winced at her full name, but sat in the chair.

"Where were you?" Peter asked quietly.

Beth thought that her father looked weary and sad. What she really wanted to do at that moment, was to crawl onto his lap, give him a hug and tell him the whole story. She was tired of carrying the burden, and she desperately wanted his help. A vision of Cindy's frightened face suddenly flashed in front of her eyes, though, and so she simply said, "Up in the tree house."

"All this time?" Peter asked, suspiciously.

"Well, no, when everyone cleared out of the Bakers, I went over and sat on the patio to talk to Meg," Beth replied.

"Where is Cindy?" Peter asked, bluntly.

"She left," Beth said.

"I can see that, but how and when?" Peter demanded.

"This afternoon. On her bike," Beth offered.

"Well, you seem to be the only one who knows that," Peter said, and then looked at Beth seriously. "Listen, Elizabeth. Things aren't looking too well for me right now. I have 2 police citations for wayward sons breaking the curfew and Cinderella driving laws. Pete and Andy are in danger of being charged with vandalism. On top of that, I've been unknowingly harboring a runaway. This is serious trouble, honey. Is there anything you can tell me that would help us out?" he asked solemnly.

Beth sighed.

"According to Cindy, her parents are treating her poorly. She has some real questions about both of them. She didn't tell me where she was going from here, but I don't think she's ever going home," Beth said, thinking to herself, "That's true. It was me who told her where she was going from here."

"How do you know her?" Peter asked.

"I don't really know her. She's only going into 8th grade," Beth said honestly.

"Then can you explain why she was staying at my home?" Peter asked.

"Uh, No. I found her in the hall two mornings ago. I didn't even know who she was. I thought maybe she came with Mr. Towers. Cindy said she wasn't with him, but honest, Dad, I didn't invite her here. I was just trying to be gracious," Beth said.

"Well, I'm sure that either Andy or Pete invited her, Beth. I'm not concerned with who invited her, I want to know why," Peter said.

"I don't think I know the whole reason behind that," Beth said evasively.

Peter realized that Beth was holding back information, so he decided to ask a different question.

"How did she carry all those clothes she had with her on the bike?" he asked.

"What clothes?" Beth asked.

"The drawers in the dresser of the children's guest room are full of clothes. If she brought them here on her bike, why did she leave them here this afternoon when she took off on her bike again?" Peter asked.

Beth panicked a little. Obviously, her father and the police had come back to the house to look for Cindy, and had searched the guest room while they were here.

"She didn't have even a single change of clothes when I found her in the hallway on Wednesday morning. She wanted to take a shower and didn't have anything to change into, so I loaned her some of my clothes from last summer," Beth said.

"She ran away from home without taking any extra clothes?" Peter asked.

"Apparently," Beth said.

"It doesn't sound to me as if she planned to run away from home then. Pete brought her and her bike here in the middle of the night. Is she the reason that the boys were out in the first place? Is she the vandal?" asked Peter, looking directly at Beth.

"I don't know, Dad. I'm pretty sure she's not the vandal, though," Beth said cautiously.

"Do you think Josh and Andy are the vandals?" Peter then asked.

"I know for sure they aren't," Beth assured her father.

Peter sighed and stood up. Beth stood then, as well.

"Good night, then, Beth. I hope you sleep better than I will," he said, following her up the staircase.

"Good night, Dad. I love you," Beth said gently, when they had reached the top of the steps.

Peter smiled, and gave his daughter a hug and a kiss on the forehead.

"Thanks, sweetheart. I love you too," he said.

Beth disappeared down the hall, turned the corner and went directly to Pete's room. He lay on his bed, while Andy sat in a recliner.

"Well, did the package get mailed?" Pete asked, after Beth had shut the door.

Beth laughed. "Why do I feel like I am living in the Underground Railroad era? Yes, the package is mailed. To Mrs. Griffith," she said.

"Well, to top off this lovely evening, Mr. Beslinger called. His plane comes in at 10:40 Saturday morning," Pete said.

"Whew! That's good. It's only a day away," Beth sighed.

"Yes, but who is going to take Cindy to the airport to meet him? It sure isn't going to be me," Pete said.

"Let her figure it out," grumbled Andy.

"We can't. That man holds the key to the secret that has gotten you and me and Josh into deep, deep trouble. We can't let him out of our sight," Pete said adamantly.

"I'll see if either Paul or Dale can take us," said Beth, and then asked, "What did Dad say to you, Pete?" asked Beth.

"Not much. I wouldn't answer his questions, so he just sent me flying home," Pete said, and then moaned, "and I don't expect to see the light of day for years to come."

Beth sighed. "Dad has a couple of messy problems on his hands right now," she said.

"That we made," Pete added sadly.

"We made them, and we'll just have to solve them," said Beth.

"Slow down, Beth. We should have most of the answers on Saturday morning," Pete said, seeing a look in his sister's eyes that made him urge her to be cautious.

"I'll check with Paul and Dale tomorrow about driving to the airport," Beth said.

She then wished her brothers a good night, and went to her own room to try to get some sleep.

CHAPTER 16

The next morning, Dale, Paul, Beth, Meg, and Di met on the Ganderson's patio. Beth asked Dale or Paul if they could get Cindy to the airport.

"I can. Diana and I are on the right side of the story for once," Dale said.

After the group discussed Cindy's dilemma a little further, they split up to go home and do their chores. Later that evening, the BBGs who were not under their parents' version of a house arrest, gathered at the Ganderson's once again to eat their Friday night pizza and to watch a movie. It was not quite the same without Pete, Andy, and Josh, so the teens made an early night of it. Directly after the movie, everyone went home.

On Saturday morning, Dale drove Paul, Meg, Di, and Beth to Mrs. Griffith's home to pick up Cindy. Cindy carried a small backpack out to the van. Inside the pack were the pictures that she had found in her grandmother's attic, as well as the faded card with the missing child information.

"Goodbye, Mrs. Griffith! You've been so kind!" Cindy said, hugging the older woman before taking her place in the van.

"And you've been a tremendous help getting these strawberries taken care of. Thank you dear, and God Speed today," Mrs. Griffith said, waving as Dale pulled out of the driveway.

The teens were too nervous to speak on the way to the airport, so Dale turned the radio on to the Christian music station, and turned the volume up. Other than the music playing, the van was silent as Dale made his way to the airport. When they arrived inside the airline's terminal, they checked the monitors for the arrival status, and found the plane carrying the Beslinger brothers was on time. They made their way to the lounge area to sit and wait for several minutes before the plane was due. Beth took her video camera out of her backpack and got it ready to capture the moment for Cindy, just in case the man really was her birth father.

After the teens had waited several minutes, the loudspeaker announced that the flight had landed. They picked up their things and went to stand near the exit where the passengers came into the terminal. It took a few minutes, but finally a steady stream of people began to come through the exit door. Beth spotted two men who seemed to be searching the crowd that was waiting for the passengers. One of them had a photo that he would look at, and then look out among the people. It was obvious that he was looking for someone specific.

"Look!" Beth whispered as she tapped Cindy's shoulder. Cindy looked where Beth was pointing.

"Do you think that's him?" she asked.

"I don't know, but they're definitely searching the crowd for someone," Beth answered.

Cindy was too frightened to move. The crowd thinned out as the passengers either found who they were looking for or moved on to the baggage claim. The BBGs hung back just a little so that the two men who were still looking through the remaining crowd could see Cindy. Suddenly, the man with the photo got a full view of Cindy, and he stood still, looking at her. When he saw the BBGs standing around her, his eyes welled with tears that spilled down his face. Beth now had her camera rolling, but there were tears running down her cheeks, too.

The man started slowly toward Cindy. "Cindy? Cindy? Cindy Rathers? Oh, my wonderful Lord, it really is Barbie!" he sobbed.

The few people who were still left in the waiting area turned to look at the sobbing man, and they smiled at him in a confused sort of way.

"Daddy?" Cindy was now sobbing hysterically herself, as the man enveloped her in a hug.

The other man picked up the photo Charles had dropped as soon as he spotted Cindy, and handed it to Meg.

"Charles took the last picture he had taken of Barbie and had it computer enhanced to age the baby's face. Pretty good job, isn't it?" he asked.

The BBGs gathered around the picture and gasped in amazement. It was a very good likeness of Cindy, indeed.

"Criminys," Dale breathed.

"She was right," was all Beth could say.

Finally, Cindy and her father stopped crying and hugging and turned to face the others.

"What do we do now, Phillip?" Charles asked his brother.

"Well, I think we've made a match, Charles. Let's get our luggage and then we need to get the whole story from these kids," Phillip suggested.

"Is there a restaurant around here that we could go to for lunch?" Charles asked the BBGs, as he grabbed his suitcase off of the conveyor belt.

"We'll treat," added Phillip, grabbing his.

"There are several restaurants near our home that we could go to," suggested Dale, and then added, "On a Saturday around the airport the restaurants are going to be crowded. We're better off heading out of town."

"That's a good point, son. Charles, let's rent a car and follow the kids to a place where we can talk," Phillip said.

"Fine. Show the way to the car rentals, then," Charles said.

After getting the rental car keys, Phillip said that he would bring the car around to the parking garage exit and wait for Dale to drive his car out.

"Can I ride with you, Dad?" Cindy asked. She was so sure that this man was her birth father that she started calling him 'Dad' as soon as she met him.

"That's not a very good idea, Cindy. You don't know us, and I think we should just play it safe and keep you with your friends," Phillip said.

Cindy's face fell, and tears appeared on her cheeks again.

"I'll be in the car right behind you, honey. I'm not letting you get away this time," Charles said softly.

True to their word, the men followed Dale to a restaurant near the BBGs' homes. They all settled into a large booth and Phillip ordered hamburgers all around.

"Now tell me this story," he said, after he had ordered.

"I've gotten these guys into a terrible, horrible mess," said Cindy, sadly.

"I'm very good at straightening out terrible, horrible messes," smiled Phillip, and then added, "but I can't help you straighten it out if I don't know all the pieces."

"Well, last Sunday I met Andy and Josh at the mall," began Cindy.

"You guys Andy and Josh?" interrupted Phillip, looking at Dale and Paul.

Dale and Paul laughed.

"No, I'm Dale Ganderson, and this is Paul Baker, Josh's brother. Andy and Josh are, shall we say, currently under our parents' version of house arrest," Dale said, chuckling.

"I guess I'll find out why in a minute," said Phillip with a smile.

Cindy continued on with her story, as the group ate, with Beth and Paul filling in details. When they had finished eating and telling the story, Charles said, "That's the most amazing story I've ever heard. What's next, Phillip?"

"The first step, I think, is to meet with these guys' parents. You should have never, never done all this without going to them with it. They're the ones who are legally responsible for you, and they deserve to be told the truth," said Phillip sternly, looking at the BBGs.

The BBGs hung their heads.

"It's all my fault, Dad. I told, or I mean, I demanded that they keep all of this a secret. I was afraid that Mom and, and, Tim would find out what I was up to before I met you," Cindy said.

"Well, we can certainly understand that, honey, but we need to get this fixed with their parents. Now," Charles agreed.

"I'll call Dad. Maybe we can all meet at our house," suggested Beth, getting up to use the pay phone.

She dialed her number, and when Suzi answered the ring, she asked for her father.

"Dad?" Beth said.

"Yes, Beth?" Peter said.

"Could you call the Bakers and the Gandersons, and if you want, Justin and Lori and see if they will meet us this afternoon? It's really important,"

Beth said.

"Elizabeth, what are you up to?" Peter asked.

"We're coming clean, Dad. Can you get everyone together, please?" Beth begged.

"To talk and resolve this issue, no holds barred?" asked Peter.

"No holds barred, Dad. It's over," Beth said happily.

"All right. We'll plan for an hour from now," Peter said.

"Great! See you!" Beth said and hung up.

She rejoined her friends and told them the news.

"That gives us just enough time to stop off at a hotel and put the luggage in our rooms." Phillip said, looking at his watch.

"Why don't you lead us to a good hotel around here, and we'll check in. Then we can follow you to Beth's home. I think that will work better than trying to figure out directions," Charles suggested.

The BBGs happily did as they were asked, and were soon on their way to the Bradfords.

"Oh, I can hardly wait until I see Dad's face!" squealed Beth.

Her squeals turned to a loud gasp, however, as they pulled into the circular drive at the Bradford's home. Directly in front of the van was a parked police cruiser. As soon as Dale put the car into park, Beth jumped out and ran for the door of her home. She raced into the reception room just in time to see a policeman finish putting handcuffs on her father's hands.

"Daddy!" screamed Beth, and lunged forward. Carl grabbed her arm as she passed him.

"Beth, wait, honey," he said gently.

Beth looked up at Carl, a mixture of anger at being stopped and fear flashing in her eyes. She tried to yank her arm away from Carl, but he held tight.

"What's going on, Dad?" asked Dale as he walked in, only a little behind Beth.

"Cindy's parents are pressing kidnapping charges against Mr. Bradford to try to force him to tell them where she is," Carl said, for Dale's benefit, as well as Beth's.

"How can they do that? Dad was never anywhere near Cindy!" said Beth.

"Honey, it was obvious from the tapes that Cindy was not happy when Pete arrived at the convenience store. The tape shows Pete taking her bike away from her, putting it in the van, and then opening the side door of the van for her, and motioning for her to get in. Now you and I know that Pete was just showing off his Sunday manners, but to someone who doesn't know Pete, that is, the strangers who are looking at this tape, it could look as if he were forcing her into the van. Since the tape doesn't show her carrying any clothes or any other personal belongings that night, it doesn't look as if she had planned to run away. In fact, it doesn't really look as if she came willingly at all," Carl explained.

"But that's Pete, not Dad!" said Beth.

"I know we've tried to tell you all this many times, Beth. Until you and your brothers and sister turn 18 years old, your parents are responsible for you. That's the way the law is," said Carl.

Just then, Cindy and the Beslinger brothers walked into the house.

Phillip Beslinger looked at Peter Bradford, and then thought hard for a moment.

"Peter Bradford! Why didn't I recognize that name when your daughter introduced herself?" exclaimed Phillip Beslinger.

Peter looked with embarrassment at the strange men. Phillip looked familiar, but he couldn't place him.

"Aren't you the CEO of Firestorm International?" Phillip asked.

"Yes," Peter said.

"I'm Phillip Beslinger, the attorney for the Detroit branch of Firestorm, and this is my brother, Charles, who manages another branch in Michigan," Phillip said excitedly.

Recognition came to Peter's eyes as he remembered the names of the men from company conventions.

"Phillip Beslinger," Peter sighed. "These aren't the best conditions for meeting the CEO of a company you represent."

Phillip seemed to realize for the first time that Peter was handcuffed and that there were policemen in the room.

"Officer, I'm a lawyer, possibly representing Mr. Bradford. Can you tell me what's going on here?" he asked, after looking around the room.

The officer patiently explained the charges to Phillip.

"Could I have a word with the Rathers before we continue any further?" Phillip asked.

The policeman thought for a moment, and then gave his consent. He knew Peter Bradford was an upstanding citizen, and firmly believed that the Rathers were taking advantage of him with bogus claims because of his wealth.

"Cindy, what's your number, sweetheart?" asked Phillip.

Cindy stepped out from behind her father to give Phillip the information. Everyone who had not been at the airport gasped in shock. Cindy Rathers, the alleged kidnapping victim, was standing in that very room.

"Before I make this connection, officer, would you be so kind as to radio your dispatch center and have a patrol car go to the Rathers' home? I have a feeling that they won't be sticking around much longer after their conversation with me, and you're going to want to at least be able to tell them Cindy's been found," Phillip said.

The officer frowned at Phillip.

"I don't have any reason to stop the Rathers from going anywhere. They're the ones pressing charges, not the ones being charged," he said.

"For now they aren't the ones being charged. If you'll trust me on this, you'll save yourselves a heap of trouble later," Phillip said.

The officer decided to give Phillip the benefit of the doubt. After all, he had brought Cindy back home. He went out to his patrol car and radioed for the back up. Phillip waited for the officer to return and then put the phone on conference mode and dialed.

A boy answered the phone with a tired sounding "hello?".

"Hello. Is your mother at home?" Phillip asked.

"She's not feeling well. My sister's been kidnapped and Mom's not taking any calls," the boy said in a monotone voice, as if he was reading from a script.

"Tell her that I have information about Cindy for her," Phillip said.

"Oh, all right. Mom! It's somebody else about Cindy!" the boy called loudly.

"Hello? Are you a journalist? I knew with such a prominent name as Peter Bradford involved, we'd be getting lots of media requests. But really, I wish you'd give us some privacy," Melissa said.

Cindy gasped. What had gotten into her mother to get her to act that way?

"I realize that you're terribly distraught, and I am sorry for intruding on your privacy. I'm a lawyer, though, not a journalist," Phillip said.

"Do you want to take our case? I'll need references, you know. I'm sure that the Bradfords will have the best legal team money can buy," Melissa said.

"I'd be taking the case free of charge," Phillip said, winking at Peter. He grinned back.

"That's not necessary. We didn't ask for a court appointed lawyer," Melissa said.

Phillip laughed. "Only defendants get to request court appointed attorneys. There hasn't even been a hearing to decide those kinds of things. That's neither here nor there, though, because I'm not a court appointed lawyer in this case. My name is Phillip Beslinger, and I'll be representing my brother, Charles, and perhaps my friend Peter Bradford as well," Phillip said slowly, making sure Melissa understood who he was.

"Phillip and Charles Beslinger?" Melissa's voice suddenly sounded faint.

"Bingo," Carl whispered to Peter. He grinned.

"Yes, and by the way, I'm also representing my niece, Barbara Beslinger. You might know her as your daughter, Cindy Rathers," Phillip added.

"No!" Melissa screamed, and the people in the reception room heard the clunk of her phone as it hit the floor.

"I gather that your names upset her. What does all this have to do with the alleged kidnapping of Cindy Rathers though?" the policeman asked.

Phillip took a faded missing child flyer out of his pocket, along with the computer enhanced picture of Cindy.

The officer stared for a moment at Cindy, and then back at the pictures.

"It appears that you've already been listed as a missing child 12 years ago," he said very slowly, looking at Cindy.

Cindy smiled and looked up at her birth father. "Can't you tell we're related?" she asked sweetly. She had not been able to take her eyes off the man who had tragically lost touch with her so many years ago, and she began to realize that she shared many of his facial features. That was a fact that pleased her greatly.

Before the officer could comment on that, his radio squawked.

"The Rathers just threw 2 kids in the car, and they're heading towards Rt. 83," the policeman on the other side of the radio said.

"Pull them over and have them come to the station. This is going to take some unraveling," the officer said, and then turned to Peter.

"There is an apology to you in here somewhere, Mr. Bradford, and I promise I'll be the first to say it when we figure this out. I never really liked the Rathers' idea. It seemed almost like blackmail to me. Can I ask you to come to the station now, under your own steam this time, and help us get this straightened out?" the officer asked apologetically. He unlocked the handcuffs on Peter's arms as he spoke.

Peter sighed a deep sigh of relief. Then he stepped over to his wife, and wrapped her in a hug. "Oh, Peter!" Emma said, tears of relief spilling from her eyes. When he released his wife, he turned to Beth.

"My little savior," he whispered, and gave her a tight hug.

Pete and Andy were standing silently on the steps, and Peter went over to them and embraced them as well.

Finally, he turned to the officer. "I'll be glad to drive over to the station, officer. But I think my wife and my older children should be there with me. I also think that the Bakers need to be included, too," Peter said, looking at Paul and Meg standing by his children.

"You're probably right," agreed the officer. "Would you mind calling them before you leave? If they could meet us at the station in half an hour, that would be perfect," he continued.

"I'll call them for you, Peter, as soon as I get home. Paul and Meg, why don't you head home now. By the time you get there, I'll have spoken to your Dad. You all just need to get to the station and get this bizarre case settled. Come on, Dale and Diana, let's take the car home," Carl said, turning to leave.

"Do you mind if Lori and the boys and I tag along to your house?" Justin

Towers asked Carl. He had been standing, unobtrusively along the wall, taking in all the activity.

"We'd love to have you. Come over as soon as you're ready," Carl said, smiling at Justin.

"Mr. Beslinger, do you have a car here, or do you need to ride with us?" one of the officers asked Phillip.

"You lead, we'll follow in our rental," he answered.

"Great. We'll see you all over there shortly then," the officer said, leaving the house.

Emma asked a maid to keep an eye on the 3 younger Bradfords while they were gone, and then went to tell the children that they were leaving.

When she returned to the group in the reception room, Paul and Meg were just walking out the door after giving Mr. Bradford a quick hug. The Bradfords then walked to the garage and got into the van. Peter drove them all to the police station, where they were immediately ushered into a conference room.

When Carl, Dale, and Diana arrived home from the Bradfords, Justin and his family were right behind them. Carl made a quick phone call to the Bakers, and then sent Kristen and Steve out to play on the playground with Justin's sons. He then invited everyone else into the family room to have a seat.

When they were all seated, Carl looked sternly at Dale and Diana.

"Do you realize what almost happened over there?" he demanded, pointing to the Bradford's home.

Dale and Diana looked at the floor.

"A very fine, Christian man was within minutes of having his life ruined. That officer had already read him his rights, and had put the handcuffs on him. It was only by the grace of God that you kids came in when you did, with the answers that you had. Do you understand that? Mr. Bradford has a reputation of integrity. There are people out there who would delight in bringing down someone with such a reputation. If they had taken Mr. Bradford out of his home in handcuffs, the news would have spread like wildfire. Even a trumped up charge of kidnapping would have damaged his reputation. This man's life, and that of his family, was on the line here, today," Carl said firmly.

"I understand," said Dale quietly.

"I do too," squeaked Diana.

"How could you two have known what was going on and still watched silently as three of your best friends were suspected and nearly charged with crimes you knew they didn't commit?" Carl asked.

"We let Cindy talk us into staying silent. It all seemed so reasonable at the time, Dad, and it seemed as though her life hinged on our silence," Dale said.

"Didn't any of you think that your parents deserved an explanation?" Carl asked.

"We were afraid you'd tell the police, and then Cindy wouldn't have been able to meet Mr. Beslinger. We had to make sure that she had the chance to do that," Diana said.

"Shouldn't you have gone to the police to begin with?" Carl asked.

"No, Dad. Don't you see? They accused Josh and Andy of vandalizing the school because we couldn't prove that they didn't do it. We couldn't prove that Cindy was the little girl who had been kidnapped so long ago, either. Do you really think that they would have listened to our ideas? Things weren't right at home for Cindy, Dad. She was afraid of being alone with the man who called himself her father. That's why she ran. All she wanted to do was get away from Mr. Rathers. The BBGs are the ones who pushed for the solution of the mystery father," Dale said passionately.

Carl sighed.

"I'm sorry, Dale. I didn't realize that her home life was so difficult. That would make a difference in the way you thought. You have to look at the whole picture, though, son. Because of your silence, three of your friends faced having criminal records for the rest of their lives, and a man who means so much to all of us was about to be hauled off to jail. Now tell me, does being silent through all that seem worth it to you?" Carl asked.

Dale and Diana looked at each other forlornly.

"I, I don't know," said Di, "It seemed like a heavy price, honestly. But if you could have seen Cindy reunited with her birth father, you would have thought it was worth it," Di's voice trailed off.

"By the time we got to the airport this morning, we really had no choice," said Dale. "It was either go for broke or lose it all. If our theory didn't turn out to be right, we all would have lost a lot. Cindy's life was hanging in the balance. If Mr. Beslinger didn't turn out to be her Dad, I don't know what Cindy would have done. She wouldn't have gone home, though. She didn't look at that as one of her options," he finished.

"We were all so confused, Dad. We knew what we wanted to do, and what we hoped the outcome was going to be, but man, this was way out of our league," said Diana.

"Now you see my point, Di. You were all confused. You had good reason to be confused, for goodness sakes! There are a lot of issues tied up in Cindy right now that you aren't familiar with. It must have been frightening for all of you. Here's the catch, though, kids. We don't expect you to know it all. You're teenagers. You can't possibly know how to handle some of life's bigger issues, because you don't have the experience with them that an adult does. It's plain and simple, you have to stop expecting that you can do it all. You have lots of resources available to help you through the confusing times. You have parents who love you. You have a youth pastor who loves you. This time, you even had the benefit of a nationally known youth speaker at your disposal. There is simply no excuse for not taking this to an adult who could have helped you think it through," Carl said sternly.

Dale and Diana could tell by the sound of their father's voice that their fates had been sealed.

"I'm sorry Dad. You're right. We should have gone to someone, even if it meant going over Cindy's head and risking everything," Dale said.

"I'm sorry too, Dad. I really, really am," Di said contritely.

"Well, Diana, I hope you've learned something. I want you to go to your room and write me at least 2 pages on what you think a real friend is. I'll discuss it with you before church tomorrow morning. Understood?" Carl said.

"Yes, Dad," Diana said, getting up.

Carl got up to embrace Diana, and Kelly joined him. They prayed over Diana for wisdom and maturity, and then sent her off to her room with a kiss.

Carl then looked at Dale, thinking. Finally, he shook his head.

"There's no getting around this one, Dale. I'll see you in my den," he said quietly.

"Yes, sir," Dale said.

Carl and Kelly prayed for Dale as well, and then father and son walked into the den and shut the door.

"You know, Dad, this is ironic," Dale said, as his father removed a belt from a hook behind his door.

"What's that, son?" Carl asked.

"Well, it's ironic that I come to the Lord, and then get my backside burned more often than when I wasn't a true believer," Dale said.

Carl chuckled. "That is ironic, isn't it? I think it's because your conscience is cleaning up your life just a little bit. It's like a refining fire in your case. A refining fire that is going to bring forth the pure gold," Carl said, giving Dale another hug before meting out his punishment.

The Ganderson's den was just off the family room, and Justin Towers cringed at the sound coming from that room.

"Wow. I wondered how you parents managed to raise kids like the BBGs. Honest, I've never seen anything like them in all my ministry days. Your children are blessed, Kelly, and you have a treasure in them. I never dreamed when I asked to come here that I'd be in for such an adventure! God bless what you're doing here," he said, sincerely.

Kelly smiled at him, while tears ran down her cheeks.

"It's not easy," she said quietly.

"I can see that," Justin agreed.

In a few short moments, Carl and Dale came out of the den. Dale went directly to his room, and Carl came to sit wearily beside his wife. She put her arm around him and gave his shoulders a squeeze.

Tears filled Carl's eyes.

"I'm sorry, Justin, that you had to be a part of all this," he said.

“Oh, I’m not!” Justin said. “I told Kelly that I thought you had extraordinary children. I wanted to see real life when I came here, not a picture perfect family show put on for my benefit. I really wanted to see the environment that the BBGs came from. Well, now I’ve seen it, and you’ve done nothing but confirm the message that I’m trying to put out there now for parents and teens. I can only thank you for that,” he added.

Carl smiled. “Are you trying to tell me that I’m doing something right? That giving my son a strapping isn’t against every parenting experts’ advice?” he asked.

Justin laughed. “It may be against the world’s parenting advice, Carl, but then again, the world isn’t turning out children like Dale and Diana,” Justin said.

Carl nodded, and looked towards the steps as he heard Dale coming down them. Justin studied Dale’s face. It was peaceful, and he was smiling as he came into the family room.

“Justin, I apologize for that scene,” Dale said.

Justin smiled. “No problem, Dale,” he replied.

“I’m going out to take care of the trimming and the weeding, and watering, OK, Dad?” Dale asked.

“Sure, Dale,” Carl said.

Dale disappeared, and Kelly offered everyone a cup of coffee. The adults sat back and enjoyed their coffee, and had a relaxed chat. It had been difficult for everyone to focus on pleasant conversation during the past few days, when they knew something was very wrong in the BBGs’ lives. Finally, Lori Towers sighed and put down her coffee cup.

“I’m sorry, Justin, but we need to get back to the Bradfords. I wanted to run to the mall this afternoon, and I promised that the boys could tag along and play for a bit in the arcade there,” she said.

“OK, hon. Thanks, Carl and Kelly. I guess we’ll see you tomorrow?” Justin said, getting up to leave.

“Tomorrow it is,” Carl said, shaking hands with Justin, while Kelly gave Lori a hug.

While Lori gathered their sons, Justin walked over to where Dale was watering the flowers along the church building.

“Hey,” Justin said quietly.

“Hey,” replied Dale, with a smile.

“How are you?” Justin asked sincerely.

“Me? I’m fine,” Dale said, and then smiled again. “Oh. You mean what happened back at the house. My Dad’s got a pretty good backhand, I’ll admit. But I’ll tell you what, compared to being grounded, it’s a piece of cake. It’s done in a matter of seconds, because Dad rarely ever gives me more than one strike. It’s pretty painful for those few seconds, but then I’m finished, and I don't have to think about it any more. I can get on with my life. Dad forgets the offense immediately, and our relationship becomes clean and closer than before. On the other hand, take Diana. She's up in her room, rehashing the whole event. She's still thinking about it, trying to come up with a paper for Dad, who won't read it until tomorrow morning. She'll be beating herself up over it until then, you know. Sometimes I think that dragging the emotional pain out for days like that is a lot worse than a few moments of physical pain," Dale said.

Justin chuckled. "Maybe I need to take lessons from your Dad," he said.

"For the sake of your boys, I hope not," Dale laughed.

Justin patted Dale on the back. "I'll see you tomorrow," he said, turning to leave.

"I'll be there. Front and center," Dale replied, with a grin.

"I don't doubt that you will," Justin agreed, and waved as he walked back to the Bradfords with his family.

CHAPTER 17

When the Bakers got the phone call from Carl, the entire family headed to the police station. They were immediately ushered into the conference room with the Bradfords and the Beslingers. A detective came in shortly after that, and put the mini-mart's security cam videotape on the table.

"We've finally finished reviewing this tape," he said. "and several things are now apparent to us. First, we've identified the bikes that we could see being put into the van. One is Cindy's, the other is Andy's. We've studied Josh's facial expressions, and his gestures. He's obviously agitated about something throughout the tape, and we found the spot where he discovers that his bike is no longer where he left it. For several frames, he points to that spot Unfortunately, the shadows next to the building where he is pointing are too dark for us to see the person who took the bike. Finally, we now have a time frame for the vandalism, and it appears that the vandalism happened while Pete was in the mini mart parking lot. The silent alarm at the school went off about a minute before the security cam shows Pete leaving the mini mart. This means that between the security cam tapes, the alarm at the school and the astounding discoveries today, your kids have an air tight alibi. We've dropped the charges of suspected vandalism against Josh and Andy."

"Oh, my gosh," breathed Josh in relief.

Andy sunk down in his chair with his eyes closed. The adults looked at each other and smiled. Things seemed to be looking up at last. Another officer then poked his head into the room.

"We're expecting the Rathers to be here in about 5 minutes," he announced.

The look of relief on Cindy's face turned back to one of fear.

"Dad, I'm scared. What's going to happen when they get here?" she said, clinging to her father's arm.

Charles Beslinger had to sigh with contentment at the sound of the word, 'Dad'. How long it had been since he had stopped hoping to hear that word from his little daughter once more?

"I'm not leaving you this time," he said firmly

"Andy, before they get here, will you please tell us now what this is all about?" Peter Bradford asked his son.

Andy looked at the table, unsure of what to do. Phillip Beslinger spoke up. "Fill everybody in, Andy. I'm going to need your testimony anyway. This way, I can hear it before things get crazy," he said.

Andy then quietly recounted the whole story. Emma and Peter, along with John and Patti, stared at their sons. Cindy stood up and faced the elder Bradfords and Bakers.

"I am so sorry for causing you all this trouble. But I just don't know what I would have done without these two. They believed my story, and saved my life," she said, sincerely.

"I'm not going to deny that they're heroes, Cindy. However, saving your life almost cost them their parents' lives. I'm going to say this one more time, so Pete, Andy, and Josh can hear me too. Don't any of you ever try this again without letting an adult in on it. Do you understand me?" Phillip said sternly, looking at each teen until they shook their heads in agreement.

Suddenly, the atmosphere in the room changed as Tim and Melissa Rathers walked in with 2 officers. Cindy shivered and drew closer to her birth father, hanging onto his arm for dear life.

"Cindy! Are you OK? What have they done to you?" Melissa cried, running over to give her daughter a hug. When Cindy only lightly returned the hug, and did not release her birth father's arm to do it, Melissa stood up and glared at the others in the room.

"Which one of you is the mighty Peter Bradford? You're going to jail for this!" Melissa said angrily. None of the adults answered her, but Pete couldn't help but speak up.

"No, he isn't," he said hotly.

"Money is not going to save that man this time," Melissa hissed at Pete.

"No, but the truth will," said Andy.

"That's enough boys. Don't say another word unless I tell you to," Phillip said.

"Who are you?" Melissa demanded as she turned to face Phillip.

"Don't you know these men?" the officer asked, pointing to Phillip and Charles.

"I've never seen anyone in this room except my daughter before," stated Melissa.

"Not even your ex-husband?" the officer asked.

"I have never had an ex-husband," declared Melissa, and glared directly at Charles.

The officers exchanged glances. Was it a mere coincidence that she chose to glare at the man who was indeed her ex-husband?

Realizing that glaring at Charles might have been a serious mistake, Melissa then announced, "Thank you for catching up to us and telling us that our daughter had been found, and her captors arrested. I had no idea that so many people were involved in the plot. Now Cindy, honey, come along. We're going to go on a nice, long family vacation to help you to forget this traumatic experience," she said, reaching for Cindy's hand.

"No, Daddy!" Cindy cried, tightening her grip on Charles' arm.

A female officer in the room walked over to Cindy, and put her hand on her shoulder.

"Don't panic, honey. You're not going anywhere, and neither is your mother," the officer assured Cindy.

"And just what do you mean by that?" Melissa asked angrily, and then said in a calmer tone, "Of course, we have to fill out the paperwork saying that we're pressing charges. After that, though, Cindy, we're going to go far away from this horrible place and its memories. We might just go up to enjoy the cool weather in Canada," she said, frowning as Tim tried to get her attention and stop her from saying anything further.

The officer who had spoken to the BBGs parents when they arrived at the station, now stepped in front of Melissa.

"Melissa Rathers, I want to inform you that kidnapping charges are being filed against you. For the forced kidnapping of Barbara Jeanette Beslinger, 12 years ago," the officer said, and then turned to Tim. "Timothy Rathers, you are being charged as an accomplice to the kidnapping of Barbara Jeanette Beslinger, 12 years ago."

The female officer then read them their Miranda rights. When she was done, Tim said,

"This is an outrage! I had nothing to do with this! My only apparent crime was marrying this lovely woman and adopting and raising her daughter as my own. I don't know anything about kidnapping!"

"Better watch what you're saying, Tim. It can all be used against you now. I have an eye witness and a good police composite sketch of you from 12 years ago," Phillip said.

"This is foolishness! I don't know these men! And I never heard of any Barbara Jeanette Beslinger!" Melissa said, angrily.

"Mom, quit! I have pictures from grandma's attic. Pictures of me with the name 'Barbie' written on the back," Cindy said, close to tears.

"Oh, honey! I've already told you that those aren't pictures of you. They're pictures of your aunt and cousin!" Melissa said.

"You've lied to our daughter for 12 years, Lynn? How could you?" Charles finally spoke.

Melissa paled at being called 'Lynn'.

"That's not my name! See, officers, he thinks I'm someone else!" Melissa hissed.

Phillip stepped into the fray one more time.

"Officers, I think an emergency meeting with a judge is in order. My client is not willing to release his daughter into her mother's custody, and I doubt that Mrs. Rathers would be willing to release Cindy into my client's custody, although he is the legal and custodial guardian. I propose that we arrange state custody for Cindy until we can get hearings started," he said.

The female officer agreed, and stepped into the hall to make the necessary phone calls. Meg stepped into the hall with her.

"Excuse me," she said quietly, and waited for the officer to turn to her.

"I was wondering, we have a friend who used to be a foster parent, and Cindy's been staying at her house for the last 2 nights. Do you think Cindy could go back there? I mean, it's quiet, and there aren't any other kids there right now," Meg asked.

The officer smiled, "I don't know if that's possible. What is your friend's name?" she asked.

"Mrs. Griffith," Meg replied.

The officer smiled again. "I'm sure we can arrange that, if Mrs. Griffith will come out of retirement long enough to do it for us," she said.

Meg thanked the officer, and went back into the conference room while the officer made her calls. When she got back into the room, Cindy was clinging tightly to Charles, sobbing.

"I can't leave my Dad!" she hiccupped.

"Cindy, he's not," started Melissa, but was interrupted by Cindy's angry voice.

"I'll go into state custody, Mom, if only to get away from you and Tim!" she cried angrily.

Meg and Beth both unconsciously moved closer to their mothers and put their hands on the women's arms for comfort. Emma and Patti looked over their daughter's heads and smiled at each other. Both were grateful at that moment for the love of their daughters.

An uneasy silence lasted for a moment, and then the female officer finally spoke.

"Cindy? If you'll come with me, Officer Edwards and I will take you home to get some clothes, and then we'll drop you off at Mrs. Griffith's home. Will that be OK?" she asked.

"Back to Mrs. Griffith's? Can I really do that?" Cindy asked in a hopeful voice.

"Yes, but don't let her 'sweet little old lady' persona fool you. She can take care of herself and she's no dummy," the officer said, more for the benefit of the Beslingers and Rathers than for Cindy.

Cindy stood, looking uncertainly at Charles. "Dad?" she asked.

Phillip stood up, and put his arm around Cindy's shoulders. "Don't worry, Cindy. Your Dad promised that he was not leaving you this time. Going to Mrs. Griffith's home is for your safety, honey. I'll see if we can get the judge to set some visitation times for us, and also for your mother, if she chooses. It'll probably have to be right there at the Griffiths, but at least you can use the time to catch up with each other. All right?" he asked, kindly.

Cindy still didn't look too sure.

"We'll call you on the phone at 9 tonight, OK?" Phillip added, giving

Cindy something specific to hold on to.

Cindy sighed. "All right. I've waited 12 years to see a father that I didn't know I had, so I guess a few more days isn't going to hurt me," she said.

"Atta girl!" said Charles, standing up to give her a warm hug.

"You'll be home with us in a few days, honey. Don't worry, you're not going anywhere with these strange men," Melissa said.

"If you choose to contest this, Lynn, we'll only be here longer. Remember, you're now charged with kidnapping," Phillip said.

"She's my daughter!" cried Melissa, hotly.

"And she's also Charles' daughter. You've deprived the man of his child for 12 years now, and at best, I think you're going to find that you'll have to share her," Phillip replied.

"Cindy, are you ready?" broke in an officer.

Cindy nodded, and followed the two police officers outside.

Another officer then took Tim and Melissa Rathers to another area to see about posting bail for them. Finally, the chief of police came into the room. He stood in front of John and Peter, and said, "Mr. Baker and Mr. Bradford, I sincerely apologize for this huge mix up. We're dropping the curfew fines for all of your boys, and we're dropping the fine for driving after hours with a Cinderella license for your oldest son, Mr. Bradford. We're totally expunging the whole record here. Is there anything else we can do?" he asked humbly.

John and Peter smiled at each other.

"No, I'm happy to finally get to the bottom of this," said Peter.

"That goes for me, too," agreed John.

"Well, you're all free to go home, then, and again, I am terribly sorry for all of this," the chief said.

"It wasn't totally the fault of the police, sir. These kids were acting mighty strangely all by themselves," said Peter, looking at Pete, Andy, and Beth.

"Yes, there was a lot of secrecy going on. Even as parents, we didn't know what was going to happen next," said John.

"Well, I hope you kids take Mr. Beslinger's words to heart, then. You could have avoided a lot of this mess by speaking up first," one of the officers said, looking at all the teens.

"Yes sir," they said in unison.

The chief grinned at them, and waved as they left the building. Out in the parking lot, Peter put his arm around John's shoulders.

"Thanks for being here with me," he said warmly.

John smiled at his long-time friend. "You've been more than a friend to me and my family for many years, Peter. There's no way any of us would have just stood by and watched your life be ruined without at least trying to do something about it," he said.

Peter smiled back at his friend and quietly said, "Thanks."

When the adults reached their vans, all of the teens were already waiting. They all looked miserable as well.

"I think I need to settle my emotions before I commence the judicial proceedings for those 3," Peter said, looking at John with a grin and nodding towards his children.

"I think I'll exile them to their rooms until tomorrow after worship, and then bring down the judge's robes. Right now, all I want is a relaxing swim in my pool, a good dinner, a quiet evening, and then a good night's sleep. What about you?" Peter continued.

"I agree. I definitely need to unwind first," John said.

"Then you'll join us? For a swim and dinner?" Peter asked.

John laughed. "I wasn't trying to invite myself over, Peter," he said.

Peter laughed too. "I know that. I meant, that since your intentions seem to be the same as mine, why not do it together? I'll call Carl and Kelly, too," he said.

John looked at his wife. Patti smiled and nodded.

"Great. Just come over when you're ready," Peter said, getting into his van.

It was a quiet ride home for the Bradfords, except for an apology started by Andy.

"Dad, I am really, really sorry," he said, as Peter turned the car out of the police station lot.

"Me too, Dad," Pete said.

"Me too, I was so scared!" said Beth.

"Apologies accepted. When we get home, though, you three are confined to quarters until church time tomorrow. I'm not trying to drag this out for you, or be cruel, but I need to take some time for my own attitude adjustment," Peter said quietly.

"Sure, Dad," Pete said, for all the kids, thus ending the conversation in the car.

Back at the house, when the kids had gone up to their rooms, the three of them met in Pete's room.

"We are in deep, deep trouble," sighed Pete.

"Dad has got to be awfully angry at us, if he needs an attitude adjustment," agreed Beth.

"Yeah, and I, at least, deserve every bit of his anger." sighed Andy.

"Don't beat up on yourself, Andy. I'm the oldest, and I'm the one who took the van out in the middle of the night. It's my fault, too," Pete said.

"I could have told him all about it when he asked me to, but I didn't, either," Beth said.

"Well, at least we agree that whatever happens tomorrow, we deserve it," Pete said, as his brother and sister made their way back to their own rooms.

A few hours later, a maid brought them some dinner trays.

"Thanks, Celia," Beth smiled as she set the tray on her desk.

"This seems to be happening a lot nowadays," Celia teased.

"Yes, it does," sighed Beth.

"Leave the tray in the hall when you're done," Celia said, grinning at Beth.

When John and Patti Baker got into their van at the police station, John immediately turned to his sad and forlorn looking children in the back.

"That's over, thank goodness. You 3 are confined to the house until church tomorrow. Your mom and I are going over to the Bradford's for an afternoon and evening of rest and relaxation. We'll talk about this whole mess tomorrow after church. Ok?" he said.

"Dad, I'm sorry," Josh said.

"Me, too," agreed Paul.

"Me, three," said Meg.

John smiled at them. "Hey, guys, I said it's over. I forgive you."

When they got home, the teens went to their rooms, and John and Patti went to their room to change into swimsuits. Patti also put some clothes to wear for dinner in a small traveling bag. They met Carl and Kelly at the bottom of the Ganderson's driveway.

"Wow. Isn't this a switch? I mean, us old people going to a swim party?" Carl chuckled.

"I think it's about time we got to do it, but watch who you're calling old," agreed Patti with a grin.

CHAPTER 18

That afternoon, the adults relaxed around the pool, swimming and laying on the lounges drinking fresh lemonade.

"This is exactly what I needed after these past few days," sighed Patti.

"It's definitely been tense," agreed Emma.

"That's for sure," added Kelly.

Early that evening, Justin and Lori Towers joined the adults around the pool.

"Micah took our boys up to his room. Is that OK?" asked Lori, sitting down beside Emma.

Peter smiled. "Don't let any of the kids know this, but right now, any thing's OK," he said.

"Hmmmm, what's in this lemonade, anyway?" chuckled Justin, and then added seriously, "How did everything go downtown?"

"I've been freed," Peter said.

"Peter and the kids all had the charges against them dropped. Even the curfew fines were dropped," added John.

"Thank you Lord," Justin breathed, and then asked, "And our teens? How are they?"

"Right now they are serving an in-house, pre-sentencing detention," Peter said.

Justin laughed. "Pre-sentencing?" he asked.

"Formal sentencing is set for tomorrow after church," said Peter, glancing over to Carl.

"Could we use your office and the Youth room?" he asked.

"Of course. I think Dale and Diana can sit in on these judicial proceedings, too," Carl agreed.

"Would you care to join us?" John asked Justin.

"For real? I'd love to," Justin said.

The adult's conversation then centered around other things, and finally, everyone went inside to get ready for dinner. After a delicious meal, the Gandersons and the Bakers said good night, and returned to their homes.

Before Sunday school the next day, the BBGs met in Dale's "office", which was really a Sunday school room.

"Dad says we're supposed to meet in the Youth room after church," sighed Pete.

"Yeah, Di and I are supposed to be there, too. I sure hope there's no 'double jeopardy' in this case," Dale said.

"Huh?" asked Josh.

"I mean, I've already seen Dad's judgment in this case. I don't want to meet it again," Dale said, grinning.

"Do you think that means that it's just lecture time?" asked Josh.

Dale shrugged, but Paul shook his head. "Sneaking out after midnight? Getting your bike stolen and then not saying anything about it, while you tried to deceive Dad by putting Andy's bike in your rack? You were suspected of vandalism, and then you wouldn't reveal the information the police needed to exonerate yourself and the others? I think you're dreaming about lectures, Josh," he said.

Josh paled, but the other teens didn't notice it because Dave walked into the room at that moment.

"You guys making waves again?" Dave chuckled.

"Why? What makes you say that?" asked Beth.

"Why? Because I just got done praying with your dads. And when they pray for mercy and wisdom, I know what's coming. Honest, you guys, don't you ever take a break?" Dave said, smiling with affection at them.

The BBGs all laughed. All but Josh, that is. His stomach just got knotted. After Sunday school, the BBGs stepped outside for a few minutes to chat with friends before the church service began.

"I heard Dad say that Justin has agreed to give today's message for him," Diana said.

"Really? I thought he was supposed to take the evening service," Pete said.

"He's still going to take that one. Justin just offered to do this morning's message, too, since Dad has been preoccupied with things this week," sighed Di.

"Well, let's get in there then," suggested Dale, and the BBGs went and found seats in the front pew.

As the worship band got up to do the last song before dismissal and ministry time, Josh slipped out of his spot and left the sanctuary.

"Where's he going?" Meg whispered to Beth, who was sitting beside her.

"Maybe the bathroom?" suggested Beth.

Right after the song was finished, Paul slipped out of the sanctuary, too. When he couldn't find Josh in the bathroom, he stepped outside. Finally Paul looked toward his house, and there he saw Josh get up from the picnic table and go inside.

"Josh went home," Paul said, as the BBGs gathered in the lobby.

"Let's hope he gets back here pronto," Meg worried.

The BBGs said good by to their friends, and then made their way into the Youth room. They sat around the tables until Dave, Justin, and their parents arrived.

John Baker immediately noticed that Josh was missing. "Where's Josh?" he asked the teens gathered around the tables.

"I saw him go home," Paul said quietly, and then added, "Maybe he's not feeling well?"

"John, do you want me to run home and check on him?" Patti asked.

John smiled, and said, "No, Patti, it's OK. I know why he went home."

"Well, guys, I've asked Justin to speak to you for a few minutes regarding what just happened around here," Carl said, sitting down beside Kelly.

When all the adults were seated, Justin got up to speak. The teens listened intently to him speak about honesty, trust, and true friendship. When he was finished, they all looked miserable.

"Now that was a winning speech," Justin teased as he sat down beside Lori.

"I'd say it was a convicting one," Carl said, getting up again. "I don't really have anything to add to Justin's speech, but Dale and Di, I wanted to be sure you heard what he had to say. You already know how I feel about everything that happened, but let me just push this one point home to all of you. If any of you ever run into a problem that you don't know what to do with, remember that my office door is always open to all of you. I may be Dale and Di's dad, but I'm also your Pastor, and part of my job is to help you get through life's little crises. It's Dave and Anne's job, too. Please don't be afraid to come to any of us if something like this should ever come up again. All right?" Carl admonished them so gently and with such compassion, that the teens knew in their hearts that the adults in the room cared deeply for them. They all nodded their agreement to get help when they needed it.

"Good, now Dale and Diana, you're excused. Please run home and make sure that Kristen has a sandwich for lunch, and not a bowl of ice cream, okay?" Carl asked.

Dale jumped up so fast that his chair fell backwards. "Sure Dad," he said, picking the chair up.

Carl laughed and said, "Don't feel so bad about leaving, Dale."

Dale was already in the doorway to the hall, but he turned momentarily with a grin on his face.

"You said, 'run' home," he teased.

After Dale and Di left, John Baker stood up and looked at Paul and Meg. They squirmed under his stern look.

"Loyalty to friends is a good thing, don't misunderstand me," he started. "But it can be misused, and harm can come to your family and other friends because of it. Do you understand what Justin and Pastor Carl just spoke about?" he asked.

Paul and Meg nodded solemnly.

"Well, Megan, suppose you write out what you understand. I want 2 pages done by the time I come home from work tomorrow, and you'll stay inside the house until I see it. Is that understood?" he asked.

"Yes, Dad," Meg squeaked.

"You're excused, then, sweetheart," he said, smiling at her and opening his arms for a hug. After giving her father a tight hug, Meg also hurried from the room.

"Paul, I'm really up in the air about you. I know your part in this entire fiasco wasn't very active, but you did know what was going on. Even if you weren't actively involved in the activities, you certainly had a hand in covering them up. So much secrecy when so many lives were at stake was a very dangerous game to be playing. Do you understand that?" John asked.

"Yes, Dad, and just for the record, I did tell Josh and Cindy to come clean a long time ago," Paul answered.

"But when they didn't, don't you think you should have stood up and said something?" John asked.

"Dad, believe me, I would never have willingly let Mr. Bradford go to jail on those crazy accusations. But I was pretty sure that Mr. Beslinger was Cindy's real Dad, and we had to follow through with the plan so they could be reunited. I do understand that we should have brought an adult into it, and I guess I thought that Mr. Beslinger and his brother served that purpose. I thought we did the best we could," Paul said.

John looked affectionately at his oldest son.

"But didn't Mr. Beslinger say on several occasions that you needed to go for help as the story unfolded, not after the facts?" John said slowly, standing up straight after leaning on the piano.

"I know, Dad, but I still think we did the best we could, and God brought all of us through it," Paul said.

"For future reference, however, even if you know you have it under control, you need to be accountable to an adult that knows you as well as knows the situation. Agreed?"

"Agreed," sighed Paul, standing up.

John put his arm around Paul's shoulders and walked out of the room with him.

Watching them leave, Peter Bradford stood up to speak to his children.

"Beth, I'm disappointed that you skirted the truth when I asked you about this whole thing the night Cindy went to Mrs. Griffith's. Life as we now know it was just seconds away from being over. Do you realize what your evasiveness brought about? I had a guest in my home that I knew nothing about. That little unknown fact brought us all great pain. One thing I am going to insist on from here on in is that I will be told when someone other than the BBGs comes to stay for the night, even if I'm in bed when they arrive," Peter thought for a moment and then laughed out loud at his thoughts. "With the BBGs, it's hard to tell who belongs to me and who doesn't, and I truly feel blessed by that. They all have the run of our home at any hour of the day. Please don't inform me about every single time I have a BBG in the house, OK? I'll never get any work done if you do. Any others I will be told about, and that's not negotiable, understood?" Peter looked sternly at Beth, and his look brought tears to her eyes.

"I'm sorry, Dad, and you're right. I will make sure that you know who our house guests are from now on," she said.

"Thank you, honey. Now Pete, I'm astonished at what you did. Not just sneaking out after midnight, but taking the van, too! I'm taking your set of van keys from you as soon as we get home, and you'll start asking permission to drive from now on. What you did was illegal, Pete. I hope you realize that," Peter said, looking at his oldest son.

"I know, Dad, and I'm sorry," Pete said sadly.

Then Peter turned to Andy, and thought for a moment about what he was going to say to him. He couldn't think of anything else except, "Andy, what were you thinking of?"

"I wasn't thinking, Dad. I offered to have you pick Cindy up that night, but she wouldn't hear of it. She doesn't know how Dad's are supposed to be, and she didn't trust you. She was so afraid, and I was afraid she'd run if she saw you driving. I just wanted to help her," Andy said, and then added, "I'm sorry."

At that point, John returned to the room. "I need to borrow our friend when you're done with her," he said quietly to Peter.

"We'll be just a minute, John. Come on, kids. We'll finish this in Pastor Carl's office," Peter replied, standing up.

Beth groaned as she realized that her punishment was not going to be in the form of an essay or being grounded. Peter smiled at her groaning.

"I'm sorry, honey, but this is just too serious to let slide with just essay writing," he said, putting his arm around her, he walked with his children to Carl's office.

After the Bradfords left, Carl turned to John.

"Was there a problem, John, that you need to borrow Old Faithful again?" he asked.

John chuckled. "Oh, there's no problem. One of mine is just waiting for home delivery," he said.

Carl laughed, too. "I understand," he said softly.

It wasn't long before Peter brought Old Faithful back into the youth room and handed it to John.

"I'll see you all tonight," Peter said wearily.

"Sure. Peter, you need to take it easy this afternoon. Remember, friend, this ordeal is over," Carl said, standing up to give his friend a hug and a good natured slap on the back.

"Well, I guess it's not over for me. I need to get home to finish it so I can relax too," sighed John, getting up and walking to the youth room door with Peter.

"OK, John, we'll see you tonight as well," Carl said, and then turned to Justin and Lori. "You two up for lunch at the lake?" he asked.

Justin grinned. "Sure, but I've got 2 rascals who would need to come along," he said.

"Don't worry about them. They're with Micah and Kristen over at our home," Peter said turning in the doorway to speak to Justin.

"But, with all this, surely you don't need to be babysitting as well," Lori argued.

Peter laughed. "Have you seen me or Emma babysitting this week?" he asked.

"Well, no, not exactly. I mean, you were in the house with the kids, but, oh, I guess it'll be alright then," Lori stammered.

"With 6 children, Lori, the youngest ones get looked after quite naturally, and with 6 kids, your house tends to be pretty child proof. They'll be fine," Peter assured her.

Justin and Lori both thanked Peter, and then followed the rest of the adults outside.

In the meantime, Meg had gone directly home after her father's dismissal, and made herself a sandwich. She had just finished eating it when Paul came into the kitchen through the patio doors. He leaned against the counter and looked at his sister.

"Man, I've got to quit giving Dad practice with his backhand swing." he said sadly.

Meg got up sympathetically and got him a glass of iced tea. She gave it to him with a hug, and a softly spoken "I'm sorry".

Paul, surprised at his sister's reaction, put an arm around her and rested his head on her head.

"It's OK," he said gently.

Meg suddenly let go of all the emotions that she had kept inside all week long, and the tears came fast and furious.

"Come on, Meggie. I'm OK. You're going to make me feel worse by doing this," Paul said, feeling a lump rising in his throat at his sister's sobs.

At that moment, Dale let himself into the Baker's kitchen.

"Can I join this pity party?" he asked, and put his arms around Meg and Paul. After a strong and solid group hug, the 3 teens released each other, and Meg dried her eyes.

"I came over to see if you wanted to come over in an hour or so and put the worship set together for tonight. I caught Pete as he was heading home, and he's game," Dale asked.

"Sure," agreed Paul.

"OK, then I've got to run. See you then!" Dale said, slipping back out the sliding glass doors.

"I'm going upstairs to change clothes," Paul said to Meg as he headed for the back staircase.

"Can I make you a sandwich?" Meg asked quietly.

"Thanks," said Paul.

"I'll bring it up when it's done," Meg said, getting the bread out.

"Throw some potato salad on the plate, and some more iced tea, would you please?" Paul asked.

"You got it," Meg answered.

Paul changed quickly and then knocked on Josh's door. When he didn't get an answer, he opened the door a crack.

"Josh?" he called softly.

Josh sat up on his bed. "Oh, Paul. I thought you were Dad," he said.

Paul grinned. "That explains the welcome," he said.

"Is Dad really angry with me?" Josh asked.

Paul laughed as Meg came into Josh's room after putting Paul's lunch on his desk.

"That's hardly the word," he said.

"You made it worse by running," Meg added.

"That sounds like the advice they give for angry bees or dogs," chuckled Paul.

"I'd rather face those things," Josh said, his voice cracking.

"Josh?" Meg asked in alarm, hearing the fear in her brother's voice.

"I'm scared," Josh admitted and choked on a sob.

Before either Meg or Paul could comment, the teens heard the sound of the sliding glass doors opening and their parent's voices downstairs.

"We'd better go. Take heart, Josh, Dad's not an ogre," Paul said, pushing Meg out of the room.

"I put your lunch on your desk," Meg said in a stony voice. Paul looked at Meg in surprise.

"Thanks. Meg, are you OK?" he asked sincerely.

"No, I'm not," she replied and stomped down the backstairs.

She ignored her parents in the kitchen as they made themselves some lunch, and walked into the family room and turned on the TV. Some time later, John walked through the family room on his way to his den. Seeing his daughter in front of the TV, he said, "It's fine for you to chill out for a little bit in front of the TV, Meg, but I want you to get started on that paper this afternoon, OK?" he said.

"Yes," Meg said curtly, not taking her eyes off of the TV set.

"Megan?" John looked at her, and feeling his glare, Meg finally turned to face him.

"What?" she demanded.

As she turned to look at her father, she noticed Old Faithful in his hand. She jumped angrily off the couch and demanded, "What is that thing for?"

"Megan, change your tone with me," John said sternly, and then Meg lost it.

"What kind of father are you? Don't you know that Josh is scared silly of that thing? You can't use that on him! I hate living here! I hate that stupid Old Faithful!" she yelled.

"Meg, please, honey. Don't push me into punishing you again," John said quietly.

Meg looked directly at her father and defiantly stated, "I hate it!".

John sighed and took Meg's arm, leading her into the den.

"Listen to me for a moment, please, Meg?" he asked softly.

"I won't!" Meg said loudly, surprising herself as well as her father.

"I guess Peter made the right decision after all," John said to himself, and then gave Meg a firm but gentle punishment.

Afterward, as she sat sobbing in his easy chair, John got down on his knees in front of her and took her hands in his.

"Can you listen now, sweetheart?" he asked kindly.

Meg wouldn't look at him, but she nodded, and so he continued.

"I know that Josh ran today because he's afraid of Old Faithful. But honey, his fear is worse than Old Faithful's bite. What is the difference if I use her or my belt?" he asked.

Meg thought for a moment, and then shrugged.

"If I continue to give in to Josh's fears, Meg, they'll just grow and grow. If he faces it now, he'll see that it's not the thing he envisioned it to be. He's got to find out for himself that he can take it, or he'll be walking in fear of the unknown forever," John said calmly.

Meg stopped crying.

"Don't you think that I love Josh, Megan?" John asked.

Meg sat thinking about what her father was saying. Suddenly, she understood the concept that he was trying to get across.

"It's like when I was 5, and afraid to put my head under water because I was sure I'd drown immediately. I remember you promised me I'd be OK, and then you held onto me and went under the water with me to prove it. This is like that, isn't it? Josh's fear is out of control and making a big deal out of it," she said softly.

"That's it, Meg," John said.

"And the longer he puts it off, the bigger and worse it gets, doesn't it?" Meg added thoughtfully.

"That's right, Meg, but you didn't answer my question. Don't you think I love Josh dearly?" John asked.

Meg quietly thought some more. She thought about the relationship between her brother and her father, and finally had to quietly say, "Yes, I do know that."

"He means the world to me, Meg, just like you, Paul, and your mother do. I mean that with all my heart," John said sincerely.

"I know," Meg answered, in a humble tone.

"Is life really that bad here, sweetie?" John asked Meg in a quiet voice.

Meg looked at her father, and realized by the pained expression on his face, and the tears in his eyes that her careless remarks earlier had hurt him. She threw her arms around him and enveloped him in a bear hug.

"Oh, Dad, I'm such a doofus! I'm sorry I hurt you by what I said before! Living here with you and Mom and the boys isn't hard at all, at least 90% of the time! I'm a kid, and of course I'm going to push the envelope sometimes. Can you forgive me?" Meg asked sincerely.

John kissed the top of his daughter's head. "I forgive you, Megan. Can you forgive me for my ways of discipline?" he asked.

"Sure Dad. It's my fault anyway," Meg said warmly.

"And can you forgive me for what's about to happen to Josh?" John asked.

Meg looked at her father seriously, and said, "I understand what you said, Dad, and you're right. As hard as it is, Josh needs to face the fear."

"Oh, Megan! I really, really do love you, kiddo!" John said, giving Meg another quick hug and opening the door for her.

"And by the way, Meg," he added as she slipped past him into the hallway.

"Yes, Dad?" Meg asked.

"Forget writing the paper, sweetheart. You're home free," John said.

"And you're terrific! I don't deserve that, but thanks, Dad!" Meg said, grinning.

John watched as Meg settled herself back on the couch to finish the show she had started to watch. He sighed and then took himself upstairs to Josh's room. This was turning out to be a very long day.

CHAPTER 19

"Josh?" he called as he knocked on the door.

"Come in, Dad," Josh answered, and when his father entered, the boy immediately burst into tears.

"I'm so sorry, Dad! I was just so scared!" he sobbed.

John went over and took Josh into his arms. "I know, Josh, I know. It's alright," he said and held him until his sobs subsided. When Josh had calmed down, John said quietly, "Let's take a walk to my den, son."

Father and son made their way downstairs to the den. John closed the door, and then stepped in front of it as Josh saw Old Faithful laying on his father's desk, and made a run for the door.

"No, Dad! Please!" Josh cried.

"Put your hands on my desk, Joshua," John said sternly.

After receiving his punishment, Josh sat down in his father's easy chair.

"That was for sneaking out of the house at night, trying to deceive us, and for letting that whole thing go on for so long. Do you understand that what you did was wrong, Josh?" John said, standing in front of his son and leaning on the desk.

Josh nodded, trying to swallow the lump in his throat.

"And it was also for you to face your fear of Old Faithful. Are you ready to add your name to her?" John asked.

Josh suddenly grinned. "I did it, didn't I, Dad?" he asked.

John smiled and said, "Yes, Joshua, you did. And you did it honorably."

He handed Josh the marker, and watched as Josh took the marker and paddle and solemnly looked at the names of his friends and brother and sister that were already written there. He ran his fingers over each one. Dale, Pete, and Paul had written their names in large and bold letters. Josh noticed that the most recent marks were bright compared to the older, more faded ones from previous encounters. He shook his head at the sheer number of marks that his brother had racked up. Then he looked at the girlish signatures of Beth, Meg, and Di. He gave a little gasp as he noticed that there were bright, new marks next to both Beth and Meg's names.

"I had no idea," he whispered to himself. Finally, his eyes hit on Andy's new signature. The lump came back into his throat, and he quietly said, "I'm sorry, Andy," as he signed his name underneath Andy's. When he had finally finished, he handed the marker and the paddle back to his father.

"Now, Joshua, tell me. Were your fears warranted?" John asked with a grin.

"Dad, your back hand is your back hand, regardless. I'm in no hurry to repeat the performance, but at least I'm not scared to death of it anymore," Josh said, smiling back at his father.

John hugged his youngest child tightly. "Mission accomplished then, Josh," he said.

Josh flashed him a grin and took off up the steps.

Standing in front of Paul's door, Josh knocked and quickly opened the door, barely giving Paul time to answer the knock.

"I did it! I did it! I'm not afraid anymore!" Josh said excitedly.

Paul was laying on his bed reading a book, and looked up at his younger brother.

"Congratulations, I think," he said with a laugh.

Meg heard the commotion in Paul's room from downstairs, and went to see if Josh was all right. Seeing Paul's door open, she let herself into his room.

"I did it, Meg! I'm not a coward anymore!" Josh exclaimed when he saw her come in.

Meg gave him a hug. "Joshua Baker, you have never been a coward, and I won't hear anymore of that nonsense. Do cowards go around rescuing young ladies at wee hours of the morning?" she said sternly, but with a grin.

Josh thought for a minute.

"Maybe cowards don't do that, but man, I sure am sorry now that I was so brave back then," he said.

"Yeah, so are the rest of us," Paul teased.

"I never dreamed that Dad would use Old Faithful on you for this, Meg. I'm awfully sorry for that," Josh said sadly.

Paul looked at Meg, questioning her with his eyes.

"What? At the meeting this afternoon, Dad let you go with a paper to write," he said

Meg hung her head. "It wasn't from Josh's adventure," she said.

"But there was a new mark next to your name. I saw it," Josh insisted.

"What did you do and when did this happen?" Paul asked, anger touching his voice at the thought of Meg being punished with Old Faithful.

Meg chuckled. "Funny you should use that tone of voice to ask that question, Paul. Just don't make my mistake and do it in front of Dad," she said.

"What do you mean?" Paul asked.

"I went off on Dad for Josh's sake when I saw him carrying Old Faithful into his den this afternoon. That's what got me my new mark," Meg replied.

Josh moaned. "It was still my fault, then. I'm sorry, Meg," he said sadly.

"My mouth is not your fault, Josh. Dad gave me plenty of chances to turn it around. I just wouldn't," Meg said.

"Well, I still don't think its right to hit girls," Paul said.

"Beth has a new mark, too," Josh said quietly.

"No!" Paul and Meg said together.

"Somebody's going to hear about this! First my sister, and now my . . ." Paul stopped mid-sentence, suddenly becoming embarrassed.

"Your what?" Meg teased.

"My good friend," Paul finished, and then added, "Now come on. We have worship practice at Dale's."

Without another word, he put his book down and left his room, leaving Josh and Meg grinning at each other.

The 3 teens stopped in the doorway of the family room to get permission to go to the Ganderson's home for practice.

"Mom, Dad, we're going to get our worship set ready for tonight over at Dale's. Is that OK?" Paul asked.

John lay on the couch with his eyes closed, resting. Patti sat in the recliner, reading the paper.

"Of course," Patti said, smiling.

John sat up, and looked at his children.

"Everybody OK?" he asked.

Josh grinned from ear to ear.

"You bet!" he said happily.

John laughed at Josh's response, and then turned his gaze to Meg.

"I'm fine, Dad," she said, warmly.

John's eyes then lingered on Paul. "Paul?" he asked quietly.

Meg glanced at Paul carefully, trying to warn him silently to be respectful.

"I'm OK for myself, Dad. But I have a real problem with the girls adding marks to Old Faithful today. I just don't think that's right," Paul said, carefully and slowly, so he could keep his anger in check.

"The girls?" John asked, confused.

"Meg and Beth," Paul said.

John smiled, and said, "Impressive, son, very impressive. It makes me feel good to know that the girls are under your loyal protection. Especially now at your age, when they're with you guys so much more now than they're with us parents. Thank you for standing up for them."

"But Old Faithful?" persisted Paul.

"Son, someday you may be a parent, and have to make some tough judgment calls. This was one that I questioned and tried to work around. Don't you agree, Meg?" John asked.

Meg smiled and said, "I told them you gave me every chance to turn it around, Dad."

"Thank you for seeing that, Meg. The bottom line is this, though, Paul. I don't mind answering your tough questions as long as we can keep it respectful, like you've done just now. Meg, on the other hand, was anything but respectful, and just couldn't give up her anger without some help. I don't enjoy disciplining any of you," John said kindly.

Paul nodded to show he understood what his father was saying, but then added, "It's just that they're girls."

"Keep thinking that way, Paul, it's honorable. Try to remember, though, that there is a difference between the women we are pledged to protect as Christian men, and the daughters we are pledged to raise into Godly women," John said.

"But Cindy's dad treated her badly, and even hit her sometimes. Wasn't that wrong?" Paul asked.

"Yes! From the little that I've heard, I'd call that abuse," John said.

"I don't see the difference, Dad," Paul said sadly.

"Meg, you and Josh run over to Dale's and let the gang know that Paul will be there shortly. Paul, would you mind sitting down here for a minute?" John said, sitting up completely and making room for Paul.

As Meg and Josh left, John put his arm around Paul's shoulders.

"This is a hard thing to understand, son, and there are some who would say that corporal punishment at any time is abusive. In fact, some countries have outlawed it altogether. I guess where I see the difference is in the way it's administered. In my opinion it should never be done in a parent's anger or out of revenge for something the child has done. It has to be spelled out as a specific consequence for specific actions, not childish mistakes or childish irresponsibility. Its goal should be to bring the child to repentance, or to bring them out of a rebellious state. It's meant to be discipline, to get the child to turn from their ways and towards the better way," John said cautiously, watching Paul's face. When he saw understanding in his son's eyes, he went on.

"We've all seen parents in stores, restaurants, or other public places swinging at their small children or swearing at their teens. That is wrong, and humiliates the child rather than teaches them. If you have children one day, Paul, you will have to make these kinds of discipline decisions for yourself. I will support you in whatever method of discipline you choose for your children, but can you understand that this is my way?" John asked sincerely.

Paul nodded. "Yes, Dad. Thanks for making that a little clearer. I guess I never understood all of that before," he said.

John smiled and said, "Well, you're not a parent, so I guess you didn't need to understand our angle just yet."

"But Dad," Paul said.

"Yes, Paul?" John replied.

"I still don't like Meg or Beth or Di being punished like that," Paul said.

"I understand," John said.

"Dad?" Paul asked again.

"Yes, Paul?"

"Come to think of it, I don't like it for myself either. I want you to know that I understand that you're acting the way you understand a good father should act. When I have my own kids, though, and if it's up to me, Old Faithful will burn in the fireplace," Paul said adamantly.

John smiled, and tucked that information away in his heart. Paul would indeed have children one day, and raise them well. He would also be true to those words. Old Faithful would remain in Carl's desk drawer, only to be taken out and shown as a relic of the BBGs childhood to their own children.

John hugged Paul, and said, "You're a wonderful son, Paul. Thank you."

"Thank you, Dad, there's a lot of your handiwork residing in me," Paul said warmly, getting up and heading for the Ganderson's.

At Dale's home, the teens were sitting around talking when Paul walked in.

"Paul! Good to see you! Everything OK?" asked Pete.

Paul grinned. "I'm fine, and no, I'm not interested in discussing it. Let's get to work on this worship set," he said.

The other teens took his cue, and got to work.

That evening, the children joined the adults for the worship part of the meeting. Justin sat in the front pew as the BBGs led the adults into a soaring worship time. After worship was over, all the children separated into their own classes, and Justin gave the adult message.

The teens were outside playing volleyball when Justin finished the adult service. Justin walked outside and watched Dale, Paul, and Pete play aggressively.

"Whoa. Those guys know how to beat that ball," Justin remarked to Dave, who was standing on the sidelines.

Dave smiled. "That's their way of releasing pent up emotions," he said, and then added, "The last time they played so hard, a ball took out the screen in the men's restroom."

Justin grinned. "Well, at least that's better than taking it out on another person," he said.

"Well, that's been done, too, although it happens much less often now that the Lord is in their lives," Dave said.

Justin's eyes grew wide. "You're kidding? These guys fight?" he asked.

Dave looked over at the boys, who had sweat dripping down their faces.

"Yep, they're tough. Nobody walks on any of them. But you know what? The last guy that Dale gave a bloody nose to turned around and came to Lord from it. He couldn't relate to anybody else except a kid who had a tough crust like he did. It was really very amazing," Dave said, proudly.

"Wow," was all that Justin could say.

"Oh, it gets better. That kid brought 4 of his tough buddies along, and they came to the Lord, too," Dave said.

Justin chuckled. “And how do Carl and the other parents feel about that?” he asked.

“Carl, John, and Peter don’t tolerate violence. The boys were punished for it,” Dave said.

“So that’s where all those marks on that paddle came from,” Justin chuckled.

“Not all of them, but a good many,” replied Dave.

Just then one of the leaders yelled “game point!” and Dale leaped for joy, slapping his friend’s outstretched hands on the way down.

“Come join us for snack,” Dave said to Justin, as the teens hurried inside for a treat.

“Thanks,” Justin said, following Dave and the teenagers into the building.

After getting his snack, and speaking to several other kids, Justin made his way over to the BBGs.

“How’s it going, kids?” he asked, pleasantly.

“Great,” replied Pete, who was the only BBG who didn’t have a mouth full of food at the time.

“And the rest of you?” Justin asked, laughing.

They all swallowed their food and said “great” together, laughing at themselves.

“I really enjoy your worship,” Justin said.

“Thanks,” replied Dale.

“Do you think that I could talk to you all for a few minutes? Lori and I expect to leave tomorrow morning, and I’d like to sit down with you before that, if I may,” Justin said seriously.

The BBGs looked at each other, and then Pete said, “We usually go for ice cream after youth group. If you want, we can go get it and bring it back here.”

“Let’s bring the ice cream back and then sit in our garden and talk while we eat,” suggested Beth.

“Great. Let me quick tell Lori. I’ll be right back!” Justin said, finding his wife in the lobby, talking with new friends.

The BBGs joked and laughed with Justin as they walked to the Pizza Place, and then sat quietly as they ate their treats in the Bradford’s formal garden. They sensed that Justin had something important to share with them, so they patiently waited for him to begin.

Finally, Justin said, “Have any of you heard from Cindy today?”

All of the BBGs shook their heads, no.

“I want all of you to know, and especially you, Andy and Josh, that what you did for Cindy was heroic. To keep all that information inside and in the balance until the timing was right, was just downright awesome. While it wasn’t exactly right, standing up against the pressure from the police and your parents took a lot of courage, too. And in the end, when you truly believed that you did the best that you could have done, to take the punishment that your parents dished out and to take it without bitterness, well, that just blows me away," he said, looking at them with deep affection.

"Ummm, I don't want to tarnish my halo too badly, but I didn't exactly take it all without bitterness. In case you're wondering what I am doing sitting with you all right now, instead of being locked in my room writing a paper, well, the truth of the matter is that I too met up with Old Faithful because I was so mad at my Dad and that stupid paddle that I just went off on him," Meg said contritely.

"And I had to deal with some resentment, too. Not for myself, but for Meg and, well, Josh saw your new mark, too, Beth. Dad tried to explain himself to me on that issue, but the thought of your new marks on Old Faithful makes my skin crawl," Paul added.

"Well, look at me. I was such a coward that I ran from it," Josh said sadly.

"You stop calling yourself a coward right now, Joshua Baker. If I hear that again, I'll haul off and practice my self defense skills on you!" said Beth, with anger in her voice.

"I tried to tell you about that earlier, too, Josh," said Meg.

"Can I throw something in here?" asked Justin, with a grin.

"Sorry," said Meg and Beth together, turning their attention back to him.

"Now listen to me carefully one more time, all of you. Josh, I just said that your actions were heroic. They were absolutely amazing. Your fear of punishment didn't even stop you from doing what you thought was the right thing to do. The fact that you ran this afternoon only makes what you did for Cindy all the more heroic. Now there will be no more thoughts of cowardice from you. Do we understand each other?" Justin looked firmly at Josh, and he blushed, but nodded in agreement.

"I also wanted to tell you what I've told your parents. You guys are incredible, and your parents are blessed to have you in their care for a little while longer. God is calling young people all over the world, and I definitely see His calling in you. It doesn't mean that you're perfect. It doesn't mean that this will be the last time your fathers will pull out their more persuasive techniques. It doesn't mean that your attitudes are going to be perfect from here on in, either. It means, and I hope that you'll let me pray for you about this in a minute, that you find favor with God, and so long as you seek Him, He will be found by you," Justin said.

The BBGs sat quietly, letting Justin's words sink in. How different their lives had become in just the few short months since school had let out for the summer! They could see the change in themselves, and in each other. The love that they had for each other seemed to grow overnight. Life seemed to have so much more joy and freedom in it, even with the recent trouble they had found themselves in. Their worship music had grown into something that they loved, and needed to do for their own spiritual walk, as well as doing it to bless others.

"Wow," Pete finally sighed, shaking his head.

Dale grinned. "You've brought the BBGs to a place that not many people have been able to bring us to," he said to Justin.

"Where is that?" Justin asked.

"Quietude," replied Dale.

Justin laughed. "Well then, this seems to be a good time to pray. May I?" he asked.

The BBGs all nodded and then basked in God's presence as Justin prayed for them. They all hoped that Justin's prayer would never end, but of course, it had to. After he finished, the BBGs all rose slowly, and with quiet good nights, each family went home.

CHAPTER 20

The next morning, all the BBGs were out in force to see Justin and his family off.

Later that afternoon, Phillip Beslinger called the Bradford home. The BBGs were watching TV in the family room when the call came in, and Andy answered it. He paled, and then put the phone on hold to dial his father's office extension.

"Dad?" Andy said as his father picked up the phone in his office. "It's Phillip Beslinger on line 1. He needs to talk to you."

The BBGs looked at each other in fear.

"Can't this all just be over?" asked Andy, as he flopped back down into his chair.

The BBGs waited anxiously until they heard Peter's footsteps coming down the long hall from his office. He stood in the doorway of the family room, chuckling to himself over the worried faces of the teens.

"Take it easy, kids. They aren't coming to take any of us away in a squad car today. Mr. Beslinger is just preparing the court case. He's going to need to talk to everyone, but he's decided to only put Andy, Josh, Pete, and Beth on the stand," Peter said.

"You mean the witness stand? In a court room?" squeaked Beth.

"Yes. Cindy's mother and stepfather are fighting Charles' custody rights. Phillip thinks it's going to get pretty ugly, and you witnesses are going to have to be tough out there. Truthful, but tough. The Rather's lawyer is going to do everything he can to confuse you," Peter said.

"Oh, man, that sounds too scary for me," Beth whispered.

"You'll be fine, honey. Phillip is coming tomorrow to get all your statements. When we get closer to the trial hearings, he'll come again and help you get ready for it," Peter assured her.

"If you say so," said Andy, doubtfully.

"I know you'll do just fine," Peter said, turning to go back to his office.

"Yeah, right. How come the BBGs have suddenly become super heroes?" moaned Josh.

"That's a good question, but it doesn't have an answer," Andy said.

The group finished watching their show, and then split up to do their afternoon chores.

The next day, promptly at 1:00 in the afternoon, the BBGs lined up in the Bradford's family room to give Phillip Beslinger their statements. Phillip brought along a small tape recorder, and recorded what was said. He informed them that the court date was set for 3 weeks from that date, which would make it shortly before the new school year started.

After recording their statements, the group decided to relax by taking a dip in the pool. Dale floated on a giant puppy raft in the middle of the Bradford's pool.

"Did you hear Mr. Beslinger say that school starts again in 4 short weeks?" he moaned.

"No reminding us!" Di replied, splashing her brother.

"Hey, watch the splashing!" complained Dale, splashing his sister back.

"Children! Children! I've had a most difficult day. Take your family squabbles elsewhere!" chided Beth, in such a perfect aristocratic tone, that they all burst into gales of laughter.

"Yes, Miss Jekyll, or are you Mrs. Hyde at the moment?" Dale quipped.

Beth pretended not to hear, but instead, swam underwater to tip the raft that Dale was floating on. He in turn, took after her in strong, clean strokes. They were both excellent swimmers, and it took Dale some work to get Beth into the shallow water. To his astonishment, she quickly ran up the steps and out of the pool. It was her mistake. She was no match for his long legs, and he caught her easily and scooped her up into his arms.

"Put me down!" she squealed.

"I can't hear you!" Dale said, carrying her to the side of the pool by the diving board.

"Put me down!" Beth squealed again.

Dale dropped her legs, but kept a tight hold on her wrists.

"You'll walk the plank for this, matey," he said, leading her to the diving board.

"Oh no! The sharks and crocodiles!" Beth cried in mock horror.

"The plank! The plank!" all the others in the pool chanted except Paul.

Paul suddenly appeared behind Dale. "I'll save you!" he cried.

"Oh, now everything will be alright. My knight in dripping swimsuit has come to save me!" panted Beth.

"Sir Drippy Suit at your service, ma'am. Now let the lady go, you cad!" Paul said, grabbing Beth's free hand.

"I won't! She has insulted the great captain of the spotted puppy raft!" Dale said.

"Then, I will defend her honor!" called Paul.

"The plank! The plank!" the rest of the BBGs continued their chanting.

Peter and Emma stood at the open hall windows, enjoying the impromptu acting.

Paul, with Beth's hand in his, gave Dale a playful shove with his other hand.

"A duel, then?" Dale asked, pretending to be shocked.

"A duel to the dunk!" agreed Paul.

"The lady still walks the plank," Dale insisted.

"Never!" shouted Paul, over the chants of the others.

"'Tis no use, my valiant knight. I will walk the plank, only do not go through with this senseless duel. One of us must live," Beth said, dramatically.

"Then it shall surely be you, my fair lady! I shall walk the plank in your place!" Paul said.

"I call the duel on the plank!" said Dale.

"Then release the fair lady!" Paul said.

Dale abruptly let go of Beth's wrist. "Of course. The crocs and sharks wouldn't get anything but a nibble off of her anyway," he said, with a wink at Beth.

"Oh, thank you, my rescuer!" Beth said, turning to Paul and giving him a hug.

Paul blushed beneath his tan. "Ahhhh, I shall go to my dunk a happy man," he sighed.

"Let the duel begin!" Dale said, leaping onto the diving board.

Paul followed suit, and a mock battle began. It ended with Dale losing his footing, and falling into the water, pulling Paul with him.

All the BBGs were laughing so hard that it was hard to stay above the water, and they all quickly swam to the shallow end. They were still sitting on the wide pool steps giggling when they heard a round of applause coming from behind them.

"Bravo! Bravo!" called Emma from the deck.

"Splendidly done, my friends, Splendid!" called Peter.

The BBGs stood up and took a bow. Paul chanced a look at Beth, only to find that she was looking at him. Although the acting was all done in the spirit of fun, there was a seriousness to it for Paul. He was beginning to feel that although he would go to the ends of the earth for any of the BBGs or their families, Beth was different, somehow. There was something else there, in his heart, for Beth that was more than just his loyalty to his family and friends. When their eyes met, Beth's immediate smile was warm, and Paul dared to hope that there was something different in her heart for him as well. He gave her a friendly wink, and then grinned as he saw a blush rise up from under her tan.

That Wednesday night, both the Senior High youth group and the Junior High youth group put their finishing touches on their retreat plans, and on Friday night, they packed the big bus and several pick up trucks and headed off to the retreat center.

"Three whole days of rest and relaxation!" exclaimed Josh, as they stood outside the bus at the retreat center.

"And just who is mainly responsible for all of us needing some R and R?"

Paul laughed.

Josh grinned back at his brother, and said, "Thank you," while taking a bow.

"I don't know," said Dale to Paul in a voice that only the 3 of them could hear, "but I think that Old Faithful must have jarred something in his brain."

Paul laughed again, and Josh took another bow. "I am a changed man," he said dramatically.

Dale patted him on the back. "It's good to see," he said sincerely.

Josh grinned and said, "Thanks."

The camp out was exactly what everyone needed after the chaos of the previous weeks. For the first time during a retreat, Dale, Pete, and Paul were able to spend hours in quiet reflection around the grounds and on the small pond located on the grounds. They brought tremendous worship to the campfires in the evenings. Dave, Anne, and the other chaperones found that they had a lot of free time on their hands as well, since they did not need to spend extraordinary amounts of time keeping the boys in line. Without the instigations of the "terrible trio" as Dale, Pete, and Paul had been nicknamed, trouble seemed to keep its distance from the camp. At first, the adults waited cautiously for the first sign of a problem, but ended up giving up their vigil when nothing bad had happened by lunchtime of the second day.

The BBG girls also seemed to be enjoying a catch up time of their own. No one could seem to remember the last time that they had seen Beth, Meg, and Di doing any kind of crafts. The girls even brought a sign language book along so they could practice signing to each other.

"I sure hope that that's a good thing," said Dave, nodding to where Beth was signing something to Di and Meg.

"Maybe one of us should learn signing as well, so they aren't talking behind our backs right in front of our faces," laughed Anne.

The retreat ended without any trouble all weekend, from any of the teens. As the church bus pulled into the church parking lot Sunday night, Dave walked back to the rear of the bus where the BBGs sat.

"I want to thank you guys," he said.

"For what?" asked Pete.

Dave looked out of the bus window. Several parents waited in their cars for their returning teens, but there were no BBG parents standing in the lights of the church entryway this time.

"There's something, or should I say, someone, missing out there," Dave said, grinning.

"Somebody's parents? Dave, do you need us to take someone home?" Dale asked.

Dave laughed. "Well, you're half right. It's somebody's parents, all right. Specifically some fathers of certain boys. I can't remember many times that we came home from a camp out or conference without seeing 3 very irritated fathers standing in the entryway, ready to do some serious talking with their sons," he said, smiling.

Dale, Pete, and Paul looked at each other, and then understood exactly what Dave was saying to them. Huge grins spread across their faces.

"So for that, I thank you," Dave repeated.

"You aren't half as grateful as we are," laughed Paul, "Believe me."

"I suspect that is a very true statement, Paul," Dave said, as he stood and patted Paul on the back.

After the retreat, school preparations began in earnest. The older boys took their cars to the high school to get them registered so they could begin driving to school in a few weeks. The girls shopped, and Andy and Josh worried about the changes about to take place. Andy worried about starting high school, and following in such big footsteps that Pete and Beth had already made there. Josh worried that he would be left out of everything. All their school concerns, though, seemed like nothing compared to the court hearing preparations that Phillip Beslinger put them through shortly after they came back from their camp out.

CHAPTER 21

The first morning of the hearing, Phillip Beslinger met with Pete, Beth, Andy, and Josh one last time.

"Just please, remember one thing, all of you," Phillip said seriously.

"What's that?" Pete asked.

"Please, whatever you do, keep calm and be polite. The other lawyer will do his best to paint you guys as juvenile delinquents. He wants the jury to think that you guys influenced Cindy into thinking that her home life was terrible, and also led her to think that the answers that her mother gave to the questions she asked were implausible. He wants the search for Cindy's father to be strictly your idea, and he wants it to look like you convinced her that she was unhappy. He's going to try to paint a picture of a loving daughter that was brainwashed by you all into being a rebellious teenager. He's going to do everything he can to make the jury dislike you. If that happens, the jury could decide the case with their hearts and not the facts," Phillip said.

"We didn't have anything to do with Tim and Melissa Rathers kidnapping Cindy," said Beth.

"That's true. But you had everything to do with solving this case. Without you and your help, it would have never happened," Phillip answered. "and that's what the lawyers are going to focus on. Ideas that they say you put into Cindy's head," he finished.

Phillip then told them they would be sitting in the audience with their parents until they were called by him to the stand. Pete, Beth, Andy, and Josh gladly went to sit with their families while the preliminary proceedings and the opening remarks from both sides began. Finally, Phillip called Josh to the stand. Nervously Josh swore to tell the whole truth, and then gave the court recorder his full name and address. Phillip expertly led him through the basics of the story, and then sat down for the opposing lawyer's cross examination.

On the stand, Josh licked his dry lips, and the sympathetic bailiff brought him a glass of ice water. The Rathers' lawyer then allowed Josh to take a few sips before beginning his questioning.

"Joshua, how well do you know Cindy?" he asked.

"Not very well," Josh admitted.

"Is she part of this crowd that you run with?"

"Objection!" cried Phillip.

"Rephrase the question, counselor," the judge ordered.

"Is Cindy part of your normal circle of friends?" the lawyer tried.

"No, sir," Josh answered.

"Did you ever do things together, you know, like sports, movies, and clubs in school?"

"No sir."

"But you did know her name?"

"Yes, sir."

"Can you give us an explanation of why she would pick you, then, to tell this bizarre story to?"

"No, sir, except that we happened to be there in the mall when she was trying to figure it all out," Josh stammered.

Phillip tried to get Josh's attention to calm him down, but Josh was looking only at the opposing lawyer's face.

"Did you find the story she told you odd?" the lawyer pressed.

"Yes, sir."

"Is there any reason why you would have put any stock in this story at all, coming from someone you say you didn't know?"

"I don't know. She had pictures and pieces of information that seemed to prove her case."

"So what you are saying is that Cindy approached 2 strangers in a mall and then proceeded to give them this outlandish story about her life. You're saying that those two strangers took her story as truth and then went to the police with it?"

Josh frowned. "No," he said, "that's not it at all. First of all, Cindy was sitting on a bench outside of a skateboard store that we were coming out of. She didn't approach us, we recognized her from school and approached her. We weren't strangers, really, we go to the same school. And she didn't tell us the story of her life. She just had some pieces of information that she was confused about, and the answers her mom gave her weren't connecting with the things she found in her grandmother's attic."

Phillip tried again to get Josh's attention. He was giving the lawyer too much information that could eventually be twisted around to the other side's advantage.

"Oh, so it wasn't a story that she gave you? It was just pieces of information? Well, then, tell us, Joshua, just who put these pieces together and who straightened poor, confused Cindy out?" the lawyer smiled at Josh, but Josh saw it as a sneer, and realized that the lawyer was doing exactly what Phillip had said he would do. Josh looked over at the jury, and they leaned forward in their seats to hear Josh's answer.

"No one," Josh replied.

Phillip winced quietly.

"So would you say that Cindy is still confused and unsure about this whole situation, then?" the lawyer asked triumphantly.

"No, I guess I meant that she figured it all out on her own," Josh said, with a tinge of anger showing in his voice.

"She figured it out on her own, without your help, or the help of your friends?" the lawyer asked.

Josh knew that the lawyer was now trying to trap him in a lie, and he fidgeted nervously, not knowing what to say. John Baker got up from his seat quietly, and walked to the back of the courtroom. He wanted Josh to see him and know that he was behind him all the way. Josh did catch the movement, and looked at his father's smiling face.

"What I'm trying to say, is that if you think I sat down with Cindy and told her what all the pieces meant, or that any of my friends might have done that, you're wrong. If anything, we tried to make sense of what Mrs. Rathers had told Cindy. No one, not me or my friends, or even Cindy herself knew the whole story until Mr. Beslinger got off the plane that Saturday," Josh said firmly.

The jurors sat back in their seats. The lawyer decided to change tactics.

"Can you tell us where you were on the night of July 29th?" he asked.

"I was in bed until early in the morning of the 30th," Josh answered.

"All right, then, did you go somewhere early on the morning of the 30th?"

"Yes, sir."

"Where did you go?"

"To the mini-mart on Shepherd's Town Road."

"Was there a crime that also occurred early that morning at the elementary school near the mini-mart?"

"Yes, sir."

"What was the crime?"

"The school was vandalized."

"Do you know what was used to vandalize the school?"

"Some sort of paint"

"Did the police come up with a suspect?"

"Objection! This is irrelevant!" said Phillip loudly.

"Counselor, where are you going with this questioning?" the judge asked.

"Your Honor, I'm attempting to prove the type of influence this young man had on my client's daughter," the lawyer said, innocently.

"Continue then, for now, and get to the point," the Judge said.

"Who was the suspect named in the vandalism?" the lawyer asked Josh, with that smile that looked like a sneer.

"Me," Josh answered truthfully, and then winced at the gasp from the jurors and the audience. The judge hit his gavel and called for order.

"Was the case resolved, Joshua?" the judge asked.

"I don't know," Josh said, his face flaming when he realized how silly that sounded.

The opposing lawyer chuckled. “Do you expect us to believe that the prime suspect in a vandalism case doesn’t know whether or not he was charged with the crime?” he asked.

“Bailiff, find the records of the case, please. Counselor, I will remind you now to stick with the current case,” the judge said.

The lawyer did not even attempt to hide his sneer under a smile, now.

“So Josh, why were you at the mini-mart that night?” he asked.

“Because I was asked to ride along with a friend to meet someone there,” Josh said.

“And who asked you to ride with them?”

“Andrew Bradford.”

“How did you get to the mini-mart?”

“On my bike.”

“The same bike that was used in the school vandalism?”

“The police said it was the one that was used.”

“Why would they say that?”

“Because it had specks of paint on the tires that matched the paint used on the school.”

“I see. Well, then, just who did you find was the person Andrew wanted to meet at the mini-mart?”

“Cindy.”

“Was she there?”

“Yes,” Josh had dropped the ‘sir’ a few questions back. He knew his father might not approve, but he disliked this lawyer, and did not feel he deserved the respect of that title.

“How did she get there?”

“I guess on her bike”

“And did the 3 of you go somewhere else that night?”

“Yes, we went home.”

“Did Cindy return to her home?”

“No, she went home with Andy.”

“Do you know why she was asked to meet the 2 of you there, and why she went home with Andy?”

“I don’t believe that she was asked to meet us. I think she asked us to meet her.”

“Did she ask you?”

“No, she called Andy and asked him.”

“If you did not hear the conversation, son, it’s called hearsay, and it’s inadmissible in court. Were you in the room when the call was made?”

“No, of course not.”

“Then Andy could have called her and asked her to meet him.”

“No.”

"Why not?"

"Because he didn't know her or her phone number."

"But Cindy had a reason to have Andy's?"

"I guess she looked it up. It was the second time she called him."

"And Andy couldn't have looked up her phone number?"

"No. I mean, he wouldn't have. Besides, Cindy was scared when we got to the mini-mart, not just sitting there waiting for us to come get her."

"She was scared? Of what?"

"Being alone with Mr. Rathers," Josh said, and the jurors once again moved to the edge of their seats.

"Had she spoken of being afraid of Mr. Rathers before that?"

"Yes, at the mall."

"That must have been some conversation at the mall, especially with 2 young fellows she didn't know."

"Yes, it was."

"How did the three of you get home that night?"

"Pete Bradford came to the mini-mart in their van and drove us all home."

"Why did Pete become involved?"

"Because my bike was stolen while we were at the mini-mart, and we only had 2 bikes for 3 people then."

"Is it possible, Joshua, that the 3 of you met at the mini-mart, vandalized the school, dumped your bike, and then called Pete to pick you up? Is it possible that that's the reason Andy called Cindy to meet you there? Was Cindy coerced into committing a crime because of a crush on Andy? Did the two of them have a romance going? Andy is a wealthy young man, did that fact influence Cindy to do what he wanted her to do?" the lawyer was on a roll.

"No, to all of that," Josh answered simply. Phillip silently cheered.

"You're asking us to believe that this all sort of happened. It was all a twist of fate? I don't mind telling you that it's mighty far fetched. Won't you please just tell us what really happened, and what's really behind all of this?"

Anger now raged inside of Josh. The lawyer was not only just hammering him, but also falsely accusing his best friend. Phillip coughed softly to try to get Josh's attention.

Josh seemed on the brink of playing right into the lawyer's hands.

"I didn't ask for all of this to happen to me. I simply tried to be a friend to a classmate who seemed to be in trouble. While I was just trying to help, I got my bike stolen, and got accused of a crime. I almost ruined my best friend's family, and I made my Dad angry with me. Everyone keeps telling us that we should have brought adults into this from the beginning, but now you can see why we didn't do that. You're a prime example of why we didn't," Josh said a little too quietly.

Phillip sighed and leaned over to speak to his brother, who was sitting beside him.

"We've got to get Josh off of the stand. Larry's breaking him down," he whispered.

"It's not my job to molly-coddle spoiled young teenagers," the lawyer snarled at Josh.

At that point, the bailiff brought in some papers and handed them to the judge to read.

"Counselor," the Judge said, after looking through the papers quickly, "I want to remind you to treat the witnesses in a civil manner. The court would also like to bring to the jury's attention the fact that the witness has been cleared of all charges against him in the vandalism case. It appears that there is substantial evidence in the security video tapes of the mini-mart and the school's alarm system that prove Josh's innocence. You are directed to disregard that line of questioning. Counselor, do you have further questions for this witness?" the judge said sternly.

"No, your Honor," the lawyer said.

"Fine. Mr. Beslinger, call the next witness," the judge said, dismissing Josh with a smile. Phillip called Andy next, giving Josh the thumbs up signal as he returned to his parents.

In the cross examination, the lawyer again tried to frustrate and anger Andy.

"Did you have any prior contact with Cindy before she spoke to you at the mall?" he asked.

"No, sir," Andy said.

"She came to you out of the blue, just like that?"

"No, we came to her."

"Did you find her story odd?"

"Yes, sir."

"And what did you do after she left the mall with her father?"

"We told our brothers and sisters about it."

"Did they find it odd?"

"Yes, sir."

"What did you all do about it after that?"

"Nothing."

"Nothing? You did not speak to Cindy about it again?"

"She called my house right after we got back from the mall to ask me to keep the whole thing quiet, and then I spoke to her again when she called to ask us to meet her at the mini-mart."

"She asked you to keep what quiet?"

"Her fears about who she really was."

"I see. And what was your reply?"

"I told her that it would stay between Josh, me, and our brothers and sisters and two friends."

"Why all those people? Is that how you treat secrets entrusted to you?"

"No, sir. But she never got a chance to ask us to keep it between just the three of us before she left the mall."

"How did you feel about Cindy then?"

"I felt sorry for her."

"Do you consider her attractive?"

"Objection! Irrelevant!" shouted Phillip.

"Your Honor, I'm trying to establish a motive, here," the opposing lawyer said.

"Proceed," the judge said.

"Do you consider Cindy an attractive girl?" he asked again.

Andy stalled. He looked at Phillip, who shrugged his shoulders slightly.

"I never really thought about it," Andy said.

"She didn't catch your eye, then?"

"We weren't even in the same grade. I really never thought about it." Andy insisted.

"But you did feel sorry for her?"

"Yes, I did."

"Are you a popular boy in school?"

"I don't know."

"Do you ever feel like the other kids are just being friendly to you because your parents are wealthy?"

"No."

"Have you considered that a girl might be interested in you simply because of that wealth?"

"No."

"You do know that your parents are very wealthy, don't you?"

"Yes, of course."

"And you do realize that money can be quite a draw to people?"

"Not to my friends, sir," Andy was also starting to get upset, but he was trying his best to remain steady.

"So tell us, did you ever have occasion to call the Rather's home?"

"No, sir."

"Not even to ask Cindy to meet you somewhere?"

"No, sir."

"Do you know how she might have gotten your phone number?"

"No, sir."

"Do you know how many Bradfords are listed in the phone directory?"

"No, sir."

"Well, there are 23 of them. How do you suppose Cindy picked the right one?"

"I don't know. Maybe she knew where we lived."

"How would she know that, if you didn't know each other?"

"Lots of people know where I live. The house is kind of hard to hide," Andy said.

"Oh, so you are popular because of your wealth."

"I didn't say anything like that. Lots of people know where Cindy lived, too."

"Did you?"

"I knew the general development, yes."

Phillip shook his head. Andy was getting too far off of the course.

"You didn't know Cindy, but you knew where she lived?" the lawyer asked doubtfully.

Andy sighed. "Look," he said, "I don't know why this is so important, but most of the kids at school know where you live if they know your name. I really don't know why that is."

"So you were at least interested in her enough to find out where she lived?"

"I didn't find out. I mean, I never asked anyone about it."

"And you figure that's the way Cindy picked the right Bradford out of the phone book as well?"

"I told you that I was only guessing. I don't really know how she figured it out."

"All right. So the 3 of you met at the mini-mart. Why did she call you? Why didn't she call any of her other friends?"

"She said she couldn't reach anyone else. It was after midnight, you know."

"Then why wasn't she afraid of calling your home after midnight?"

"I don't know."

"What did she say when she called you?"

"She said that she was at the mini-mart, alone, and couldn't reach any of her other friends."

"What was she doing out at that hour?"

"I think she said that she had to leave her friend's house earlier because the friend had to go stay with her grandmother or something. She didn't want to go home because her mom was out of town on a business trip."

"What about Mr. Rathers? Wasn't he at home?"

"She was afraid of being alone with him."

"Afraid of the man who raised her? Why?"

"She never really said. She only said that she didn't like the way he treated her."

"So this stranger calls you at 1A.M. What were you doing? Sleeping?"

"We had family company staying with us. I was just going to bed."

"Didn't the phone wake everyone up?"

"No, sir."

"And why was that?"

"Because we have several phone lines. The only line that rings in my parents room is an unlisted emergency number. The line Cindy was calling on is our teen line, and it only rings in my room, my brother's room, and my sister's room. My sister never hears the phone once she's asleep, but it did wake my brother up. He just didn't get to answer it before I did."

"So you answered the phone, and found out that Cindy was at the minimart. Why didn't you suggest that she go home?"

"Because, she's a young woman, alone late at night, on a bike, and she's afraid of the adult that is in her house."

"Why didn't you suggest that your parents go for her, then?"

"I did."

"Why didn't your parents go pick her up?"

"Because Cindy panicked when I suggested it. She was afraid of most of the adults in her life, remember? She didn't want my parents involved."

"And you're going to tell us that after the phone rang and woke up your brother, you managed to get out of the house, get your bike, and get Josh out of bed and onto his bike without anyone in either house hearing you?"

"I told you that my brother heard me."

"But he didn't do anything?"

"He didn't know what I was doing."

"How did you manage to get Josh out of his house without anyone hearing you?"

Andy blushed and paused for a moment. John and Patti Baker were sitting right there, along with his parents and the Gandersons. The BBGs had methods that they used at every house, and had used them very successfully. To reveal the method now would render it useless if the need to use it again ever arose.

"Have you done this sort of thing before?" the lawyer pressed, sensing that this was something he could get Andy in trouble for.

The judge grinned at Andy's discomfort, and called Phillip up to the bench.

"Might I suggest that you inform your witness about taking the 5th amendment?" he said quietly.

Phillip smiled, and thanked the judge. He said something quietly to Andy, and Andy relaxed again.

"On the advice of my counsel, I respectfully take the 5th amendment on that question," Andy said, a triumphant grin on his face.

A ripple of laughter went through the audience and the jurors box. Peter shook his head at Andy, but smiled at him as well.

"Fine. You and Josh arrived at the mini-mart on your bikes. Cindy was already there. What happened next?" the opposing lawyer seethed at Andy.

"We had to put air in Cindy's tires. While we did that, someone stole Josh's bike."

"And you didn't see this happen?"

"No, sir, not until we were ready to leave."

"Then what did you do?"

"We called my brother."

"Another phone call? How many people were in your home that evening?"

"There are 8 members of my family, and a family of 4 were our guests."

"Twelve people in the house, and nobody was awakened by the phone ringing all night?

Andy sighed, he was losing patience.

"I called my brother on the teen line. He was awake, because he knew I had left. He picked up the phone, knowing it was going to be me, before it finished the first ring. The only other person who could have heard that phone ring, was my sister. I already told you that she sleeps soundly."

"But even if the phone isn't in anyone else's room, do you mean to tell me that no one else in the house can hear it ringing in your room?"

"No. The way the house is set up, our rooms are not near my parent's room, or the guest rooms. The only other possibility for hearing the phone would be my younger sister or my younger brother, if all the bedroom doors or the connecting bathroom doors are left open."

"Rather convenient that way, isn't it?" snarled the lawyer.

"Should I answer that question?" Andy asked innocently, but with a smile at the lawyer.

"No. So Pete also now sneaks out of the house, and," the lawyer thumbed through his notes. "oh, yes, and now, Pete gets in the van, and drives away, still without waking anyone. Where was this van parked?"

"In our garage."

"And the garage door opening, the van starting, the lights, nothing woke anyone here, either?"

"No, sir. The house was made so that the cars and the garage door wouldn't wake anyone up."

"And so Pete just drives over to the mini-mart, picks you all up, and then drives you all home again?"

"Yes. He took Josh home first, and then the rest of us went across the street to our house.

"Where did Cindy stay that night, if you had 4 other guests in your home?"

"She slept in the kids' guest room."

"The kids' guest room?"

"Yes, sir."

"Which is located, where?"

"Next to my sister Suzi's room."

"Who else was sleeping in the kids guest room?"

"No one at the time."

"And you just politely said good night and then you and Pete went to your room and fell asleep."

"Pete and I have our own rooms, and yes, that's what happened."

"Nothing else happened?"

"No sir, not that I can recall."

"Will Cindy say the same thing when I ask her that question?"

"Of course."

"Did your parents find out about what happened that night?"

"Eventually."

"But not right away?"

"No."

"Oh, come on, they had a girl that they had never seen before in their home and they didn't ask questions about why she was there?"

"Yes, they asked questions."

"But you didn't give them truthful answers?" the lawyer grinned. He thought for sure that he had Andy now.

"We didn't lie, if that's what you're getting at. We just didn't, we just evaded their questions."

"Is that standard operating procedures for your circle of friends? Evading your parents' questions and deceiving them?"

Andy glared at the lawyer. Then he looked at his parents sitting in the courtroom. Finally he looked toward Phillip. Phillip used his hands to motion for Andy to calm down.

"Do you play these games with your parents often, Andrew?" the lawyer pushed, knowing that he had Andy over a barrel.

"No, sir. Not often. In this case, we thought that we were protecting a young woman. We knew what our goal was, and that was to get Mr. Beslinger here to see if Cindy's fears and theories were true. None of us thought about what would have happened if the end result wasn't what it turned out to be. Cindy was really, really scared. We were way out of our league in trying to help her by ourselves, and we've admitted that. When we make mistakes, sir, we learn from them. This won't happen again."

"Those are noble words, son, but you already demonstrated several times to this court that you have done this sort of thing before. To say now that it won't happen again seems awfully trite and redundant. No further questions." the lawyer said, ending his examination so that Andy couldn't contradict him.

Andy stared at him for a second, and then went to sit down.

CHAPTER 22

Pete was called next, and the opposing lawyer fairly danced up to the witness box to cross examine him, so confident he was that he would be able to fry Pete on the stand easily.

"It says here that you are 16 years old. Is that true?" the lawyer started.

"Yes, sir."

"And you have a junior driver's license?"

"Yes, sir."

"Are you aware that a junior license is only good between the hours of 6 AM and midnight?"

"Of course."

"Do you know what the penalty is for ignoring those restrictions?"

"Yes, sir. A fine and your license suspended until you are 18."

"Did you give those penalties any thought as you snuck out of the house at 1 AM and took your van to the mini-mart?"

"Yes, sir, I did."

"But the law did not restrain you? Isn't that what the law is supposed to do?"

"Sir, I also knew that an exception could be made for an emergency. I was thinking primarily about my brother's safety."

Phillip smiled. Pete was doing a fine job so far, and he was the one everyone had seemed to be worried about.

"Did you know Cindy Rathers before the night you picked her up at the mini-mart?"

"Not at all."

"But you had heard her story?"

"Yes, sir. From my brother."

"Did you know that your brother knew Cindy?"

"Not before he mentioned seeing her at the mall."

"Would you consider your brother to be close to you? I mean, does he talk to you, share secrets, that sort of thing?"

"Andy is one of my best friends," Pete said, looking directly at Andy in the audience.

"That's unusual for brothers so close in age. Did or does Andy discuss his romantic interests with you?"

Pete's anger flared, and Phillip held his breath.

"If he had them, I'm sure he would talk about it with me," returned Pete as calmly as his seething emotions would allow.

"You mean to tell us that at 14, your popular brother, the son of a wealthy man, has no string of girls and dates in his life?"

"It's obvious that you have little understanding of me, my family, or my friends. We don't want to play the 'love them and leave them' game. And there's no need for Andy to center or focus on one girl right now. We have sisters, and our friends have sisters. That's all the female company we need right now in our lives," Pete spoke with deep conviction. The lawyer frowned, and tried to think of a way he could get Pete to contradict himself. He looked at the jurors, some of whom were nodding in agreement to what Pete just said.

"Well, then, Pete, do you know how old Cindy is?"

"No, sir."

"Do you know whether or not she is under the age of 18?"

"Yes, I know she's under 18."

"Do you also know, then, that under the law you cannot take a minor female anywhere without her parents' permission?"

"No, sir. I was not aware of that law."

"Do you now realize then, that you broke another law that night by taking Cindy away from her home?"

"That may be, sir, but if I have to go to jail for protecting, or trying to protect a young lady, then I guess I'll just take what's coming to me and then get on with my life. I don't regret going to pick the guys up, and I don't regret bringing Cindy home with us."

"You don't regret breaking the law?" the lawyer was now sneering at Pete.

"I have enough faith in our legal system to know that getting Cindy away from someone she feared was the right thing to do."

"You speak like a knight in shining armor from the dark ages. Do you know, or did Cindy tell you exactly what it was that scared her about Tim Rathers?"

"No. I told you that I had never seen her until I picked them up that night. That isn't something you discuss with a guy that you don't know or know whether you can trust him or not."

"Then how did you come to the conclusion that you were rescuing her from something?" the lawyer sneered again.

"Because I trust my brother," Pete said simply.

"But even he says that he doesn't know what Cindy was afraid of."

"No, that's not what he said. He said that all he knew was that Mr. Rathers did not treat her well. And that was good enough for me."

"Pete, I've spoken to some of your classmates in preparation for this trial, and they've given me some interesting facts about your family. Tell me, do you think your parents treat you well?"

Pete glared, wondering if the lawyer was trying to call his bluff, or if he really had spoken to some of the kids from school.

“Yes, sir. They treat me very well.”

“How about your friend’s parents. Do they treat them well?”

“As far as I know, yes.”

“Are your parents very strict?”

“On some points, yes.”

“Then you have family rules or laws?”

“Boundaries, yes, sir.”

“All right, boundaries then. Are they reasonable?”

“Yes, sir.”

“What happens when you step out of those boundaries?”

“There are consequences.”

The lawyer was trying to portray the Bradfords as strict, unyielding, and abusive parents, and at the same time, trying to make Pete appear as if he was rebelling against their strong hold on his life. Pete was catching on to the little scheme, and while he was determined to be truthful, he was just as determined to thwart the lawyer’s plan of attack.

“All right, then, are following the laws of the state in those boundaries?”

“Of course.”

“Well, then what were the consequences of you sneaking out of the house and taking the van at a time when your license had expired for the day?”

“I had to give back my set of van keys, and now I have to ask for the keys whenever I want to go somewhere.” Pete was not about to give the lawyer the satisfaction of knowing the rest of the story.

“Did that seem fair?”

“Yes, sir.”

The lawyer was clearly frustrated with Pete.

“What I’m trying to get at Pete, is that just because a teen thinks she isn’t being treated fairly at home, whatever that means, doesn’t mean it’s a crisis situation. Haven’t you ever thought a punishment handed down from your parents was unfair?”

Pete thought about the BBGs and the revocation of their pizza privileges earlier in the summer. He remembered how unfair that had seemed then.

“Yes, sir.”

“Did your friends come and take you away to an undisclosed location then, because of that?”

Pete smiled. Yes, his friends had absolutely done just that. They had taken him out to dinner as a surprise.

“Well, once they did do that. They took me out to dinner as a surprise.” he said.

A gleam came to the lawyer’s eyes. “They took you away without your parents’ knowledge? Just like you did with Cindy?” he asked.

“No, of course not. My parents were in on the surprise.” Pete had to smile at the lawyer's confused expression.

"Could you then, have been acting a little too hastily on Cindy's behalf?" the lawyer asked, trying now to get back on his line of questioning.

"I don't think so. Thinking your parents are unfair, or not treating you the way that you think you ought to be treated, is far different than being afraid to be alone with them."

"You said your parents are strict. Aren't you ever afraid of them?"

Pete laughed and relaxed. "Plenty of times, when I've done something that I shouldn't have done, and the consequences are looming ahead of me."

"And have you sought refuge at a friend's house during those times?"

Pete laughed again, a fact that endeared him to the judge and jury, but flustered the attorney.

"Sir, you're comparing apples to oranges. My parents don't abuse me. I'm not afraid of being hurt by them. I have absolutely no reason to question whether or not I am the biological son of either one of them. I have a sense of security with them, that, by the way, was horribly lacking in Cindy."

"Are you an expert at being able to spot abusive situations with other children?"

"No," Pete sighed for a moment, then looked at Phillip. Phillip smiled at Pete, giving him the courage to say what he had been wanting to say.

"No, I'm not an expert, I'm just another kid. But I'm not just some rich, naïve, spoiled brat, either. I'm not afraid of my Dad. What I fear sometimes are the consequences of doing something wrong. But isn't that what discipline is all about? A deterrent to get us to stay away from trouble? My Dad is predictable and stable. I know he loves me dearly, and I also know that he will punish me when I deliberately step outside the limits. I am, however, allowed to make mistakes, and I make plenty of them. Let me tell you what I do know, though. I know, I know," Pete paused for a moment, trying to phrase his words tactfully in his mind before he spoke them.

"I know that my sisters are not afraid of being alone with our Dad. They go to sleep every night knowing that their father has done everything he can to protect them. They know that they have brothers who are there for them. When my Mom has to go away in the evening, or overnight somewhere, my sisters don't risk their lives trying to bike to a convenience store at 1 in the morning, rather than stay at home with our father. And I find it quite odd that you don't see the difference, sir," Pete finished.

The opposing lawyer was flabbergasted. Phillip wanted to stand up and applaud.

"No further questions," the lawyer said quickly.

He was so flustered, that he did not even cross examine Beth at all.

After Beth's testimony, the court took a one hour lunch break. The BBGs and their parents shared tables in the courthouse cafeteria with Phillip, his helper, Charles, and Cindy.

"You kids were magnificent!" Phillip said warmly.

"You think so?" asked Josh.

"I sure do. His tactic of trying to make it sound like you all influenced Cindy, and planted the story in her mind, fell flat on its face. When he tried to make it sound like you were after her and using her, the jurors actually were frowning. I firmly believe that Cindy is coming back to you, Charles, and I suspect that Melissa and her husband will be spending time in jail," Phillip said.

Cindy's face clouded at that thought. She was angry at what her mother had done, at the lies she had been told, and angry at what Tim had done. But Melissa was still her mom, and Cindy still had a younger brother and sister who meant something to her. She wasn't sure what was going to happen to them if both Melissa and Tim were put in jail.

Charles looked at his daughter's troubled face.

"What your mom did was wrong, Cindy, and you can't imagine the pain I've been through all these years. But I can see that you love your Mom, and that's something that I don't ever want to try to change. When you get your chance on the stand, tell the judge how much she means to you, and don't hold back on my account, OK?" he said gently.

"Dad, she lied to me! She tried to pass Tim off as my dad! I don't understand why she did what she did, and I don't ever want to live with her and Tim again. But what's going to happen to Matt and Katie? They're innocent in all this mess," Cindy said.

"That's true, Cindy, and they are your half brother and sister. Believe me, the court will take all of this into consideration, and try to do what's best for them," Phillip said.

The BBGs looked at each other. How glad they were for the security they had in their homes!

Six days later, the trial ended. There were no BBGs in the courtroom when the double guilty verdicts for the kidnapping of Barbara Beslinger were handed down. Cindy sat with Matt and Katie during the sentencing part of the trial. Charles was called back to the stand to make an impact statement. His eyes filled with tears as he looked at Cindy, seated between two very scared children. He realized that he could influence how they spent the rest of their childhood, and he couldn't bring himself to add to the fear and confusion already written on their faces. He cleared his throat, and told the jury about the pain he had been through for the last 12 years, longing to know how his daughter was doing.

Finally he finished by saying, "I'd like the court to know that I have a job offer in this area that I intend to take. I'd like to relocate here by next month so that my daughter can remain close to her friends, and her siblings. I can say that I'm forever grateful to the jury for the verdicts that they handed down, but there is no way to reclaim the last decade in my life, or in Cindy's. I'm simply asking that the court uphold my total custody of Cindy, and allow only supervised visits with her mother and siblings in a place of my choosing. I have no desire to see the other children in the home have their lives and hearts ripped apart as mine was. Thank you again," Charles said, and wiped his eyes as he sat down.

Cindy beamed at him. It really did look like everything was going to be OK.

After one last phone call from Cindy telling the BBGs about the outcome of the trial, they lost track of her. Her father bought a house in a neighboring school district, so that Cindy could start a new life but not have to face the challenges that would have come with a move to a new state and a totally new environment.

As for the BBGs, they threw themselves into school preparations as hard as they could. School was going to be a challenge. Their teachers and their classmates had known the BBGs for years as students who could be difficult. The BBGs were no longer the same students that had left the buildings that spring, however. Adjustments were going to have to be made on both sides of the desks this school year. How hard will it be?

• • •

Stay with the BBGs as they begin a new school year, and continue their adventure in the Land of Grace. You will find them all back again in the next novel, ready for action, and trying hard to prove to everyone that their hearts belong to the Creator of the Universe.

See you then!

Contact Sheryl Malinics
iamsherylm@netscape.net

or order more copies of this book at

TATE PUBLISHING, LLC

127 East Trade Center Terrace
Mustang, OK 73064

888.361.9473

www.tatepublishing.com